BLADES
OF DEMON

ANTON ZVOLINSKYI

MILTON & HUGO L.L.C.
4407 Park Ave., Suite 5
Union City, NJ 07087, USA

Website: *www. miltonandhugo.com*
Hotline: *1- 888-778-0033*
Email: *info@miltonandhugo.com*

Ordering Information:
Quantity sales. Special discounts are granted to corporations, associations, and other organizations. For more information on these discounts, please reach out to the publisher using the contact information provided above.

Library of Congress Control Number: 2024903300
ISBN-13:   979-8-89285-037-7   [Paperback Edition]
                    979-8-89285-039-1   [Hardback Edition]
                    979-8-89285-038-4   [Digital Edition]

Rev. date: 04/08/2024

PROLOGUE

Heinrich came to his senses again. He no longer knew how many times consciousness left him and returned again. Henry was sure of one thing: there wasn't much left. Death will not be long in coming. The first time, Henry lost consciousness from the pain caused by his own spear. Piercing right through, it pinned him to the ground, preventing him from falling. Afterward, he fell into oblivion from the heavy loss of blood. Heinrich wondered every time why he was still alive. Apparently, the spear had blocked most of the torn arteries, preventing the blood from rushing out in a violent stream.

Heinrich was a brave commander of his army. He led his trained warriors onto the field with a thirst for victory. Fight for your idol. Instead, half buried in the ground, burned in their shells, they looked with cranial eye sockets at their commander, asking the question "Why?" Heinrich asked himself the same question. Being killed by one's own weapon is not exactly what a brave warrior wants when going into battle. He looked at the one he fought for, at his idol, floating in the air a few meters above the ground. It seemed like he was completely weightless, woven from air. However, he confidently held his blade, pointing the tip at his sworn enemy. Heinrich knew that thanks to the owner, many soldiers were spontaneously killed. Despite the help, Heinrich failed his idol. Only he remained alive, and very soon he will follow his brothers-in-arms into oblivion. Heinrich wanted to devote the short time now allotted to life to contemplation.

The Master was in the air, looking at the enemy with hatred. The earth around was moving, promising to take you into its arms if you just touched it. He was in no hurry to attack, because he knew that at a distance, he had an advantage with a huge curved katana, reaching the size of Henry's spear itself.

The Idol called on the elements to help, which answered the call, thickening heavy clouds, forming sparkling lightning. Several of them immediately hit the ground, trying to incinerate the enemy. They both moved at a speed beyond Heinrich's eyes. Having stuck the katana at his feet, the enemy immediately began to cast spells in response, calling on another element for help. She answered, and a tongue of flame burst out of a hole in the ground toward the lightning, reaching the thunderclouds. The owner was almost able to get it at that moment, taking advantage of the enemy's lack of weapons, with a powerful blow of the sword without a guard—the tanto cut the body in half. However, the enemy was not inferior in speed. Without taking the blade out of the ground, he simply shielded himself with it, crouching on his knees, meeting the blow. There was a deafening ringing sound.

The subsequent ringing of weapons echoed across the scorched field, indicating the location of the combatants, because Heinrich, with a clouded consciousness, could determine their location only by ear.

They were elemental enemies who had been fighting for decades—Flamentia and Reiza. Despite the length of the blade, Flamentia was not inferior in speed to the lightning-fast Reiza, who constantly tried to find a gap in the defense. He carried out his attack from the air, inspired by the elements, gaining an advantage in movement. Like a sting, Reiza pierced the air just a few millimeters from Flamentia, who warmed up to his opponent's attacks with unique agility. There was another reason why Reiza did not descend to the ground. Flamentia could control the element of earth, creating a shifting surface around himself, ready to swallow anyone if he just touched it.

Flamentia's next attack pierced the air with a powerful wave of fire. Reiza released the element of lightning with a few swings of his blade, cutting the streams of fire, turning them into harmless shreds.

"Your attacks are slow, as always," said Reiza, Heinrich's master, who was again unconscious, in a superior tone. "You are still using primitive weaving structures with both hands."

Flamentia said nothing as he created a rain of fire toward his opponent. Reiza did not even think of giving in. With barely noticeable manipulations of one hand, he created a dome of lightning streaks, protecting himself from the destructive elements. This is what Flamentia wanted. With a powerful jerk, he pushed off the ground and closed the distance to the enemy, who was busy defending himself. Ignoring the bolts of lightning, Flamentia brought his blade down onto the dome of lightning with a wide swing, pinning Reiza to the ground. Having created the final weave, Flamentia revealed the quicksand into which his enemy would fall.

Reiza, waving his hand, destroyed the weaving of the dome, reducing the distance to the enemy in order to reach the body with the sting of the tanto. The blade was not long enough, but this was not necessary. Passing the element of lightning through his sword, Reiza pierced Flamentia through. At the last moment, he managed to dodge; so the lightning struck not his heart, but his shoulder, tearing apart all the muscle and bone tissue.

Without touching the ground, with powerful leaps, Reiza increased the distance between them. Of course, this was not the outcome he expected, but he was still pleased with the result.

"Without one hand, now it will be difficult for you to weave, huh?"

Flamentia, gritting his teeth in pain, barely warmed up with the insidious attacks of the enemy. A bloody veil covered his eyes, making it difficult to come to his senses; but he still confidently held the blade in his other hand, keeping Reiza away from the body.

They fought for a long time. As often as Heinrich regained consciousness, he observed the two moving at inhuman speed. Lightning flashed around. Clots of hot flame melted. Drops of blood watered the ground. Heinrich did not know how it would end, who would win. He fought for his master, Reiza, but now he didn't care anymore. He knew that his end was near. With the last of his strength, he looked at the battle, which defied any explanation.

With the hot blade of his weapon he cauterized the wound on his shoulder. It was clear that in the near future, the arm would hang limply along the body. The fire was still with him. He could, just like Reiza, free him through the blade. They were both tired, but no one showed it on the battlefield. The elements were in the air all around. During that day, so many weavings were created that the air had a persistent smell of ozone.

Creating a powerful attack from thunderclouds, Reiza rained down a sheaf of lightning on the enemy. Flamentia had no choice but to move, not to fall under the sizzling string of the elements, looking at Reiza, hovering in the air.

"Look around, Flamentia!" Reiza shouted to him from above. "What is all this for? Why did so many good fighters die? For the sake of your ambitions or a nonexistent credo that eats you up from the inside?" Reiza looked behind the enemy's back, expecting the end of the fight any minute.

"Your betrayal set this all in motion," Flamentia said, barely audibly, feeling a vibration in the ground that was not caused by magic.

Reiza's surviving accomplices destroyed the dam that held back the flow of water, which was now rapidly filling the dry riverbed where the two fought. Before Flamentia realized the ruse, it was too late. Water enhanced the effect of lightning. As soon as water reached his ankles, a powerful discharge pierced his entire body. Releasing fire from his blade, Flamentia tried to deflect the damage as much as possible. Taking advantage of the enemy's inattention, Reiza fell from the sky, hitting the opponent's crown with the handle of his tanto. Flamentia, dropping his sword, fell like a sack into the water.

"Without the demon's blade, you are nothing," said Reiza, watching the streams of water carry away the weapon.

Dark water gradually filled Flamentia's lungs. The last exhalation came out of his mouth in bubbles, and Flamentia slowly sank to the bottom. The river increasingly filled the bed with its waters, absorbing the fighting fighters, taking the cooling Heinrich into the abyss, who never knew the outcome of the battle.

Reiza stood in the air several meters above the water, completely exhausted, but pleased with himself. He dealt with it. It was he, the adept of the element of lightning, the owner of the demon blade, who put an end to it.

Chapter

1

The final stages of equipment testing were coming to an end. Time was running out; it was necessary to move forward. Avalsa checked for the last time how the oblong knife fit in the vertebral sheath and set off.

She was dropped off from the van a few blocks from her destination. Dressed in all black, she easily disappeared into the darkness of the night, merging with the wall of a residential building. Avalsa listened into the silence for several seconds, trying to catch the slightest suspicious rustle.

The time of day was chosen appropriately. At this time, residents of houses slept the most soundly. Shaking her tousled blonde hair, Avalsa began a silent climb up the sheer wall of the building. She needed an overview. Climbing onto the roof, she leaned against the still-warm tiles, moving on her belly. Precaution is never too much. The light of a laser sight flashed very close. It was unclear whether she had been spotted or whether this was the sentry's standard review route. Avalsa began to count. Exactly twenty seconds later, the laser appeared nearby again.

"What a responsible mercenary," she whispered under her breath.

As soon as the light appeared again, with the grace of a cat, Avalsa exploded from her spot and jumped to another roof without making a sound.

Now she was separated from her goal only by a stone fence, stuffed with modern technology. There were watchtowers at the corners of the protected area. From the top of each, snipers watched along their own observation routes, covering distances of a good three hundred meters.

Avalsa would bet they had night-vision scopes or thermal imagers. And this was only the first line of defense.

Avalsa chose a place where she could jump over a guarded fence from the roof of a neighboring house, which stood three meters away. The alarm prevented her from doing it at that moment. Into the void, she spoke barely audibly. "I'm ready."

The microphone in her ear, crackling slightly, answered in a confident male voice, "Then I'll go."

Without thinking, Avalsa took a short run. Gently pushing away from the tiles, she caught the edge of the stonework with strong thin fingers. In one jerk, she jumped over the fence. The de-energized network several blocks above helped her do this silently. The building alarm switched to the generators, but with a slight delay. It was enough to penetrate the first line of security.

Avalsa pressed herself against the inner wall of the courtyard, catching her breath and listening to extraneous sounds. The timing was perfect: the patrol inspecting this area had passed forty seconds earlier. The next round will be in a minute and a half. This was more than enough.

The facade of the building was illuminated by soft light coming from the parapet around the house. There was no lighting in the area. It became clear that the guards were using night-vision devices. So much the better for Avalsa. Focusing only on the sound in the pitch darkness, she crossed the lawn, covered with a delicate grass, warming up with the placed "traps"—laser threads crossing the entire yard.

Her movements resembled the jumps of a wounded hare. Avalsa found herself at the entrance to the basement unnoticed. She was happy that the owner of the house did not have dogs. She couldn't stand them.

Checking her digital watch, barely moving her lips, she began to count the seconds. On the tenth, the door opened, forming an even rectangle of yellow light in the darkness. The cleaner came out and was accompanied by a security guard. After cleaning out the kitchen after a heavy day's cooking, he unceremoniously dumped the slop onto the lawn. Cursing and muttering, the cleaner hurried back. The guard stood at the very entrance, blocking the passage, but the height of the opening was sufficient to enter the house through the top, directly above the guard. The minimal equipment made no noise, so Avalsa easily found herself behind the guard. There was a great temptation to knock him out, but the promise she made to herself made her turn on her heels and, bypassing the kitchen tables, move to the next room.

"I'm inside," she whispered briefly to her partner, closing the doors to the bathroom. Wasting no time, she opened the small ventilation window and climbed out. There were no response sensors installed on the window. Only a small boy could squeeze through it; there was no way for an adult to go up here. For Avalsa, this was not a problem. Having a petite build and flexible posture, she deftly found herself on the windowsill next to the drainpipe.

Carefully studied plans and diagrams of the building made it possible to choose exactly this route. She left behind many traps and avoided the possibility of being spotted by a wide-range surveillance camera. Avalsa was considered a high-class specialist, so her decisions were never questioned.

Wrapping her arms around the pipe, she began a leisurely climb, trying not to loosen the outdated fastenings. When she reached the Venetian balcony, thirty meters above the ground, Avalsa paused, standing on the threshold to catch her breath.

The balcony was three meters from the pipe. She needed to get there, because the master's quarters began outside the window. This distance did not bother Avalsa. She just looked back at the ground, making sure that no one suspected anything. Exhaling briefly, in three leaps along the wall, she barely had time to catch her hand on the edge of the Venetian balcony when the force of gravity pulled her down. She watched as small crumbs of whitewash fell onto the lawn.

Avalsa easily carried her slender body in her arms over the balcony railing. There was pitch darkness all around; but her nostrils caught the salty smell of the Tyrrhenian Sea, her ear heard the sound of waves crashing on the rocks, and her tongue tasted the slight bitterness of citrus fruits blooming in the garden. Perhaps at other times, Avalsa would like to be here at sunset or dawn, but now she did not allow the alluring aromas to distract her from her work.

The last frontier: mineral window. The bolts opened from the inside. On the outside, there was only a hollow window frame made of quality

3

wood. For many burglars, this window was an impossible task. With modern progress in engineering, there were a number of devices that can cope with the mineral. Avalsa was not eager to raise half the house with such devices, so she chose ventilation a few centimeters higher.

This was general ventilation for the entire house. Often in spacious rooms, a hood is installed under the ceiling, driving air, forcing cold air to mix with heated air. A tall man will not fit through such a "gut," but for Avalsa, it's a piece of cake.

Carefully prying up the motion sensors on the grille, she removed it from its mounts, carefully leaning it against the wall. Avalsa crawled into the ventilation like a snake. Fear of confined spaces was not one of Avalsa's weaknesses, so she moved like a worm through the "guts" with forward movements.

She moved quite carefully, listening every time. She heard someone walking around the room below her, but she was sure that the owner of the house was sleeping. This means that the master's room was much farther away, along the ventilation pipe.

Finally, the right grate for the right room was underneath it. The closed curtains did not let in any light from the street, so it was dark inside. Avalsa had the plan of a building in front of her eyes, which she had studied a good hundred times. Directly below it was the master's bed. There were guards behind the door, and somewhere next to the bed there must be a dog that belonged to the owner's mistress. Avalsa hated animals. They heard too well. She had to spend a lot of time unscrewing the grille screws so that the dog's ears would not hear the rustling. Avalsa was seething inside with irritation.

Through the gap in the curtains, one could see the sky outside the window beginning to turn gray. On the sea horizon, the sun rises much earlier. She didn't have any time left. Smoothly lowering the grate, Avalsa hung on the edge of the ventilation with outstretched arms. Exhaling softly, she jumped onto the noisy parquet floor without making a sound. At some distance from her, something snorted. Ahead of the bulldog's warning growl, Avalsa was next to him, at the same second plunging a neural needle into the dog's thick skin. The dog didn't even sob. The neural impulse, through the needle, struck the animal's nerve cells, temporarily paralyzing it. Not forgetting to take the evidence, Avalsa removed the needle, catching her breath. The worst was behind her. Although Avalsa hated animals, she did not kill them under any circumstances, even if they leave behind very impressive scars.

The owner did not sleep in bed alone. There was enough light from the slightly open curtain to see those sleeping on snow-white sheets. Embracing a bottle of champagne with one hand and the owner with the other lay a pretty blonde whose curls were developing on satin pillows. Her firm breasts were exposed because the blanket had slid down, and a jeweled piercing protruded from her nipple. Avalsa knew whose gift it was. Middle-aged men with grayish temples and chest hair of the same color, which rose in rhythm with their drunken breathing. He hugged his favorite, inhaling the aroma of sugary perfume. Avalsa felt them strangling her nostrils.

Without wasting another minute, she approached the head of the sleeping blonde. Taking out another neural needle from the bracelet on her wrist, she gently stuck it into the beauty's neck. Avalsa turned her voice recorder up to maximum volume so the guards outside the door could hear the recording.

"Damn you with your politics and girls!" said the voice of the favorite.

Then the countdown went on in seconds. Holding her hand in hers, Avalsa smashed the champagne bottle against the headboard, driving the rosette into the man's neck in one powerful motion. The official, bubbling with his own blood, died immediately. Adding three more blows, she hastily pulled the needle out of the blonde's neck, awakening the "sleeping" one. Hardly understanding what was happening, she screamed. The door began to open, but Avalsa still rushed toward it. Dazed, sleepy guards burst into the room and looked at the bleeding dead man, not noticing how Avalsa left the room behind them, moving to the western wing of the building.

A few more seconds and the whole house will be on its feet. There was no point in diving into the ventilation again. In the living room, on the second floor, logs were barely smoldering in the fireplace. Without stepping on the ashes, Avalsa slid into the chimney, ignoring the dirt and soot, trying not to sneeze from the smoke tickling her nostrils.

Once on the roof, she smiled with satisfaction. Avalsa saw how the house, sleeping just a few minutes ago, was burning with the lights of all the lamps. Snipers and guards were combing the area with the greed of an angry wolf. Having accelerated and pushed off strongly from the edge, Avalsa jumped into the bay in the northern part of the territory.

She flew along the rock on which the building was erected. It was a good hundred and fifty meters to the water. Barely containing her excitement, moving her graceful body, Avalsa pierced the water gap, finding herself in the saving abyss. And only the silence of the watery depths applauded the work well done.

Chapter

2

"Your methods have always amazed me, Avalsa." The tall African, sitting with his back on the bench, never stopped grinning. She read the headline of the local newspaper he held out.

"Betrayal is always punishable, and not always at the hands of the victim," Avalsa read aloud, but then her eyes skimmed over the lines, quickly reading to herself.

The article stated that an influential official of the island of Sicily, namely, the region of Palermo, was killed by his mistress. During the confusion, being out of her mind (the article noted that this happens quite often), the girl stabbed the broken bottle several times into the official's neck and chest. At the bottom of the article, there was a paragraph of speculation from several criminologists. It said that the fragile blonde could not break a tight bottle of white sparkling wine to inflict fatal wounds. It is impossible to do this without proper experience. The medical examiner's column mentioned a blow to the carotid artery, executed so accurately and fatally that the next three may have been a cover-up.

Avalsa returned the newspaper to the African, and he read the last lines of the article aloud, "One way or another, for lack of evidence, the Sicilian model, shining on chic catwalks under the Italian sun, was detained."

"I hope the Guild is happy?" Avalsa asked after waiting for her companion to laugh.

"Quite." The African became serious again. "Not only does the dirty official owe us a debt, but he has also begun to disobey orders recently."

"The Guild does not tolerate this," Avalsa said, watching the azure horizon.

She knew that debts for the Raven Guild were not a reason for murder, because you cannot extract a debt from a dead person. However, if you begin to be willful, to forget who gave you power by placing you in a high position, then the Guild will not hesitate to respond.

"You have three days of rest. What are you going to do?" the African asked, distracting Avalsa from here thoughts.

"Three whole days? Abollo, you're spoiling me." The girl's lips formed a smile for the first time. "We're in Palermo, remember? Checking the water temperature of the Tyrrhenian Sea will be my first activity."

Abollo chuckled as he rose from the bench to leave. Avalsa didn't look at him. She was still watching the crests of the waves on the horizon, looking forward to time on the beach, away from prying eyes. She knew how to hide.

***

Among the noisy streets of Sicily flooded with tourists, between stalls with various kinds of vegetables grown by the tropical sun, where everyone tried to ask the seller something louder than the other, thereby irritating the others, there was the building of the Raven Guild, which did not attract the attention of the crowd. The same cannot be said about the variety of artisan shops located in the neighborhood. Grocery stores and textile shops were completely crowded with people from morning until deep twilight.

The white building with a tiled roof and low steps at the entrance seemed nondescript compared to its neighbors. There was no sign on the door, and the walls of the house were not surrounded by a fence. Being open to everyone, the oak wooden door, with a powerful ring in the shape of a raven's beak, was rarely opened by visitors.

Avalsa looked appreciatively at the Raven Guild branch. She had been to the main residence, so she had something to compare it to. There were forged figured bars on the windows of the two-story building.

There were many of these on the streets of Palermo. There were flowers planted on the windowsills, in every residential building.

Walking across the street at a green traffic light, Avalsa grabbed the ring in the shape of a raven's beak and pushed. The door opened heavily. After the bright sun, it might seem that the building was in twilight. After a few moments, Avalsa was able to look around. The interior was made in the classic style of ancient Italy. In the center of the room was a spiral wooden staircase the color of ripe cherry. The walls were decorated with many flowerpots. Sometimes, instead of living ones, colorful compositions were observed in pots. Wide oak benches with long massive tables formed the image of an old tavern. The picture was completed by a huge bar counter, painted the same color as the stairs.

There were four chairs placed at the counter, three of which were empty. Several people were sitting on the benches, trying the traditional cuisine of Italy from earthenware. They did not even raise their heads to the one who entered. Avalsa felt that all seven visitors were watching her. But she didn't care much about that. She walked slowly to the bar counter, taking an empty chair.

A man of about thirty, wearing a worn denim jacket, with long hair tied in a ponytail, looked at her appraisingly. Avalsa was dressed in a light-beige sweater that covered her slender arms and simple jeans that hugged her thin legs. The shod moccasins visually further reduced her short stature.

The look lasted only a few moments, after which the man affably raised his half-full glass. Avalsa nodded reservedly, paying attention to the innkeeper of the tavern.

"Are you following me, Master Clark?" after a respectful greeting, she asked the head of the Raven Guild.

He was quite tall and had a truly aristocratic bearing. His hair was straight, the color of a raven's wing. His love for the color red sometimes surprised Avalsa, a faithful servant of the night shadow. Clark often dressed in red trousers and a fabric vest of the same color. True, the shirt was black, but it had a scarlet tie. His regularly shaped lips were constantly smiling, so the head of the Raven Guild could win over anyone.

"You flatter yourself, Scout." Clark smiled, holding out a banana milkshake. "You just need to run the Guild on your own, without intermediaries."

"It sounds like you are present in all branches." Avalsa took a sip of the amazing drink with pleasure.

"It's possible that I'll also be present when orders are executed." A smile touched Clark's lips.

There were rumors in the Guild that not a single business, not a single order, was carried out without Clark's personal supervision. It was as if he was behind everyone's back. Avalsa came to the conclusion that this was impossible, since the Raven Guild mercenaries fulfilled up to hundreds of orders around the world per day. However, the feeling of someone else's presence did not leave her while completing tasks. Over time, the feeling dulled but did not completely disappear.

"I see that the Mediterranean sun has done you good."

"You did me a great service by letting me warm up after ordering in Siberia."

"It's not my fault that the victim tried to hide so far away." Clark spread his arms unarmed. "By the way, your fee for the official."

Avalsa unceremoniously began to count the money, taking it out of the envelope. Taking the required amount, she put the rest into the envelope, returning it.

"As I understand it, you want to put the rest into your account?" Waiting for an affirmative nod, Clark again hid the money under the bar counter.

Avalsa never walked around with such sums in her pocket. There was no point in this, just like hoarding pieces of paper by hiding them in the "mattress."

"There is one more order for you."

"And I thought you'd give me the opportunity to choose from there on my own." Avalsa pointed her finger over her shoulder at the order board by the spiral staircase.

"This is more interesting." Clark handed her a black folder with the Guild emblem on the first page. "Besides, the tasks that hang there, you know where they come from."

"There is more honor in this," Avalsa finished her thought, taking the folder, causing an approving smile from the head of the Guild. "Confiscation?" she read the first word out loud and then went deeper into the matter, reading to herself.

Clark took his time, returning to wiping glasses and giving orders to the kitchen. The visitors present wanted to eat after their journey.

"Norway?" Having familiarized herself with the case, Avalsa again began to drink the unfinished cocktail.

"Another cold city." Clark nodded. "We need to take something from someone who doesn't want to give it up voluntarily. But without bloodshed. You should not be noticed, and believe me, the owner will not report your loss to any authorities."

"But it's just a figurine." Avalsa critically examined a photo depicting a jackal's head in a reduced form.

"This is not a figurine, but the top of a staff."

Deciding not to go into further detail by asking useless questions, Avalsa closed the folder. The terms and payment were specified in the task. Both suited her.

"When should I start?"

"As soon as you get there." Clark handed her a business-class ticket for a flight to Norway.

Avalsa took the task and the ticket, replaying in her head her actions before boarding the plane. She had already started work.

"When you have the pommel with you, be sure to wrap it in a rag." Clark took out of his pocket a knitted fabric made of coarse thread, with Egyptian hieroglyphs along the edge. "This is an additional condition of the order."

Without asking any further questions, Avalsa silently hid the fabric in her jeans pocket and left the Raven Guild branch in Sicily.

Chapter

3

Dawn had long arrived, but at the foot of the mountains, the sun will appear much later. The traveler was in a lowland, moving along a rocky ridge along a snow-covered riverbed. Snowshoes prevented him from falling into the snow, slowing down his confident step.

The cold was terrible. The crunch of snow underfoot seemed to be heard throughout the entire riverbed. White snow sparkled all around. Rocks covered with ice could be seen far above. They sparkled with dazzling light in the sun.

The riverbed was in the shade until midday, so it would be foolish to sit in camp and wait for it to warm up a section of the path. During the long journey, the traveler's eyebrows and eyelashes became covered with frost. A thick knitted scarf covered a good half of his face, protecting him from frostbite.

He left the small settlement at the edge of the mountains three days ago. Local residents collected provisions for the journey, as well as a large armful of brushwood. Dry firewood is very rarely found in snowy areas. The traveler thanked the residents for their help. He happily put on a warm tanned jacket, along with sheep's wool pants, leaving in the village his city clothes, which were of no use in places of eternal snow.

The glacial canyon began to narrow, showing the traveler the right path. The sun had long passed over the tops of the mountains, and now he squinted from the bright light, intensified by the crystal white surface of the earth.

It was no longer so cold, so he quickened his pace, slapping his snowshoes. Approaching the source, the traveler stopped, having reached his goal. The Latoritsa River, in Transcarpathia, was completely covered with ice. The winter turned out to be cold enough that the raging waters were captured by ice. However, this turned out to be beneficial for the traveler.

Not far from the slope, he barely made out an opening in the rock.

"It seems this is what we need, Hans," he talked to himself.

Entering the doorway, Hans noted that the sun was already low. Very soon night will fall on the ground, again paralyzing the limbs that have warmed up during the day.

Wasting no time, he threw the heavy backpack off his shoulders and took out an armful of firewood, forming branches for the fire. Having done the necessary, he was now sure that if he just touched a match to the paper, the fire could flare up, warming him all night.

Hans was in no hurry to light the fire.

"First things first," he said to himself, taking off his sedentary warm clothes.

He took his equipment out of his backpack, checking it again. He laid out the short curved blade, with a sharpened edge along the inside of the blade, first. A hilt of yellowing bone, with a round metal eyelet at the end, protruded from a makeshift sheath. There was no guard on the dagger. The dagger inflicted terrible wounds with the tip of the blade. He wasn't called Claw for nothing. From the bag, Hans carefully poured onto the floor a long sparkling chain with small spikes on the links. It was one of the artifact weapons—the Grail chain.

The traveler changed into comfortable fabric trousers, tucked into soft boots, and a bib made of tanned leather, worn over tight-fitting thermal underwear. After slipping the leather bracer onto his arm, he wrapped the Grail chain around his forearm. Having critically examined the equipment, Hans issued a phrase that he said every time: "Eh, that's not all."

The rays of the setting sun had not fallen into the crevice for a long time, but Hans had no use for it. He oriented himself perfectly in the darkness and slid into a gap through which he could crawl. Finding

13

himself in an abandoned mine, in the depths of which the target was located, Hans descended lower and lower.

Once upon a time, ore was mined here for metal production. Now, after a long time, the mine was considered abandoned. Local residents spoke about the location of the mine, adding that the mine could be dangerous.

There was a feeling of stuffiness in the air, but there was still movement of dust. Hans walked along the main workings, with a track laid for the movement of trolleys. The sleepers made it difficult to move quickly, so he decided to walk along the edge of the rails, managing his balance perfectly.

The farther he went from the crevice, the muffled the steps became, and the silence became oppressive. Mentally, he remembered the way back, since the branching of the workings could get confusing.

The road went farther into the depths of the rock, plunging Hans down the slope. A layer of stone could be seen overhead, with a beam fixed here and there, in which places of burning torches could be seen. Neither sunlight nor a living soul penetrated here for a long time.

The breathing was becoming too loud. The traveler stopped, catching his breath. He looked around, listening to the slightest rustle. In front of the workings, and also behind, no movement was heard; only drops from the roof broke the silence.

At a certain point along the way, Hans realized that he was no longer alone. He did not notice any danger around, but he felt that he was being watched. As if to confirm his fears, he discovered a corpse that had decomposed many years ago. The skeleton's skull was fractured. Now it is no longer possible to know the cause of death. Perhaps an ordinary piece of rock fell from the roof onto the miner, crushing his head. Hans was not satisfied with this explanation.

The workings turned into a chamber where the traveler walked bent over. The chamber connected the adjacent working, leading farther into the depths of the mine. Not reaching a few meters from the pairing, Hans heard a barely noticeable grinding sound. It sounded quite ominous in the darkness. The Claw was already in his hands, ready for defense.

The dripping from the roof intensified, indicating that he was getting closer to the source of the noise. The sound of water made it difficult to listen to another sound. Suddenly, right around the bend, at the very moment when Hans entered the next working, a clawed paw emerged, aiming for the unprotected throat. Honed reflexes made it possible to place the blade of the blade in time to meet danger.

It scraped loudly. The paw, closed on the weapon, pulled strongly toward itself, trying to snatch the dagger from Hans's hands. He held the handle tightly, so he took flight. He was flown into a neighboring excavation, landing against the wall. He ignored the pain and rose to his feet, ready to meet his opponent. The creature's retreating steps allowed him to take a break.

His heart was beating wildly. Trying to breathe evenly, Hans brought his heartbeat in order. The workings were quiet again. The stale air was felt more strongly. It was becoming difficult to breathe. Covered in sticky sweat, Hans continued moving deeper.

Increasingly, traces of three-fingered claws were found on the stone walls. Skeletons lay on the ground in various poses of horror, with outstretched hands begging for help. The excavation was no longer secured by anything, so Hans looked with caution at the roof, from which a block of rock could fall, sealing the passage or crushing him.

His nerves were tense. There is not a single hint of light visible ahead. Production began to expand. Hans found himself in a spacious chamber with a hollowed-out opening inside. The opening was uneven, as if it had been created in a hurry. Behind it was a semicircular man-made room.

After a few moments, Hans realized that this was not a room. Around the opening, there was the largest number of corpses. To see what the passable workings revealed, all the underground workers gathered inside.

In the center was a sarcophagus. Based on the lid and walls, Hans determined that it was at least a century old. Hans was familiar with the Old Norse script. The sarcophagus was empty.

It became pointless to continue further investigations into who and when the burial was discovered. The number of deaths around indicated the true reason for the closure of the ore mine.

A grinding noise behind his back made him instinctively put his hand out in defense. A huge toothed jaw closed on his forearm, instantly burning his consciousness with a wave of pain. The chain wound around the bracers prevented him from grinding his hand into powder. Howling in frustration, the creature jumped to the side, splashing bloody saliva. The Grail chain stopped glowing, burning the skin. Hans, not allowing himself to freeze in shock, went into a somersault just in time—three-fingered claws clicked above his head. He slashed with his Claw, at the level of the legs, catching the tendons with the blade. The creature scraped its claws along the stone, showering Hans with crumbs of rock. It was furious.

Waving its arms indiscriminately, the creature tried to hook its claws on the annoying victim. Having taken one blow to the blade, Hans fell to the ground. Rolling over his shoulder, he found himself at a safe distance, with his back to the sarcophagus. The creature was approaching. It felt the narrowing of space into which Hans, unwittingly, had found himself. The traveler had no chance against long arms and sharp claws in the cramped room. Quickly unwinding the chain, he took out the next artifact weapon from his hip sheath—the nail of the Savior's Cross. Having threaded it through the link, he kicked it into the excavation soil.

Hans spent no more than two seconds manipulating the nail, but this was too much of a head start for the toothy creature. The traveler barely had time to untwist the second end of the Grail chain, with a sinker, when the creature attacked, stretching out into a deadly string. Predicting the angle of attack, Hans threw the chain and tumbled to the side. He had pressed himself hard against the wall of the sarcophagus, and he raised a column of dust into the air.

The inertia of the untwisted chain wrapped the creature over its shoulders, constraining its movements. Without wasting a second, he pulled out the second of four nails. Using his free hand to draw a rune on his palm, Hans forcefully nailed the nail to the other end of the chain, pinning the creature to the ground. It howled loudly, stunning Hans. Tired and disoriented, he rose to his feet, where he was finally able to see the creature in full size.

The creature turned out to be a head taller than Hans, but its stoop and crooked hind legs did not allow such a conclusion to be made immediately. The lower jaw, with a row of sharp needle teeth closely located in the mouth, was pushed forward in the manner of a bulldog. This creature had no eyes. The keratinized plate moved onto the bridge of the nose. Hans came to the conclusion that she once had vision, but due to uselessness it atrophied, allowing the creature to be well oriented toward sound. The skin was covered with fine tar-colored fur. It could seem that the creature was dressed in armor made of steel; its fur had a metallic sheen. The hind legs with curved knees ended in short rounded plates. The front deformed phalanges of the fingers formed three-fingered claws thirty centimeters in length.

The creature howled and wriggled, trying to escape from the trap. The chain of the Grail held tightly. Shining, it reduced the body shell, opening access to soft tissues. The nails of the Savior's Cross pumped out dark energy, dispersing it into the bowels of the earth. The creature was shrinking in size. The darkness that had enveloped it in initially strong armor began to fall off in pieces of black mucus, boiling like tar on a fire. Hans waited until the pink skin on its back showed, and with one movement of his Claw, he pierced the creature's heart, driving the blade between the third and fourth ribs. At a certain moment, holding his hand on the handle, Hans felt the creature's heart stop beating. Squeezing out a groan of pain from its lungs, which could be mistaken for a human one, the creature gave up the ghost.

Hans silently took out the nails, wound the chain back onto his bracers, and stood over the sarcophagus. Approaching the front side, he read aloud, "Rothgar, Heart of a Dog. Centurion of the brave army." Turning to the Scandinavian, he said, "Your brave warriors have brought you far, Centurion."

The answer, as always, was silence. Looking inside the sarcophagus, he clicked his tongue in frustration. It was empty inside. No weapons, no armor. Hissing in pain, overcoming fatigue, Hans lifted the creature's body and placed it back into the sarcophagus.

"Rest in peace, Rothgar," said the traveler, after which he carefully closed the lid of the sarcophagus.

The journey back took longer than expected. As he was climbing out of the crack in the floor, pain pierced his side like an arrow. Hans took off his bib and saw that his thermal underwear was soaked in blood. In the heat of battle, he did not notice how the creature still left a mark. It caught on a tangent. The cut was long, stretching from the solar plexus to the shoulder blade, but not deep. The blood had long since dried, but when he crawled out of a crack in the rock, the ichor burst in several places.

Hans started the fire quite quickly. The firewood had not yet become damp. Having quickly built a tripod, he placed the pot with the collected snow. While the water was heating up, Hans looked with annoyance at the breastplate, which was no longer suitable for battle.

"What did you expect, going up against a creature in tanned leather?" he talked to himself, throwing the breastplate into a crevice on the floor.

Hans washed the wound in heated water and washed himself. The traveler was very tired but patiently waited for the morning, looking into the cheerfully flashing embers. He took the potatoes out of them, peeled them, took a piece of cheese from his backpack, and ate it all, continuing to look at the coals. Here and there lone tongues of flame were still trying to break through, fighting for the right to burn. The hands on the clock showed nine. Having spread out a sheepskin blanket, Hans covered himself with a warm blanket, not forgetting to throw a couple of wood into the fire. After watching how the fire, at first carefully and then with ever-increasing zeal, attacked the dry log, increasing in size, Hans fell asleep.

He woke up as the last rays of the sun left the horizon. Hans felt well rested, although the wound marks were a little sore. Having collected the coals of the fire and poured them into the crack in the floor, Hans began to turn off the parking lot.

The path to the nearest village was not close. As Hans expected, the tracks were covered in the snow. But the traveler knew that if he walked along the riverbed, sooner or later he would be able to get out at the desired village.

Hans hid the weapon back in his backpack, not planning to use it that night. As if in response to his thoughts, a lonely howl of a wolf was heard in the forest. First hesitantly, and then with ever-increasing numbers, other wolves joined in the howling. Each time it came closer and closer. The young moon, hidden behind the clouds, completely plunged the area into darkness.

The distinct howl of a wolf was heard along the left channel of the river. They felt Hans, he knew it, but he couldn't do anything about it. Wolves were the masters of this forest. His ear caught a single crunch of a branch not far away.

Orienting himself in the darkness, Hans turned his head toward the sound, trying to see the danger. The pack was already visible, partially hidden near the tree trunks.

Hans saw the leader almost at the same time that he saw him. With an ominous roar, the wolf jumped out of the bushes into the middle of the river, a few steps from Hans. At that moment, the world seemed to stop. He did not pay attention to the wolf pack, hidden a few meters away in the undergrowth, or to the snowshoes, in which he could not escape from the wolf's paws. The wolves were waiting for the leader's command to tear apart the defenseless man. They simply looked at each other, their predatory eyes shining in the night.

The leader and Hans felt that no danger should be expected from each other. Without a single gesture, the seasoned wolf turned his pack along the riverbed to look for other prey for his children and mothers. Hans looked after them. Smiling at his thoughts, he continued the interrupted path.

Hans arrived in the village in the morning. The sun had not yet dawned, so the people in the houses were still sleeping. Having crept along the street so as not to disturb the dogs, Hans left warm clothes on the doorstep of the people who had given him shelter. He stuffed a letter inside his pocket with words of gratitude and a small amount of cash. With a sense of accomplishment, Hans left the village without looking back.

It's dawn. Standing by the road, he stopped the first shuttle bus that morning. In the salon sat a grandmother with huge bags at her feet, a man with a basket of eggs, and a woman with cans of morning milk. At such times, people went to the market to sell their modest supplies. Hans found an empty seat and placed his backpack next to him.

With his appearance, he attracted the attention of passengers—a long cotton jacket with a hood, with a light scarf tied over it to hide the lower half of his face. Comfortable all-season shoes with a strong tread, along with distressed jeans, completed the traveler's look. There were a lot of tourists in this area, but not this early. Hans tried to be kind to such views. Combing back his long hair with shaved temples, he lost interest in the passengers and stared out the window. The predawn scenery in the hilly areas was amazing.

When they reached the city, Hans thanked the driver and headed toward the highway. Walking through the noisy streets, periodically adjusting his backpack, he watched the passersby. Once out on the road, Hans again began to catch a ride that would take him in the right direction. The traveler had a long route ahead of him again.

Chapter

4

Mornings in Norway are always unpredictable. You can't tell by looking at the sky what the weather will be like during the day. Avalsa was irritated by this fact all the time.

Having left Oslo a few hours ago, she got off the bus in a small town with just one hotel. Surprisingly, there were free places, even a lot. Apparently, the season for tourists has not yet arrived.

The beauty of hotels in small towns is that there is no requirement to present documents at the check-in desk. Avalsa was greeted by a nice older couple who handed over the keys immediately after she filled out the form. They accompanied her to her room, talking about the vicissitudes of life.

Avalsa left her personal belongings in a cozy small room and went outside, wrapping herself tightly in a scarf. The gusts of wind seemed especially prickly when you left a warm room.

She crossed the street, finding herself on the outskirts of the city. After walking a few meters at a leisurely pace, Avalsa turned off the road and began to run. She decided to take a shortcut through the forest, starting just a kilometer from the city.

Stepping on dry spruce needles, wide areas of moss under perennial trees, she moved silently. It wasn't necessary, but habits are stronger than Avalsa. The sun had difficulty finding a hole through the dense crowns of trees, illuminating the mighty trunks covered with rough bark.

The twilight in the forest did not bother Avalsa at all. It even liked her. There were many animal trails around. The people of Norway cared about the lives of animals. Therefore, signs prohibiting hunting, food boxes, and bird feeders were posted in the forest. Of course, this may not be found deep in the forest, but on the outskirts, this practice was welcomed.

Suddenly the forest ended, releasing Avalsa into the open. She walked at a leisurely pace along one of the animal paths leading to the river.

The river turned out to be wide enough that it was impossible to cross it on her own. In the distance, she could see a gray monolith of rock, framing the entire coastline of a deep river. Launching was possible only from the opposite bank, on which Avalsa was located. At a distance, a good hundred meters from the coastline, there were numerous fishing boats. People came from different countries to fish in Norway's rich waters.

All this was of little interest to Avalsa. She paid much more attention to a private property built on the shore. From the outside, it looked like a medieval hotel made of logs. A fairly large area of meadow grass was outlined with a low fence, creating a corral for horses. Behind the fence, several crows could be seen walking freely around the accessible territory. Avalsa tried not to look at the horses' gracefulness. They moved so beautifully.

Not far from the fence, a stable for a dozen horses was built, from which neighing could be heard and the corresponding odors were emanating. Avalsa was on a hill, so she could see that the wide courtyard from the residential building was divided by stables.

There were several SUVs parked in the yard, and people could be seen nearby. It was difficult to determine whether they were guards or servants.

The residential building had a barn structure with three floors. There were cameras built into the walls at every corner. Satellite dishes were located on the sloping roof. There were no guard towers, a barbed fence, or a double row of walls—there was nothing like that, which embarrassed Avalsa beyond measure. Come in, take it and leave. This is what can be said about the safety of this house. However, the scout was in no hurry. Based only on external observation, she could say that the work would be easy. Having found out everything she needed to know, she went back to her hotel.

In the following days, Avalsa took care of the estate with all care, making forays for two or three hours. She did not attract the attention of the stable residents. Each time she took on a new look—changing wigs, baseball caps, hats, glasses, clothes. She tried to build a house plan in her head. Avalsa found out that this following week, a horse race was being organized at the estate, and everyone was invited to watch. The grounds even had bleachers for three hundred people around the paddock. Avalsa assumed that this was the number of people living in the city.

She needed to find out where the owner of the estate kept the figurine. The file specified that the figurine was the pommel of Anubis, one of the parts of the staff. Avalsa did not study mythology, so she did not delve into the difference.

The owner of the estate was easy to identify. Moreover, it was he who organized the event. He was a retired politician who paid a fair amount of taxes to the Norwegian government. He hid his gray hair at the temples behind a wide cowboy hat and wore a bright plaid shirt and leather shoes with spurs and pointed toes. The image of a cowboy did not fit into the mountainous landscape of Norway. Avalsa had little interest in aesthetics at the moment. Sitting firmly on his tail, she followed him around the entire estate, introducing herself as a journalist from a local newspaper.

Avalsa asked various questions regarding the social life of the retired politician and at the same time found out where his room was. It was located on the second floor, with corner windows overlooking a deep river. Having studied the habits of the owner, Avalsa assumed that this kind of relic was kept either in his room or next door. The retired politician did not want to share with anyone.

Avalsa was concerned about why such a large estate did not have security. Just a huge number of cameras and a room of monitors, with an analyst present, and that's all. No dogs, no guards, no one. Of course, Avalsa admitted that due to the low crime rate in the city, some carelessness takes place, but . . . Something was clearly bothering Avalsa. As with all orders, she decided to take her time and make inquiries.

—ᵒᵐ—

Ray Price loved his estate. He enjoyed the quiet, unhurried Norwegian life under the country's changing sun. Ray accepted that he had left the States to do charity work in a foreign country. Walking leisurely along the stables, he looked at the clear sky, squinting contentedly from the bright sun.

The toothpick in his teeth slowly rolled from side to side. Ray had the pleasure of being interviewed by a pretty girl journalist from a local newspaper, who was tactfully interested in his life. Price readily answered any questions, eagerly examining her appearance. He respected beauty. The delicate features and delicate skin excited his imagination. What a pity that Ray had to leave a country where there was much more beauty.

Price was approached by one of his men.

"We found what you asked for. We'll deliver it to the estate tonight."

Ray's mood improved noticeably. He nodded to his man as he passed the locked door to the stables. Inside was a special horse. Ray wondered if it was possible to change the artiodactyl's diet. It took a while, of course, but he succeeded.

Smiling ever wider, he more actively rotated the toothpick in his teeth. When the show jumping ended, the guests went home, crossing the gates of the estate.

Ray went up to the second floor to walk along the corridor of his fame. He liked painting. Price tried to fill the house with artworks. Only with his own. The canvases featured evening landscapes, city night lights, and raging waves of the oceans. Not having fully decided on the direction of painting, Ray tried himself in everything.

He needed rest. Age still takes its toll, as does the hair on the top of your head. Price tried to hide the bald spot on his head under a wide-brimmed cowboy hat. Ray liked the image of a farmer from his homeland. He lay down on the bed and closed his eyes. Today they will bring another canvas for the masterpiece. He needed a good rest.

The clock showed half past ten. It was deep night outside the windows. Ray first heard and then saw from the window an SUV approaching the estate. His SUV.

Slowly, barely hiding his excitement, Ray went outside. There were two people behind the wheel. They left the estate a week ago. Upon seeing the owner, they hastily opened the back door of the car, allowing them to see the prey.

It was a girl, about eighteen years old. From a completely different city, many miles away. Ray Price was no fool. The pretty face turned out to be tearstained, and the blonde hair was frayed and looked like tow. Her clothes were torn, but Ray knew that his men would not dare abuse her. Rather, she was resisting. Price liked the glib ones. Smiling widely, Ray almost dropped the toothpick from his mouth.

"To her room" was all the owner said, closing the door and going to get the instrument. Art did not tolerate delay.

Before taking her to the basement, the servants bathed the girl, changed her clothes, and combed her hair. They even applied light makeup, emphasizing her natural beauty. When the girl was brought into the room, Ray's breath caught. He loved beauty.

Her hair was braided into a spike, falling from her right shoulder to the middle of her chest, which heaved anxiously; and her breathing turned to sobs.

"Thank you. I'll do the rest," he said to the servants, taking the girl by the arm and gently pushing her toward a metal chair in the middle of the room.

The look on her blue eyes was hazy, expressionless. She had little idea of what was happening around her; her movements were automatic. The girl did not pay attention to the tools located near the chair, to the scratched floor around it. She didn't even notice that the room in the basement was best isolated from sound.

Ray Price, with childlike trepidation, sat the girl down so that her chest rested against the back of the chair. Wasting no time, he tied leather straps around the victim's arms and ankles. Price slowly rolled up his sleeves. He never spoke on such occasions; he just enjoyed it.

The girl was brought to her senses by the sound of tools hitting a metal table. For the first time that evening, she consciously looked at Ray.

"I demand to be released." She was prevented from finishing her angry speech by a treacherous sob when she saw a scalpel and a burner in Ray's hands.

"I'm afraid that's impossible," he answered in a voice full of sympathy and, bending over her, added, "I liked you too much."

He set to work with the methodical precision of a craftsman. Price could bet that the girl had never felt pain like this in her life. Behind the door, it could seem that cattle were being slaughtered in the room; such an inhuman scream was uttered by the distraught victim.

Ray liked those screams. They gave inspiration. First, he marked the contours of the future canvas, starting from the cervical vertebra and passing along the perimeter almost to the victim's pelvis. With a scalpel, he cut off tissue after tissue, pulling back the skin on the girl's back with the help of special forceps. This way the skin was cut evenly, preventing the canvas from being damaged. He stopped the flowing blood with a burner, cauterizing the bleeding places in time.

The victim came to her senses and then lost consciousness. Until her voice became hoarse, she tried to call for help. Because of the scalpel and the torch, articulate speech turned into an inhuman screech, which Ray Price was satisfied with.

"Your skin is very delicate," he whispered in her ear. "Oil paints will apply well to it."

The girl hardly understood his words, being in a state of shock.

Having separated the skin on the back, Ray stretched the "canvas" in a special frame in front of an ultraviolet lamp, allowing it to dry. The most important thing had already been done; Price had received the necessary canvas for painting. He didn't need the girl anymore. However, it was impossible to simply throw it away. After all, Norway had the lowest crime rate. Price did not intend to raise it with his actions.

Ray gave the girl an injection. He put on a plastic robe, covered his head with a plastic mask and picked up an electric cutter. Small pieces were required for food.

When the job was done, Ray felt a surge of fatigue. Sawing through human bones, even female ones, was no easy task. Having laid out the body in bags, Ray went outside and stopped at the closed door of the stable. Only this door was made of durable steel. There was a latch at face level that opened from Ray's side.

"Are you hungry, buddy?" Price asked as he opened the bolt. From the darkness, there was a whiff of animal hunger. Slowly, he began to dump the contents of the bags through the latch. At first, nothing happened. The horses around went wild, smelling blood, neighing loudly. Price didn't care much about that. He was more interested in what was happening on the other side of the door. He had not dared to go inside for a long time. Through the metal door and the wild neighing of the horses, Price heard the heavy clatter of hooves. The horse outside the door came closer. There was a crunch of bone, followed by the sounds of meat being separated. Human meat. Price taught this horse to eat human flesh. During the feeding process, certain changes occurred in the horse, so when it almost killed Price himself, he decided to feed it through the door. In one evening, a horse could devour a person whole.

Before the horse's diet was changed, it was a draft horse, one of the largest horses of its subspecies. Now Ray couldn't even imagine what the horse was like. He was content with the horse "cleaning up" after him. Curiosity sometimes required you to open the door and look at your creation, but for this, you need to have at least a shotgun with you. He promised to think about it in his spare time.

Having finished, Ray closed the valve again and began whistling a familiar song, contentedly playing with the toothpick in his teeth. Tomorrow he will paint another masterpiece on the finished canvas.

"And I'm telling you that Ray Price is a philanthropist whom Norway has never seen before," one of the bar visitors continued after the races on the estate.

"I agree with you, Sarah," a man of about fifty, wearing fishing boots, supported the woman. The fisherman was already finishing his third glass of beer. "He made roads for us, outside the city, by the way, too."

"You say that because he buys your rotten fish, Karl."

The bar's patrons burst out laughing.

"Nothing rotten! It's freshly *caught*." He was able to pronounce the last word only on the third try.

The bar laughed again.

"I can't understand why you all like him." The owner of the establishment, a portly woman, nervously wiped glasses at the counter. "Even though he plants trees in the city in the spring, donates large sums every year to our orphanage, but a stranger always remains a stranger."

"I agree with you, Elsa," another man in fishing boots supported the hostess. "It is unknown what he did in the States, since he began to spread his popularity here with charitable deeds."

Avalsa sat at a corner table, hidden from the customers by the shadow of the counter. She listened to conversations without taking sides. She just needed information. In these kinds of bars, the truth came out much more often than on the personal Internet pages of celebrities.

City residents had mixed opinions. Some considered him a godsend for a run-down town, while others were not going to take his charitable deeds at face value. They became suspicious. Avalsa understood them completely.

While talking to Price, she felt the evil lurking in his eyes. The way he looked at her also did not escape Avalsa. She considered him a preoccupied old man with a weakness for young people of the fairer sex.

After she finished gathering information, Avalsa paid for breakfast and left the bar in the midst of an argument between Sarah and Karl. She had everything she needed to sneak into the estate tonight and fulfill the order.

Avalsa opened her eyes when everyone in the hotel was asleep. The full moon was shining in the sky, illuminating the deserted streets of the city with its radiance. The lanterns illuminated only the central street; it was dark in the alleys and on the outskirts of the city.

Avalsa dressed all in black. It turned out to be cold outside. To prevent excess clothing from impairing her mobility, she donned special Raven Guild gear: a formfitting jumpsuit with thermal pads. These clothes allowed them to withstand the cold for some time.

Slipping out the second-floor window, she secured another gift from the Raven Guild on her back—an oblong knife without a guard. The handle flowed smoothly into an elbow-long blade. Throwing on a hiking cloak, without attracting the attention of random (unlikely at such a time, but still) passersby, she set off first along the street and then through the forest to the estate of Ray Price.

The night hike did not frighten Avalsa at all. The ominous silence, the lonely creaking of branches, and the bizarre patterns of the crowns illuminated by the full moon did not disturb the scout's trained consciousness one bit. She was headlong into the task, calculating her strength.

Abollo's appearance was too noticeable to get lost among the provincial Norwegians. Therefore, he stayed at the Guild residence. Avalsa will have to deal with the cameras alone.

She approached the edge of the forest. The estate was not yet visible, but Avalsa knew that as soon as she crossed the hill, it would be in the palm of her hand. The scout listened. She had to run through an open area illuminated by the full moon. Of course, the cameras were still a long way off, but she decided not to risk it. Taking off her cloak, she crawled over the hill and hid behind the nearest stone.

The ground cooled her body, slowing down her movements. Leaning against a stone, she began to vigorously rub herself. Avalsa needed a flexible body. The wind rose from the east. The horses, sensing the scent of Avalsa, began to worry. After running along the wall, she found herself on the south side, where the animals could no longer smell her.

After some time, the horses calmed down. Except one. Avalsa, walking past the end wall of the stable, felt her hair stand on end. This condition was new to her. Avalsa hadn't felt such panicky anxiety since she was a teenager. She took a few steps forward, her nervousness suddenly evaporating as her confidence surged within her again. Not understanding anything, Avalsa returned to the strange place. She looked closely but couldn't see anything. Just a wall, grass, and the full moon shining directly overhead. *Time is running out*, she reminded herself, deciding to put such an anomaly out of her mind. Business first; weirdness can wait.

She stretched out on tiptoes, grabbing the edge of the log fence. She pulled herself up. The cameras in this area were facing the other way. Ray Price saved on angular viewing by installing stationary equipment instead of moving equipment.

With the grace of a cat, she jumped over the fence, finding herself on the estate. In short runs, Avalsa moved along the wall, hidden by the shadow of the building. She deftly passed the cameras near the stables, crossed the parking lot, and stopped at the wall overlooking the deep river. The log wall was not particularly difficult, so in just a few moments, she was already looking out the window of the corridor on the second floor.

Avalsa examined the window frame, again making sure that the owner had not installed any alarms on the windows. Opening the plastic window from the outside did not cost her any effort. Barely audible, she leaked into the corridor. The already-quiet steps were muffled by the scarlet carpet. She saw paintings on the walls. Avalsa did not know the author, but she could say that the paintings looked rather strange. She did not see the characteristic thread, like on the linen canvas on which artists usually paint. She didn't notice any more oddities in the paintings, except that the landscape paintings were mediocre But when she stood by the paintings, she was overcome by a depressing feeling. Heavy. As if layer after layer of dirt, pain, and agony were sticking to her. Avalsa could not accurately describe the condition.

She lingered near the paintings much longer than she had expected. However, no one in the house showed signs of life. It was as if there was no one on the floor. Avalsa approached the door of the owner's room. Solid oak door. A classic castle with one secret. After playing with the master keys for a few seconds, Avalsa heard a quiet click in the keyhole. Smoothly pressing the handle, she opened the door just enough for her thin figure to seep inside.

The room was completely dark. Thick curtains covered the window, preventing moonlight from illuminating the room. Avalsa's sensitive ears did not need the lighting to detect that Ray Price was not in the room. She couldn't yet decide whether this was good or bad. Deciding not to waste time searching, Avalsa turned on the flashlight attached to the inside of her palm.

Lighting her feet, she looked around the owner's room. The bed was located opposite the window. A carved chest of drawers occupied most of the opposite wall. To the left of the bed, there was a floor-length mirror with a wooden frame along the edge. The carpets were made of terry pile, in which the feet sink up to the ankles.

What Avalsa was looking for was on the dresser, a few meters from the bed. Her gut feeling was right; people like Ray really do keep things like this close to them. The head of Anubis looked predatorily into the darkness. The eyes of the figurine were made of yellow stone, which reflected the glare of the lantern. Following Clark's instructions, Avalsa took a drape bag from her belt, into which she placed the "top." When she took the figurine of Anubis in her hands, it seemed that his eyes flashed for a moment. Avalsa was not sure whether it was really a flash or just a trick of light on the gem. Something strange was clearly going on at the estate.

Avalsa left the room, carefully closing the door behind her. Having gotten used to the darkness, she noticed as she left that the master's bed was made. So he hadn't gone to bed yet. Trying to figure out where he might be, Avalsa went down to the street from the same window through which she entered. Behind her, the river roared in steady splashes, relaxing her tense nerves. After taking a few steps, Avalsa felt the ground disappear from under her feet. Literally. Without giving in to panic, with long strides she reached the saving shadow from the fence of the stables and hid.

A soft light came from the ground. Whistling contentedly and fingering a toothpick in his teeth, Ray Price came out of the basement. Haste played a cruel joke on Avalsa. She did not have time to find out that the estate had a basement equipped with the latest technology. With a soft rustling sound, the doors automatically closed behind Price, and the street fell into darkness again. Avalsa saw that he had three garbage bags in his hands. She was in no hurry to move, even when Price walked toward her. She was lucky that the owner of the estate did not use the lantern, but decided to reach the island of light on his own. Price passed by just a few steps away. Avalsa wasn't even breathing.

There was nothing suspicious in his behavior. He disappeared into the garage, only to emerge a few minutes later with a shotgun in his hands. He left the garbage bags near the metal door with heavy bolts. While Price was in the garage, Avalsa changed her hiding place and hid on the roof of the stable. From here, there was a good view of the entire yard. Her instinct told her to leave, but curiosity begged her to watch for a couple more minutes.

Ray leaned the shotgun against the wall next to the bags. Having mastered the heavy bolts, he opened the doors. The creaking of the shutters seemed capable of waking up half the estate. Price didn't care much. He peered intensely into the darkness. At the far wall, he could see a scarlet haze, which contrasted brightly with the darkness reigning in the stable. The aura increased in size and looked at Ray with two lights. He felt feverish. In an instant, he was overcome by panic. Despair, pain, agony awoke. Without noticing it, Price dropped to his knees. He forgot to even think about the shotgun.

The heat became more and more unbearable. Beads of sweat flowed down his temples. Price was afraid, but he continued to look at the lights getting closer with every step. He was doused with steam from the air exhaled from his nostrils. You could hear the horse snorting. Others around were raging in fear, wanting to ride away as far as possible.

Just one hit. One blow of the hooves crushed Price's head like an overripe pumpkin. He never had time to use the shotgun. Smelling blood in the bags, the horse left the stable and began to tear them apart, getting to the remains of Ray Price's last victim.

Avalsa saw everything. From start to finish. She wanted to run, to hide away from the estate, but she couldn't. She was overcome by a feeling of fear that had already been present in her life as a teenager.

She again found herself thrown out onto the street, of no use to anyone. Hunger and cold returned to her with renewed vigor. Apathy and fear shackled her legs, making it impossible to escape. When the horse emerged from the stable, she could only watch. From being a scout for the Raven Guild, Avalsa turned into a little girl from an orphanage.

She was horrified by the horse's appearance. This simply could not exist. Instead of hooves, the horse had keratinized three-toed claws. Each breath filled the animal's chest with fire. The horse's croup was covered with tar-colored growth plates, the nature of which Avalsa could not say anything about. The bridge of the animal's nose, like coals, flickered with fire, ready to flare up. On the horse's forehead was an ornate horn, capable of piercing a mature man through and through.

Avalsa couldn't believe this. She just couldn't. It was as if the nightmares that the girl had not had for a long time returned. Having finished devouring the contents of the bag, the horse looked up at Avalsa. As if it knew where she was hiding. The sight of the fire made Avalsa feel hot, burning out her insides, shackling her with fear.

The horse moved toward her, the weight of its powerful body knocking down the log wall of the stable. Avalsa fell to the ground. She only had the strength to raise her head and see the horse's hooves lifting above her head. A picture of Price's head bursting appeared before her eyes. She closed her eyes, not ready to face death from an animal that shouldn't exist.

She was carried to the side. Something hit her forehead hard, but it didn't look like a hoof.

"Are you okay?" rang in her ears, and Avalsa had to open her eyes. She was held in the arms of a man with long hair and shaved temples. His eyes seemed strange, but he no longer looked at her.

Avalsa's confidence returned. Fear and despair had not completely disappeared but were now felt like some kind of obsession. This could be dealt with.

"Let me go." Avalsa broke away from the man's embrace.

"Take the people away and leave yourself," the man said, unwinding the chain from his forearm and drawing an unusually shaped dagger from his hip sheath.

She ignored the first but decided to use the second.

Hans no longer paid attention to the girl. He focused on the creature standing in front of him. The horses in the stables were going wild, making noise. Hans looked into the burning coals of his eyes and felt at the edge of his consciousness how obsession was trying to creep inside. It induced a nightmare and drove him crazy. Exhaling smoke from its nostrils, the horse struck with its hooves and charged. It lowered its head, aiming its ornate horn at Hans's head. Hans ran toward the creature as fast as he could. Not reaching a few meters, he pushed off from the wall and straightened up, letting the dangerous creature pass underneath him. This turned out to be quite difficult, since the horse reached the size of a well-fed bull.

Hans slashed with his Claw while in flight, but the blade only met the resin shell that protected the creature from damage. The horse entered the wall, breaking several logs, and disappeared into the garage. Hans ran after it, not allowing it to escape from the cramped space. While running, Hans pulled out one of the nails and tried to drive it under the creature's left paw. The nail of the Cross of the Savior passed along the armor with a disgusting grinding sound, unable to pierce it. In addition, Hans burned his other hand when he touched the horse's hot chest.

Ignoring the bubbles appearing on his palm, he wrapped the Grail chain around the creature's neck. Hans was a little late, as the horse, rising to its full height, shook its head, throwing off the lasso, and kicked its hooves, aiming at his stomach. All Hans had time to do was point his blade to meet the blow. Instead of broken ribs, he was simply carried to the opposite wall, hitting the back of his head hard against a car wheel.

The horse was prevented from approaching the stunned Hans by a car parked in the garage. Snorting loudly, releasing streams of smoke from its nostrils, the creature pushed the car with its hooves. Tires squeaked as it approached Hans. The toolbox, which stopped the body of the car, prevented Hans from being pressed against the wall. Neighing angrily, the horse ran out of the garage, walking around on the other side.

Hans, having come to his senses, began to climb out of the rubble. As soon as he was on the roof of the car, the wall where Hans had just been cracked, and the creature's horn appeared from it. The logs began to smoke around the horn. The first tongue of flame appeared, flaring up to ever larger sizes. The high temperature did not cause the logs to burn; they immediately melted, instantly turning into ash. A horse's head appeared from a crack in the wall, engulfed in fire. The horn on the head turned fiery white.

Hans lowered himself onto the raging horse from the roof of the car. Using his legs to push off his croup, he ran toward the shore. Hans could not allow the creature to burn everything here. The garage, engulfed in flames, created an ominous halo of a horse. Continuing to exhale coal-black smoke from its nostrils, the horse watched Hans run away. Having no other purpose, the creature rushed after him.

In open space, he had no chance of attacking the horse. Hans only had time to dodge. For a draft horse, it was quite agile.

The moon illuminated the movements of the two, making their shadows gray, stretching their silhouettes. It was a frosty night outside. Whitish steam emanated from the horse's chest and horn.

The creature rushed to attack again. Like a bull, it wanted to pierce Hans. He, in turn, like a conquistador, missed red-hot death at the very last moment. Unwinding the chain, he quickly threw it over the horn, threading the other end through a nail and driving it into the ground. Due to inertia, the horse overturned to the ground. The snow around it hissed, uselessly resisting the fire.

The Grail chain began to glow, doing its job. However, the horse had a certain amount of intelligence. Rising to its hooves, it lowered its head low; and the chain, without encountering any resistance, slid from the horn to the ground, ceasing to influence the creature.

Hans clicked his tongue in frustration. Even though the shell had become much thinner, the Claw still cannot penetrate. He turned to the gentle bank of the river, located a hundred meters away from him. At one point, one idea came along with another.

The horse neighed loudly, again attracting attention. With short zigzag runs, he regained the chain and nail. However, the horse almost crushed its head with its three-toed hooves for this. As a sinker, Hans hooked the Claw to one end of the chain.

In front of the horse, he rotated figure eights and loops, inviting him to rush into the attack again. A hungry creature shouldn't be asked twice. Flames from the chest and bridge of the nose heated the air around the horse. Hans was overcome with warmth, and at the last moment, he went into a somersault a centimeter from the horse's front hooves. He threw the chain of the Grail after the horse. Like a sling, it wrapped around its legs, knocking the monster to the ground again.

Hans fussed around the horse, walking along the sandy shore. Sand was not suitable soil to drive nails into. He found a gap in the armor by accident and, with all his might, placed a nail with a chain link threaded under the jaw. The horse neighed loudly in pain. The flame on the bridge of its nose became even stronger. With smoking hands, Hans held the other end of the glowing chain. From the pierced nose, the red-hot end of a nail was visible, which did not melt, like other metals.

Hans pulled with force. There were ten meters left to the water. For the first three steps, the horse, gripped by pain, gave in; but on the fourth, it dug its hooves into the sand. With short, confident steps, the creature began to step back. The man was clearly inferior to the horse in pulling the chain. Resisting with his whole body, Hans vainly buried his feet in the sand. The horse guessed his plan and moved farther and farther from the water.

Avalsa was running away from the estate. The fire that broke out brought everyone in the area to their feet. There was no need for her to glow. Holding the cloth bag tighter, Avalsa tried not to drop the contents as she walked deeper into the forest. At some point, she stopped. Avalsa found it difficult to overcome her interest, especially when her brain can't answer her questions. Who was this man? Why didn't he feel afraid of the creature she saw for the first time? Where did he even come from? Deciding to calm her thoughts, Avalsa hid the bag near a noticeable tree and ran back.

The fire department of a neighboring city had already arrived to extinguish the fire. Under the general panic, it was easy for Avalsa to rush past without falling under the light of the flashing lights of official cars. She followed the tracks of hooves scorched on the ground.

Hearing the sounds of battle, she fell to the ground, continuing to move more carefully. An unimaginable scene took place on the riverbank. This man fought with the fiery horse as if he was a bullfighter. Constantly avoiding collisions at the last moment, he risked cutting his stomach open in one of these maneuvers. The chain in his hands flared up with a golden light as soon as he threw it on the horse.

It was an unreal picture. Avalsa couldn't believe this was possible. She did not believe in otherworldly forces. How else to call what was now fighting with the man?

Avalsa saw the man pull off a successful move, lassoing the horse and driving a nail through its lower jaw. While an ordinary one would have fallen down dead, this creature only neighed wildly. A man with long hair pulled the chain toward himself, luring the horse closer to the water. Avalsa understood his intention. Fire doesn't like water. She was overcome by an inexplicable desire to help the stranger. As if in approval of her thoughts, the raven above her head cawed contentedly. Avalsa didn't notice any birds in the area except this one. She returned to the estate for the second time that night. As Avalsa expected, a police car was at the gate.

The horse moved back step by step, moving farther from the shore. Hans resisted with all his might, burying himself knee-deep in the sand. Suddenly there was a roar of an engine somewhere very close. An SUV appeared from behind the hill, racing toward them at full speed. A girl with blonde hair was driving. The horse was distracted by the car, and Hans took advantage of this. Pulling strongly, he regained his lost position. Hans saw the girl jump out of the car. Holding the chain taut, he let go at the last moment. The SUV crashed into the horse at full speed, pushing it into the water. A dense cloud of steam rose near the shore.

Without allowing the creature to come to its senses, Hans jumped into the water from the roof of the SUV. The ice water turned into boiling water. He drove two more nails of the Savior's Cross into the horse's smoldering chest. The horse neighed angrily. The armor fell like sticky clay into the darkening water. Hans mounted the creature. With a confident movement, he ripped open the horse's throat with his Claw, barely touching the vertebrae. The horse's wheezing turned into gurgling. In the water, the horse did not resist. The life given after death was leaving it. Hans felt how the body between his legs became Plasticine. He whispered into the horse's ear, "Rest in peace," and then jumped into the cooling water.

The cold air chilled his wet pants, slowing down his movement. Hans didn't pay any attention to it. He watched the creature disintegrate as it floated down the river. Having appeared above the water surface for the last time, the horse disappeared into oblivion. For the first time that night, Hans took a deep breath. He did not notice how tiredness suddenly set in. Turning around on weak legs, he saw the girl standing on the shore. She too watched the creature swim away with mixed feelings on her face.

With every step, Hans froze more and more. Being in the water at this time of year was a challenge. When he approached the girl, she briefly said, "We need to leave." He himself understood this: the fire on the estate attracted too many people. He didn't want to explain why the police SUV was in the water. Having mutually decided to wait with questions, Hans moved with the girl away from the shore.

"I have a camp nearby." The man turned to her after a while of moving through the forest. She looked at him in disbelief. "Away from people," he continued convincingly.

Avalsa couldn't understand why she was following this man. She took the bag with the figurine a long time ago, the order had been completed, and she can take it to the Raven Guild residence. But she hesitated. Avalsa saw him kill the horse. She also saw that the man was frozen. He had saved her life, so Avalsa wanted to make sure he didn't become numb from the cold.

They found themselves in a small clearing hidden by a dense wall of trees. Under the rolling pines, Avalsa saw a small pile of branches. Up close, she saw in these heaps a cunningly laid out hut. A firepit had been built near the entrance, hidden by a wall of brushwood.

While she was looking at the hut, the man had already brought a match, lighting a fire that had been prepared in advance. The fire burned quickly. The branches were dry, so there was almost no smoke from the fire. As she was approaching the fire, Avalsa felt that she would like to warm herself. The man was in no hurry to take off his wet clothes. To her questioning look, he replied, "My clothes are frozen. Let them warm up. I don't want to take them off along with my skin."

Avalsa watched as the man performed the ritual with the weapon. He cleaned the curved dagger of dirt and soot with a whetstone, smoothly running it along the blade. He put the case with nails and the bag with the chain in his backpack, believing that he would no longer need them. Fascinated by his movements, Avalsa pulled a long knife from her sheath. Looking at the glittering blade, she shoved it back in again. Avalsa didn't use it once during the night.

"It's a good blade." The man managed to see her weapon, hiding the dagger in his backpack.

His clothes finally warmed up, and he began to take them off. Burns on his arms and back left by that creature were visible. Avalsa didn't understand the categories, but her blush turned out noticeable. He put on a warm knitted sweater from his backpack and changed into wet jeans. Hans put his shoes closer to the fire, wrapping his bare feet in a blanket.

"What was it?" she finally asked the disturbing question. The man looked at her for a long time. Avalsa did not immediately notice that his eyes glowed in the dark.

"Once upon a time, it was a cavalryman's horse." The man turned back to the fire. "The terrible deeds of that man summoned a spirit that inhabited the horse."

"Scary things?"

"Ray Price fed the remains of the girls to the summoned creature. True, he thought that it was still his horse, and he used the girls' skin to draw perverted pictures."

Avalsa, to her surprise, believed every word he said. She suspected that something was wrong with the retired politician, but she didn't know what it could be. Now she understood why she had a strange feeling of oppression when she looked at the paintings in the corridor.

"This creature could influence consciousness, raising forgotten fears from the depths of the mind, using them against you."

"And who are you?" she asked instead of unnecessary details. Avalsa decided to get to the truth gradually.

"My name is Hans." He smiled, but from fatigue, the smile looked more like a grin. "And I would like to hear your name in response."

"Avalsa," she said displeasedly.

"The water has already boiled, Avalsa. Let's eat."

Hans's supplies were simple but filling. He treated Avalsa to a piece of dried meat and a crust of rye bread. He brewed delicious cocoa in the boiling water. Avalsa could not remember when she drank such a drink. They ate in silence, thinking on their own.

Avalsa digested what she heard. If she had not seen what happened with her own eyes, she would never have believed Hans's story. Do human cruelties and atrocities attract evil spirits? Maybe. Avalsa admitted a similar thought from a corner of her consciousness. The look of the interlocutor's glowing eyes served as proof. Avalsa had enough composure not to look away during the conversation, although it was creepy. It seemed that a hungry wolf in the guise of a man was looking at Avalsa.

Cocoa warmed their chilled body. Animals began to wake up in the forest, marking the beginning of a sunny day.

"I have a request for you, Avalsa." Hans spread the blanket on the ground, preparing for bed. "Wait for me in the room today. I want to meet your mentor."

"A mentor?" Avalsa didn't like it.

"Or to those to whom you are carrying this figurine." He nodded toward the rag bag.

Avalsa was torn by curiosity, so instead of answering negatively, she asked, "What do you need it for?"

"Conversations with new people are always useful," Hans said, covering himself with a second blanket and leaving Avalsa to think alone.

She couldn't understand why she was so curious about this man. Servants of the Raven Guild were prohibited from disclosing their affiliation on pain of death. It turned out that someone let it slip, since he knew something about the Guild. Many questions arose that she wanted answered immediately. Therefore, instead of leaving, Avalsa waited for the agreed time in her hotel room, leaving Hans to spend the night in the forest.

Hans woke up when the sun was at its zenith. The coals had long since burned out, but his shoes had time to dry. After putting on his shoes, he began to break up the camp. The branches were scattered on the ground, and not a trace remained of the cozy hut.

He came out of the coniferous forest; and the landscape around him, along with the weather, changed. The sun was covered with a gray veil, causing the colors of nature to fade. The bare branches of deciduous trees reached toward the sky with their clawed paws. The first buds will not appear soon. The soft pine needles on the ground gave way to rotten leaves, and the smell of herbal decomposition hung in the air.

After some time, Hans found himself on the road. Small neat houses of different colors significantly lifted his mood.

This creature was much stronger than the previous one. If not for an accident, Hans would not have managed it on his own. Human vices feed dark forces. He recognized the stolen figurine. It was part of Anubis's staff. But he couldn't understand why Avalsa's customer needed such an artifact. Hans had no idea who Avalsa was working for, but he suspected that the organization was extremely serious.

While walking through the streets of a Norwegian town, he found the right hotel. He adjusted his backpack on his shoulder, smiling widely at passersby. People around were discussing the fire that had happened in the estate. Hans saw how residents gathered in small groups in the square and along the streets, discussing the possible causes of the fire. As soon as Hans passed by, people fell silent; but as soon as they walked a few steps, the conversations resumed. Norwegians were reserved toward tourists.

As soon as Hans crossed the threshold of the hotel, the foggy sun reappeared in the sky, and the direct rays reflected on the stained glass windows of the room. There was an elderly couple at the registration table, discussing something very quietly. From their peaceful faces, Hans realized that they still loved each other over the years. Smiling bitterly at his thoughts, he combed his hair with his fingers, heading toward them.

The owner did not immediately notice the newcomer.

"Hello. How can I help you?" he asked when Hans was already at the table.

"Good afternoon. A friend of mine stayed with you a couple of days ago. The one with blonde hair. Could you tell me what room she is in?"

The owner exchanged glances with his wife. "You know, no one similar to your description has stayed with us. Despite the small town, we have quite a large flow of visitors. It's impossible to remember them all. Gretta, do you remember anyone?"

The old woman with curly, lush hair thought for a second. Then she took out the logbook. "Do you know exactly when your friend arrived?" Gretta asked, putting on her glasses.

"Unfortunately, no." Hans shrugged his shoulders in annoyance.

He was pleased to communicate with the elderly couple, but he knew that his description was not enough to find Avalsa. There was no such name in the registration book either. Apologizing for the disturbance, Hans turned to leave; but Gretta, having read something, called out to him. "Is your friend a reporter?"

While Hans was pondering his answer, the owner's wife continued, "On Tuesday, a girl reporter, quite nice-looking, stayed with us. Her work is completely exhausting. That's how thin she was." Gretta showed her finger. "But she was discharged in the morning. She said that she had received a report that would raise her fee."

"She was just lucky that she caught a fire in the estate," the owner muttered. "And I wouldn't have gotten anything sensational in our town."

"You know a lot, John," Gretta mimicked him, but Hans had already left them, closing the door behind him.

He realized that Avalsa was the reporter. The bad news was that she checked out this morning. So she didn't wait. Hans plopped down on a park bench, wondering where to look for her now. It was difficult to put his thoughts in order. He couldn't get out of his head the figurine of Anubis and the person who might need it. Hans had no doubt that Ray Price didn't know how to use it. One can only guess whether the customer had the second part of the staff.

Hans was pulled out of his thoughts by a familiar voice.

"You thought I didn't wait for you?"

"I didn't even think about it."

They were silent for some time. The sun warmed up, forcing him to squint. Hans watched the children frolic on the playground.

"Listen, I don't know who you are," Avalsa began, "but what happened at the river made me think about your request. This isn't the first time you've encountered something like this, is it?"

"I won't try to convince you, but 'like this' happens often in this world.'

Avalsa silently took note of this.

"The head of the Guild is now in New York."

"Guilds?"

"The details depend on whether you can convince the head of what you and I saw." Avalsa stood up. "We must hit the road. We're still on time for the last flight. We need to hurry to the airport."

"Night flight?"

"Do you have problems with this?"

Hans looked at Avalsa. There was doubt in his gaze.

"Well, we won't go on foot across the ocean."

"Then you need to stock up on coffee." Hans stood up, took his backpack, and followed his new guide.

The road to New York promised to be difficult.

Chapter

5

They landed as the last stars disappeared from the sky, although in such a metropolis, it is impossible to see anything in the sky due to powerful floodlights, huge high-rise buildings, and a thick layer of smog. Hans felt this, so he tried to breathe every now and then and not deeply.

Avalsa called a taxi straight from the airport and gave the address. The flight exhausted both of them. Hans spent the whole flight fighting sleep. Avalsa took this oddity for eccentricity. On the night flight, everyone on the plane was asleep except him.

As soon as they arrived in the city and got out of the car, their ears became blocked from the sounds of a huge metropolis—car horns, shouts of people in a hurry, barkers at the shops, voices from the speakers advertising various products. In the distance, digital banners of immense size could be seen with an endless stream of floating information. If you have succumbed to such irritants, you may not even notice how tired you are.

"How can you react to all this?" Hans couldn't stand it.

"What are you talking about?" Avalsa was completely immersed in her thoughts, and Hans's voice distracted her.

"How can you not get lost in this atmosphere?"

"Oh, you've never been to a big city," she concluded.

"I try to avoid them. Evil spirits also try to avoid such . . . noises." Hans took a long time to find the last word. "So work appears mainly on the outskirts."

"This is where we need to go," Avalsa said, going down the steps to the subway.

Hans had to strain all his attention so as not to lose sight of the girl. People seemed to be walking in one continuous stream, trying to take away, drown in themselves. Hans had to be resourceful to keep up with Avalsa. She felt like a fish in water here.

There were no empty seats in the subway car. There was no question of standing comfortably in the carriage. But Hans did not complain or show it. It seemed as if he was hearing the roar of an accelerating train for the first time.

Avalsa was annoyed by everyone around her. Her discipline was enough to stoically withstand clumsy pokes and shoves from all sides. You always need to blend in with the crowd. However, with Hans, who never parted with a huge backpack, it was impossible to be invisible. And she had to endure this too.

They came out next to one of the landmarks of New York—the Empire State Building. Hans tried to determine the height of the legendary building.

"If you stare at everything like that, then you can forget about the contents of your pockets." Avalsa was beginning to get annoyed by Hans's reaction to his surroundings. "The fluidity of the crowd allows you to rob people right on the street."

"You learned your craft from people like me, right?" Hans smiled benevolently, letting her go ahead at the green traffic light. Avalsa did not answer. She remembered her childhood, when she took her first steps in the Raven Guild.

"If you want to be the best, learn to fleece the best," Clark told the fiery, arrogant little girl, showing the rich on Wall Street as victims. Hair waxed, expensive branded trouser suits, always with leather briefcases. Almost three decades had passed, but the habits of stock exchange brokers had remained the same.

"We're almost there," Avalsa answered, walking around one of them. She gave up pickpocketing a long time ago. They reached the next landmark of the city—Central Park. It was the only oasis of greenery in a cesspool of glass-concrete skyscrapers.

Inside, the park was dotted with many paths, jogging paths, and walking sidewalks. Benches of various sizes and patterns were quite common. During the daytime, especially if the day was sunny, it was impossible to find free seating. Hans cheered up considerably, feeling the dense foliage of the crowns above his head instead of a cloud of smog.

"It's easier to breathe here."

"Of course, it is."

The building opposite overlooked the park. In front of them stood a multistory hotel that could accommodate hundreds of visitors. Made of glass and concrete, the structure was no different from others. But Hans saw a flag waving at the top that did not look like the US banner. It was impossible to see what exactly was on the flag from such a distance.

"I don't intend to stay at the hotel." Hans watched as Avalsa headed toward the spiral door of the entrance.

"Just be a little patient, okay?" Avalsa wanted to quickly enter the residence, deal with the necessary matters, and be in the restroom.

They were greeted by a huge hall in the Gothic style, which turned out to be filled with people.

"Are we in the underground again?"

"There is such movement here all the time." Avalsa had already dived into the crowd, making her way to the registration desk.

There were four performers at the table, dressed in elegant tuxedos. The clothes matched the hotel interior. In the corner, there were musicians playing live music from famous performers of the century before last. Lighting around was provided by round several-tier chandeliers suspended from the ceiling on powerful chains. The dome-shaped ceiling was buried in twilight. The marble floor was covered with a scarlet runner, dividing the hall in half, separating the elevators from the waiting chairs. Next to the musicians was the hotel bar with several dozen seats along the counter. All the chairs were occupied.

Hans's guesses were incorrect. Instead of the check-in desk, Avalsa made her way to the building's elevators. There were four elevator doors in the hotel, but only one of them had the same design as the interior. There were no buttons at the entrance to open the door. However, Avalsa stood opposite and began to wait. For some time nothing happened, but soon something clicked, and the door jingled, inviting entry.

"This is the only elevator that goes above the twentieth floor."

"Twenty floors of cover, you mean?" Hans was surprised.

Instead of answering, Avalsa just shrugged. The elevator signaled their arrival on the twenty-first floor.

"Aren't you afraid that someone might use the stairs?" Hans was curious.

"There are no stairs leading up to this floor." Avalsa walked along the corridor, where completely different people were present.

They sat in armchairs and talked loudly. Some were walking around with luggage; others were just getting an assignment. Hans saw one of them holding a pistol, the other a heavy hammer. There were those who preferred a modernized crossbow as a burden.

Hans suspected that Avalsa was one of them. To confirm his guess, those around her recognized her; some even smiled welcomingly. However, the overwhelming majority only looked at them gloomily.

Everyone noticed Avalsa in the company of a stranger. Particularly nervous people even freed their weapons from their holsters.

"Don't worry, as long as you're with me, the storm troopers won't come at you." Avalsa caught his gaze. Hans nodded no longer to her, but to his own thoughts.

Those present sat in groups, as if everyone belonged to their own clan. Hans noticed that there were few like Avalsa in the hall, with catlike grace and silent steps. There were also those who wore new-style bastard swords on their belts. He studied with great interest the high-carbon steel of the blade, sharpened by laser technology. The melee weapons really looked amazing.

Seeing that her companion was interested in people with edged weapons, Avalsa commented, "These are the swordsmen—the most useless in the Guild."

"Why is this?"

"Because there are almost no orders for them. In the modern world, people no longer cut with swords or stab with spears. Progress has come quite far from the use of hardware. They will only become cannon fodder if they are sent to order along with the storm troopers." Avalsa saw that Hans was looking at one with a terrible burn on half his face, without an ear, and added, "Although some are trying. Do you see what they look like? Like actors from some dramatic theater."

"Do they handle weapons the same way as they look?" Hans examined the leather doublets and high boots with thin soles, as if they were a stain of a bygone era in this room. He had respect for them. They didn't care about Hans.

"Avalsa!" The girl turned toward the voice at the same time as her companion. A girl a head taller than Avalsa, with the same gait and grace, called out to her.

"Chloe." Avalsa smiled in response. "How long have you been at the residence?"

The girl brushed an unruly strand of brown hair out of her green eyes, smiling radiantly. "Since yesterday. I was nearby, in Los Angeles. I even managed to visit the local beach."

"I have no doubt." Avalsa noticed the tan on the girl's bare arms. Chloe preferred crisp white tank tops, so she wore a sports top underneath.

"Who is this with you? He's not one of us." They were more like storm troopers, but they looked at him like a wolf and didn't recognize him as one of their own.

Hans smiled disarmingly. Chloe returned the smile, not understanding the reason.

"Is Clark at home?" That was Avalsa's entire answer. In her gaze, Hans saw a promise to tell Chloe everything, but later.

"He is at his place all the time. Unlike him, we work," Chloe complained, walking away. She understood Avalsa's hint.

They were about to climb the steps to the head of the Raven Guild, but Clark himself went down to the new arrivals. Hans appraisingly examined the stately man with excellent posture, slowly walking toward them. Clark was wearing a light leather coat matched with a tie of a similar color. The shirt and trousers were black. Hans concluded that such a combination of colors would not allow one to get lost in the crowd but rather stand out. He saw that Avalsa shared the same thoughts on this matter.

Clark stopped three steps from Hans. An awkward silence reigned in the hall. Strangers never came to the Guild, so everyone awaited the development of events with interest.

"Master Clark." Avalsa was the first to break the silence, addressing the head of the Guild by rank, "he asked to meet with you, claiming that he knows the true meaning of the item from my assignment." Avalsa deliberately did not talk about the figurine in front of everyone. Professional ethics.

"Then you did the right thing by bringing him here," Clark replied, smiling with his eyes. "Francis, kill him."

Avalsa wanted to object, but a burly bearded man emerged from the crowd, pushing the stranger away from the others. The crowd formed a circle inside the hall.

With one swoop, Francis drew the katana from its woven sheath. Hans dodged the blow, throwing his backpack aside. He was not going to use his weapon in front of everyone.

Swing, swing, blow. Hans avoided the attacks more and more slowly. He had exhausted his strength during the flight and wanted to lie down and rest. Instead, he was forced to dance, watching as the swings of Francis's high-tech blade passed by mere millimeters.

The swordsman held his weapon very confidently. With a deceptive movement of his hand, he almost reached his opponent's neck. His comrades considered this technique to be fatal and sure to achieve its goal. With a powerful blow of his knuckles, Hans hit Francis's hand, forcing him to unclench his hand with the weapon. However, the blade did not have time to fall to the floor. Hans caught it in the air, at the same time picking up Francis, who had lost his balance, with his foot. Taking the katana with a reverse grip, he pinned the warrior's palm to the wooden parquet. An indignant cry of pain echoed throughout the hall. Those present looked at Clark.

The head of the Guild thoughtfully tapped his finger on the corners of his lips.

"Fine. Come with me. Lucius, help Francis. And your guest, Avalsa, interested me." Clark turned to her. Avalsa nodded in agreement. Francis was considered the best swordsman in the Guild.

As soon as Hans picked up his backpack and followed Clark, Chloe approached Avalsa from behind.

"Tell me, friend."

"Which version should I tell you?"

"Tell me the truth."

"Then let's sit down." Avalsa invited her to the vacant sofa.

"And what does it turn out to be?" After Avalsa told her everything, Chloe, watching as Francis was given first aid, asked, "Does the supernatural exist?"

"Chloe, I'm not sure.

"You are not sure?" Chloe moved closer, switching to a whisper. "You saw this creature live. This Hans also confirmed that there are a lot of 'like this' walking around the world and hiding in places with no civilization. And then you say you're not sure?"

Avalsa looked at her friend. She hesitated to answer. Chloe, unlike Avalsa, believed in the existence of everything. She didn't even need confirmation. She took what she heard on faith.

"It was discouraging for me. After such news, you will begin to look at your night shadow with caution. And you know what a night friend is for us."

"Our nurse, cover, and savior. Don't think that I forgot, Avalsa." Chloe was referring to their difficult childhood.

They were silent for some time.

"I've never seen anyone do this to Francis." Chloe decided to change the subject. "Except you, of course. You won't find such resourcefulness even among our people, not to mention swordsmen."

"I saw his dexterity back in Norway. Here he only confirmed himself in the eyes of Clark. Everyone knew that the fight with Francis served as a test, except Hans.

"I'd like to hear what they're talking about."

"What, what? I don't have the slightest desire to know such things." Chloe waved her hands in protest. "It's more expensive for myself. Of the two of us, only you have excessive curiosity."

Avalsa did not answer. She just looked toward the exit where Hans and Clark had disappeared some time ago.

Chapter

6

Morning came quickly. The hum of cars could be heard outside the window. In New York, the noise of cars is 24/7.

The alarm sound brought Rick out of another nightmare. This time the sheet was wet with sweat. Rick got out of bed to ventilate the stuffy room. The hum of cars from the open window became even louder.

"Good morning, New York," he said from the fifth floor into the void. The alarm clock read six forty-four. It's time to put on coffee and take a contrast shower.

The coffee was brewing as Rick walked out of the bathroom. He now felt much more alert. Even glimpses of logical thoughts appeared. Mechanically tying his tie over his crisp white shirt, Rick thought about the day ahead. He looked at himself in the mirror. That's another view. Three-day stubble, sunken cheeks, tousled hair, a half-mad look—the best image of a criminal detective.

Already going down the steps of the apartment building, Rick remembered that he had forgotten to make the bed. It's a small thing, but it left an unpleasant aftertaste of disorganization on his soul. "The day promises to be interesting," he responded to his thoughts.

Rick walked up to his car, opened the door, but immediately slammed it shut as soon as the app on his phone showed heavy traffic on the street. He had to walk. The clock showed seven fifteen.

On the way, Rick drank another cup of coffee and ate a donut. He decided not to think about the nightmare. A screaming girl, bleeding, begging for help, kept popping into his head. Rick had been tasting blood in his mouth all morning, as if it were spraying from a severed artery. He took a larger sip, washing away the disgusting sensation.

"And how does Rick Castel himself get to work on foot?" an officer asked, standing next to him in the police headquarters.

"Traffic jams, Jerry, traffic jams," Rick greeted his colleague.

"You have a flashing light in the car. Turn it up louder and you can drive, pushing the traffic apart, like Moses.

"In New York?" Rick said ironically, and both officers laughed. "Is everything the same?"

"Everything is the same," answered Jerry, a tall middle-aged African American, as he watched Rick Castel walk up the steps to the office.

The clock on his hands showed eight thirty in the morning. The New York Police Department's workday had begun.

Rick walked past the booths where operators took emergency calls, scouting for potential crimes. He walked past the desks of detectives raising their hands in greeting, without raising their head from the table littered with papers.

Castel entered his office, on the glass door of which was the inscription "Senior Detective." Before he had time to sit down in a chair, there was a knock on the door, before someone entered.

"Rick, they gave me the case, but after reading it, I realized that this is your forte."

Rick looked at the newcomer. It was John Walk, a crime detective. He had worked in this department long enough that every conversation began with something important. Rick thought this was a good trait in a person. Without further questions, he took the file and started to read it. Both detectives stood in the middle of the room.

"A brutal murder," John commented after waiting for Rick to finish reading.

Castel looked at the photograph of the girl. There were lacerations visible on the body, as if she had been cut with a dull knife. All three cuts started from the neck, cutting diagonally across the body.

"Where and when?" Rick asked hoarsely, putting his coat back on.

"Tonight, a few blocks from the station."

"You'll come with me," Rick said, and his soul became restless. This girl was from his dream; she was screaming for help.

The gray walls of two adjacent houses hid an alley within them. Cold, unfriendly. Today there were a lot of people crowded in there. Officers were stationed around a perimeter surrounded by yellow tape. Even during the day, the alley was dark. To be sure, Rick adjusted the six-shooter Magnum in his handy holster.

"Well, what do you have here?" He asked the usual question to analysts.

"It's strange," one of them answered. "It's like a killer fell from the moon."

Castel walked along the trail of blood starting from the middle of the alley.

"This is the first strange thing," the analyst continued. "The trail starts right in the center. It's not clear where it comes from."

Rick found the victim near the trash cans. He looked at the girl for a long time. Her frozen face with wide eyes screamed in horror. What he saw made the hair on his head stand up. John, accustomed to human cruelty, swore loudly. The girl was in a pool of blood, which had already become a thin film. In her hand, she was clutching a phone with the flashlight on. What they saw turned out to be even worse than in the photo.

Rick squatted down, taking a closer look at the wounds. The edges turned out to be really torn and open.

"They were applied while the girl was conscious." John broke the silence.

"She couldn't lose him from shock." Rick nodded. "What are the reasons for the murder?"

"This is the second strange thing," the analyst answered. "Her purse was next to her. Her cash remained intact, in the wallet, along with all the credit cards."

"It turns out that a maniac has appeared in the city?" John voiced the general thought.

Rick silently returned once more to the beginning of the blood trail. He looked around. There was nowhere to hide in this section of the alley. Castel looked up. On both sides of the walls, air conditioners and hoods were visible, located on each floor. No stairs, no balconies.

"She knew the killer." Rick put forward his hypothesis when John approached him. "There's nowhere to hide in the alley, except for those tanks, but they are far from the beginning of the trail. There's no place to jump from above." He pointed to the walls. "If the killer had been a stranger and started coming at her from the beginning of the alley, she would have shined a flashlight on him from her phone, turned around, and run away. However, the wounds were inflicted from the front. This means the girl knew the killer."

"Sounds like a working hypothesis," John agreed.

"Do you want to hear the third strange thing?" The analyst approached them, taking off his gloves. He finished examining the wounds. "Judging by the edges of the cuts and the degree of blood clotting, it follows that the wounds were inflicted at the same time."

"All three at the same time?" asked John Walk.

"For a more accurate answer, an examination should be carried out in the laboratory, but according to the primary data, yes." The analyst nodded.

"We're done here." Rick turned to exit the alley. "The examination report should be on my desk by evening. John, look up the archives. Compare similar murders in nearby states." After waiting for an affirmative nod from both, Castel left the alley.

On the way to the station, Rick had an uneasy feeling. A killer maniac in the city center? If this was so, then they should expect another victim. And he was unable to prevent it. There were too few clues in this case. Just weirdness.

As soon as Rick entered the police station, someone called him in an authoritative tone. "Castel, come to my office."

Before entering, he automatically read the sign on the door: "Police Chief Jim Rober" Taking a short breath, Rick pushed the door open.

"Homicidal maniacs in my city?" The boss was indignant. He shook his strong, too-hairy hands in indignation. Castel realized that John Walk had shared the information. "It's outrageous! Tell us the details of the case."

"Chief Rober, by evening I could provide you with a written report of what happened," Castel began, but Jim interrupted him.

"To hell with the reports!" He sat down in a chair, making it clear that he was listening.

"The victim, Susan Moon, was twenty-eight years old. She worked in a nightclub, pouring drinks. According to witnesses, she left work at half past two, after midnight. She often walked home through that alley. The killer not only knew her, but also studied her habits. Residents of a neighboring house heard a scream at two forty-eight. The witness, suffering from insomnia during the full moon, came out to see the cause of the scream.

"How brave." Jim chuckled. Both realized that he was the main suspect.

"As soon as he saw the girl lying in her own blood, he vomited, and then he called the police."

"Also impressionable," Rober responded once again.

"At the moment," Rick concluded the report, "officers are interviewing witnesses, and Detective John Walk is comparing the murder with similar ones in neighboring states. Perhaps the killer is a stranger. Or he travels."

Jim Rober was silent for a while. He lit a half-smoked cigar, and the smell of expensive tobacco floated through the office.

"We need to find this maniac as quickly as possible," Rober began with the obvious. "The press is probably screaming with delight. Here's how we'll do it: you'll interview witnesses personally. I need to be sure that there will be no one else in the club except our guys. Lousy journalists distort any information they hear in their own way." After thinking a little, he added, "I'll speak to the press tomorrow. Until then, do not disclose the details of the case to anyone."

Rick realized he was done with the instructions, so he stood up to leave the office.

"Rick," the boss called to him at the exit, "we have to find this son of a bitch as quickly as possible."

Castel said nothing. Leaving the office, he plunged headlong into work. The search began.

"I tell you again, Susie was a great person. She could get along with everyone, even her bosses. She's smiling all the time, always in a good mood." Rick had been questioning the witness for twenty minutes, Susan Moon's partner at the bar, a bald man with tunnels in his ears and black-framed glasses.

The Paradise nightclub was closed and cordoned off for the questioning of employees. Castel considered this idiotic, since the interrogation should be conducted in a neutral environment, when some information could also be unobtrusively extracted from visitors. However, Rick understood why the room was being cordoned off. The journalists' tongues were of no use here. Therefore, with an impartial air, he interrogated the staff one by one.

After some time, Rick sat at one of the tables, next to the dance floor, digesting the information received.

Susan Moon was considered a cheerful girl. At least that's what it seemed to others. She's not an envious person and had no ill-wishers. She got along with all kinds of people. Rick called these people "icebergs." Nothing was visible on the surface; you needed to dig.

He rubbed his temples, relieving the tension. He really wanted to sleep. He couldn't get the image of Susan begging for help out of his head. Rick did not consider himself a psychic, much less a medium. He could not explain why he dreamed of a girl he had never seen before. Rick also couldn't say why she was killed. John was still comparing this case with others, but Rick guessed that this would not yield anything. The murder smelled "new." Jim Rober felt it too, so he sent him here to ward off the local reporters.

He was pulled out of his thoughts by a policeman's voice.

"Officer, there's a reporter on the street, trying to get in. She says she knows you, and you gave her permission. Before letting her in, I decided to check with you to see if you really know each other."

"Stacy," Rick muttered through his teeth, standing up, "and you'll go far, Suspicious Officer."

Rick went outside, where a girl in a beige coat stood near the entrance to the Paradise nightclub.

"Well, it's Rick Castel himself, surrounded by guard dogs. I just have to get inside."

"Stacy Richie, just as disrespectful to law enforcement," Rick remarked sourly, although it was clear from their eyes that both were glad to see each other. "You only have an 'obligation' to observe law and order. Why did you come?"

"Actually, I was going to Starbucks for a cup of coffee, when I saw several officers of the law at the entrance to Paradise"—Stacy deliberately emphasized the last word—"standing with a very important look. I thought that something had happened at the club and my help was needed to figure it out. After I learned from the officer that you were inside, I wanted to say hello to you. I would have killed two birds with one stone at once.

"You don't go to Starbucks with a camera." That was Rick's entire answer. He didn't believe a single word the reporter said.

"Come on, Rick, let me in." Stacy Richie's face now became pleading. "I'm broke. I need a sensational article. New York is a big city, but journalists in it, like scavengers, rake everything without leaving a trace. I need an article," she said with emphasis.

"And still no." Rick crossed his arms over his chest.

Each time he watched with pleasure the performance of one actor. Stacy Richie. Hot brunette from the Bronx. Her curly locks cascaded over her shoulders. The charming gaze of green eyes could drive particularly impressionable and unprepared people crazy. With an excellent command of facial expressions and beautiful facial features, Stacy could persuade anyone.

"Come on." She clicked her tongue. "Do you really want my premature death? The boss will skin me alive."

"If he weren't gay, you could have persuaded him."

Stacy chuckled. She did not confirm his words but did not deny it either.

"I heard a woman a couple of blocks from here claims that she saw a yeti sneak into the store and destroy all her property." Rick's eyes smiled. "Even a trace remained."

"This woman was taken by your colleagues two hours ago. You need to pay your bills, not steal from yourself by relying on insurance. Okay, if you don't want to let me in, then let me invite you to have a drink sometime." Now it was Stacy's turn to cross her arms over her chest.

"Maybe. Somehow today Robert leaves me on night duty."

"But I don't go to bed at nine o'clock either." Richie raised an eyebrow, and Rick smiled for the first time.

"I'll take that into account." Rick turned to leave, making it clear that the conversation was over.

Rick had known Stacy for a long time. They studied at the university together. Together they skipped lectures, went to the movies, and walked around the park.

Fifteen years had passed since that moment. Much had already been forgotten. And two years ago, she appeared in New York as a journalist. Each time they wanted to say a lot to each other when they met, but professional ethics and personal ego did not allow it.

With similar thoughts, Rick entered the club, continuing to guard the "sensational article."

The sun went below the horizon an hour ago. People were returning from work, the streets were bustling. Rick looked at the passersby from the second floor of the building with a detached look.

He never learned anything new about Susan Moon. No one wanted her dead, and she did not communicate with suspicious individuals. However, she was killed. Cruelly.

John Walk called, reporting what Castel already knew. "I didn't find any similar murders in neighboring states. But what's interesting, Rick," he said into the phone in a tired voice, "is that in 1956 in New York, a man was found with a torn larynx, as if he had been cut with a dull knife. Three blades at the same time. Moreover"—John did not allow Castel to object—"such killings continued for a week. The victims came from different genders, ages, and nationalities. No external resemblance was identified. I looked for what could connect them, and I found"—a triumphant voice was heard in the receiver—"all the victims were connected by the time of the murder. They were all killed between two and three o'clock in the morning. The killer was never found."

"John, you did a colossal job, bringing up archives from so long ago." Rick didn't even know where to start. "But this is nonsense. Think for yourself: if, hypothetically, Susan Moon was killed by the same maniac as in 1956, then our suspect must be over eighty. There aren't that many people living in New York. Were there any later cases?"

"No." The voice on the phone seemed muffled. Rick realized that he had offended his colleague.

"Thank you anyway for the information received." But Castel's answer was only beeps.

It sounded truly unthinkable. Rick heard his partner on the phone, who spoke about an incident from the past. It seemed to him that for a second, he believed in the veracity of the information. It turned out that the suspect was an eighty-year-old man who had retained excellent body physique? Rick shook his head, clearing his thoughts.

His wristwatch showed eleven forty-four. An officer approached the table. "Mr. Castel, Chief Robert sent us to relieve you."

Rick looked at the guy. He was from the homicide department and liked to work the night shift. Rick didn't remember his name. He nodded gratefully to his colleague, getting up from the table. He took his cloak from the chair and went outside.

His head felt heavy with thoughts. Without thinking about the consequences, Rick took out his phone and dialed a number.

"Hello?" came from the receiver after several rings.

"Can I still take advantage of your offer?"

"Have you decided to satisfy the lady yet?" The voice was cheerful. "In forty minutes at a bar north of Central Park."

"Okay." Rick liked businesswomen.

The night air was filled with autumn freshness. Rick exhaled small clouds of steam into the darkness of the park. He decided to take a shortcut through the jogging path. At such a time, all the athletes were at home and had their ninth dream, because the next day they needed to go to work. Rick raised his head, trying to see the stars. The sky was covered with a black shroud, and all that the policeman could see was the full moon hanging low on the horizon.

Three people were hiding behind a tree. As soon as Rick passed by, two went behind him, and the third came out to meet him.

"Are you walking far?" The guy smelled of fumes. Under his hat, he hid his unwashed long hair.

Rick thought he was underage. He didn't answer and decided to wait for events to develop.

"What is it? Did you shit your pants?" asked a voice behind him, and all three laughed nervously.

Rick had heard enough, so he hit one of them in the bridge of his nose with the butt of his Magnum. Blood flowed from the guy's nose, and he sank to the ground, losing consciousness.

"He has a gun!" exclaimed the second, and the would-be robbers scattered, leaving their comrade.

The guy in the hat seemed to have forgotten about everyone; all he cared about was his broken nose.

Rick squatted down and addressed him, "Can you go?" The guy heard the question for about the third time, followed by an uncertain nod. "Then I don't want to see you here. Get out of here!" With a final exclamation, Rick raised the guy to his feet, who immediately trotted off home to his parents. Rick had no desire to arrest the guy for assaulting a police officer. If something is stuck in your head, then you won't do such stupid things again. He watched as the boy ran away, holstering his Magnum.

"You're unpunctual as always, Castel." Stacy was indignant. "I've been waiting for you for fifteen minutes."

"It only makes you more beautiful." Rick smiled charmingly. He didn't want to make excuses about what happened. "The evening cold is hardening."

"That's for sure." Stacy shrugged her shoulders in her sheepskin coat.

They went into a bar located in the basement. At such times, the room was filled with a sufficient number of visitors. Many of them lived on the floors below in this very house.

Rick helped Stacy take off her sheepskin coat. The sweet scent of perfume filled his nostrils. Rick barely suppressed his desire to inhale her scent closer. Stacy Richie wore a long chunky knit dress that hugged her chiseled waist and shapely hips. For the first time, Rick felt ashamed of his wrinkled shirt and dusty shoes. After straightening his tie, he sat down next to her at the table with a businesslike look.

"You will not believe me, but today after work, I'm as hungry as a coyote."

"A late-night snack is always welcome." Stacy also took the menu. "Especially if it's harmful to your figure."

They were silent for some time. Each of them was figuring out where to start. The waiter brought their drinks. Stacy ordered a margarita, and Rick settled for a double whiskey, neat. Waiting for their order had become more fun.

"How was your working day?" she began from afar.

"Quite tiring."

"Because ours bothered yours?"

"On the contrary," Rick replied, taking a sip, "no one even came in after you. Apparently, the vultures had enough of the body in the alley, which they managed to capture. By the way, where were you at that moment?"

"Mom's." Stacy clearly didn't like this topic, because she missed such material.

Silence reigned again.

Soft music was playing from the speakers; the visitors, already tired, were finishing off the remains of their strong drinks. Some were getting ready to leave. Their food finally arrived.

"Bon appétit." With these words, both greedily plunged their utensils into the meat, cutting it into juicy pieces.

"Listen, Stacy." Rick took a second sip of whiskey. "No matter how much you bat your eyes and ask little questions, I really can't say anything about this case. Everything is too confusing and serious. What I can say with confidence is that this is not the last murder, so don't go to your mom in the morning anymore."

Stacy Richie didn't say anything. She knew how to play this kind of game. She pretended not to be interested in the information, waiting for Rick to continue. Rick read her cunning tactics, so he just smiled, taking a sip from his glass and not saying another word.

He read it. He read it like everyone else. Rick knew that Stacy valued her work above all else. For the sake of a good article, she was ready to do anything, go anywhere. The true quality of a careerist. But there was something about her that Rick liked. More than once, watching carefully, Rick tried to discern the real her, without unnecessary clichés.

"Rick, when you look at me like that, you scare me." There was not a shadow of fear in her eyes, only mischief.

The meeting passed without touching on unnecessary topics. No one wanted to seem defenseless in front of others; they valued the feeling of independence too much.

"I was pleased to hear 'nothing' from you." Stacy extended her hand as a sign of farewell.

"I was glad to share this with you." He shook her hand in response. The handshake did not last long. Unable to bear it anymore, Rick pulled the girl toward him, kissing her greedily. For the first seconds, Stacy resisted; but then, opening her lips, she responded to the passion.

The French kiss turned out to be hot and exciting for both. The autumn night no longer seemed so cold and lonely. Two figures merged under a lonely streetlight of a deserted New York street. It was two twelve.

—m—

Rick woke up in his apartment to the terrible sound of his alarm clock. He was tormented by nightmares again. The ringing phone did not allow him to collect his thoughts.

"Rick, this is John." The detective's voice sounded tense. "Another murder. This is our maniac. Come quickly. I'll send the address to your phone."

Rick mumbled something affirmative, getting out of bed. He only had enough time to wash himself and leave the apartment. There was no need to get dressed. For some reason, he slept dressed. He decided to grab some coffee on the way.

Rick walked and replayed last night in his head. After the kiss, Stacy invited her over. Everything continued there. Rick held trembling body in his hands and could not get enough of her. Exciting sighs while kissing breasts, stroking bare thighs. Rick forgot the last time he was with a real woman, passionate, insatiable. He even regretted leaving. The image of Stacy sleeping peacefully on burgundy sheets was in front of his eyes. But the vision turned out to be short-lived. There was a metallic taste in his mouth. The nightmare appeared in his head again.

A man running into the darkness from someone. He didn't look around, didn't waste precious seconds. He tried to hide in the park.

Fool. Death fell upon him from above. Splashes like a fountain watered the yellowed grass.

Rick had a headache. With an effort of will, Rick drove away the pulsating nightmare. He had never heard men scream in fear like that. The scream was in his ears when he entered Central Park and saw a large crowd of people.

Everyone was there: reporters, journalists, police. The police pushed the others back with protective tape and dispersed around the perimeter, not letting anyone in. Rick saw Stacy in the crowd. It was not clear from her facial expression whether she saw him. He approached an officer.

"Detective Castel," the officer greeted, letting him through the fence, "Detective Walk is already there."

Rick nodded silently, throwing his half-drunk coffee into the trash. His mood was bad.

The victim was under a tree. The body was in an unnatural position and looked terrifying. The blood around only increased the effect of horror. The taste of blood in his mouth became stronger.

"Rick, look." John Walk, as soon as he noticed Rick, immediately bent over the body. The entire right side, from neck to shoulder, was a bloody mess. The blue of the bone was visible from it. "The victim was attacked from above."

"I would say collapsed."

"I agree. And bones of the victim were broken, when falling."

"He now looks like a huge spider," the criminologist intervened in the conversation.

Rick turned to him. "Tell me something about the case."

"The victim was killed at three forty in the morning. The murder weapon is unclear to me. It was as if he had been cut with three knives at the same time."

The detectives looked at each other. Rick was not interested in such information. With gloved hands, Rick turned the victim's head. The victim's eyes were wide open in horror. His pupils looked up. Without explaining anything, Rick climbed along the spreading branches of the tree.

Rick noticed a footprint five meters above the ground. He observed three parallel grooves on the branch. Rubbing them thoughtfully, Rick looked down, wondering something. After descending and not paying attention to the questioning glances, he carefully examined the soil. There were no traces around to catch on. Of course, it was already too late to identify them, since too many people had crowded together.

"Was he an athlete?" Rick pointed to the sneakers.

"A lawyer. Jonathan Martello, originally from Italy."

"I heard about him," John responded, "a prominent lawyer. In addition to winning cases, he was famous for his strict adherence to a sports regime."

"Jogging is lethal for me, not to mention getting up at three in the morning," the criminologist intervened again.

"John, what's your version?" Rick didn't listen to the criminologist; he was interested in the detective's opinion.

"The guy was going for an evening jog, after which he decided to stay with his girlfriend. This is indicated by marks on the neck from kisses, and if you look at the back, you can see fresh vulgar scratches. Then he decided to take a shortcut through the park, where the killer was guarding him. He was waiting for him on the tree. As Jonathan passed underneath him, the killer came down from above, inflicting fatal wounds. I can't say where he disappeared. There were no traces on the ground."

"Did you arrive here before the police?"

"Yes." John was not in the habit of lying. "I found the murdered man on the way to work. I wanted to come earlier to finish my report. Instead, I hung around here, waiting for the forensics."

"He didn't plan to go through the park." After listening to John's version, Rick began his own. "Fear brought him here. And legs. He saw the killer and even tried to escape from him. Martello was caught near this tree. But he didn't wait for him."

"Murderer?"

"Yes, he chased after him, throwing Jonathan into panic."

"But the tree, Rick," John began, but Rick stopped him.

"That's right, the tree. The height from the ground is almost five meters. I don't think the killer could have jumped from such a height without hurting himself."

"And why even climb on it?"

It was difficult for John Walk to believe this, but he believed.

"Perhaps the effect of surprise." Rick himself hadn't figured it out yet. He needed more time.

Before his eyes, Jonathan Martello was writhing in agony, and someone was hiding in the shadow of a tree. Rick blinked a few times, and his vision went away. His headache got worse.

"Rick, are you okay?" John noticed a change in Rick's behavior.

"We're done here. John, can I talk to you alone?"

"We need to meet after work," Rick began when the detectives were alone. "The murders are quite strange, and the situation is far from under control. We don't even have any clues or traces. It's as if the killer was walking on air. Remember what happened to Susan Moon. The trail of blood began from the middle of the alley. Here, besides the blood, there is only one trace, on a branch; and I think it was left by the killer. But he's five meters from the ground, John." Rick switched to a whisper. "No person in their right mind would jump from such a height. Moreover, without damaging anything."

"Okay, Rick, we'll meet after work." The murders also seemed strange to John. "What should we say to Robert?"

"As always." With these words, Rick left the crime scene.

Chapter

7

Evening came faster than expected. Rick was heading to the appointed bar, located at the end of the street. On the way, he thought about Martello. Jim Rober didn't manage to say anything sensible. Naturally, he didn't like the fact that no evidence, suspects, or leads were found. He liked the mysterious footprint on the tree even less. Having nothing better to do, Jim sent Rick to question Jonathan's girlfriend, but she didn't say anything useful. The girl cried throughout the conversation. It was clear from the expression on her face that she loved the murdered man. They even wanted to get married.

After leaving her a business card in case she remembered something, Rick went back to the station, intending to work in his office. Just as he had closed the door to his office to read about the 1956 series of murders, there was a knock on the door.

Jim Robert entered his office. "The journalists got wind of everything about the murder." He simply stated the facts. There was no anger in his voice. "These scoundrels connected yesterday's murder of Susan Moon, and now in the newspapers on the front page you can see an article about a serial killer who appeared in the peaceful city of New York."

"It's bad" was all Rick said. He didn't want to reveal John's information that the murders of seventy years ago were similar to those of today. Jim still won't believe it. Rick didn't believe it either.

"Now the FBI will handle this case," Jim said with contempt. He didn't like the feds. "We were given the role of consultants. I just made sure that you will be the main assistant in this matter."

Rick didn't say thank you. He knew that this was the responsibility of the senior detective.

There were few people along the way. In this neighborhood, they tried to get off the streets as soon as the sun goes down. The lanterns shone through one at a time. However, there was enough lighting to see the gathering companies, who laughed loudly and shouted something out of place, frightening oncoming passersby. They didn't care about strangers. They were from this area, so they felt confident and relaxed.

Rick didn't care about petty bullies. The ringing phone interrupted him from his thoughts.

"Castel!" He heard a sharp female voice on the phone. "Do you think that you can spend the night with me as if I were some kind of cheap woman? You left! You ran away! This is vile, even for you, Castel." He heard Stacy's angry speech. He could also sense bitterness in her tone.

It was his fault. Rick didn't call or even come over when he saw her in the park.

"Did you write an article about serial murders?" That's all that came to his mind as an answer—a very good article, brave.

Stacy's angry tirade paused. But then she erupted again. "Don't think that you can change the subject just like that, do you hear? You used me!"

"But we had a good time?"

Stacy Richie didn't even hear the question. She continued, "Such a brave detective. He solves cases fearlessly, but he's afraid to wake up in the morning with a girl in the same bed! Don't think I didn't guess why you left."

Rick got tired of listening to this, so he hung up. Stacy was proud enough not to call back.

Rick himself did not know why he left then. Something took possession of him. He just packed his things and left. Only now did Rick realize that he didn't remember how he got home. Booze wasn't to blame for this, he was sure.

Lost in thought, Rick entered a bar located on the corner of the street. John Walk was already waiting for him at the table.

"I ordered us some beer."

Rick nodded gratefully. He made sure there was no one around when they started talking. "I'm seriously thinking about the 1956 murders that you talked about."

"I thought about this too. And yet I admit that this is not the same thing."

"What then?"

"Copycat."

Such a simple thought is usually the last thing to creep into one's head. At least that's what happened to Rick. It dawned on him. After all, it really could have been a copycat. And if it was the same person who committed the murders, then who could he be? And why seventy years later? Many questions arose, but not a single answer.

"And where do we start?" Rick finished his beer and looked out the window where the full moon was shining.

"Castel, you forgot that the feds are now handling this case." John also hated the FBI. "We can't even deploy patrol officers without their knowledge."

"Do you propose to let everything take its course? John, if this is truly a copycat, then the killings will happen again." Rick mentally calculated what day it was. "Today is Tuesday, which means there will be five more murders before he escapes. During this time, we must figure him out and catch him."

"Sounds great," Walk responded without much enthusiasm.

"John, we need to collect evidence." He sat closer. "This is our business."

There was silence for some time.

The detectives felt helpless due to their catastrophic ignorance. They had no choice but to wait. Wait while innocent people continued to die in the most brutal manner. And the police can only identify the victims and inform their loved ones about their death.

Rick ordered a double whiskey.

"John, let me ask," Rick began some time later, "have you ever dreamed of murders that might happen? Didn't you feel their agony and pain, fear of the killer? In this dream, you find yourself as a cold contemplator who looks at the blood with utmost pleasure."

As Rick's story progressed, John's eyebrows slowly rose. "What the hell is this, Rick? Of course not!" Walk was excited by such a question. "In all my working practice, I have never dreamed of anything like this. Yes, there were nightmares that woke me up at night, but these were nightmares of murders that had already happened. I've seen them before, you know? No supernatural nonsense. How long have you been dreaming like this?"

Rick hesitated to answer. He was frightened by such a coincidence of circumstances.

"Since the day before yesterday."

John didn't even bring the bottle to the table. "Mysticism" was all John could say, agitating Rick even more.

Before this conversation, he had not even connected the nightmares with the ongoing murders. "I thought it was just a coincidence. Professional," Rick answered himself.

"And you see in these dreams," John hesitated on the last word, "a murderer?"

"No, only victims. I see how they are being killed. They are being slaughtered. I feel their agony, and I can't do anything.

"So either this is a coincidence or there will be more dreams."

The detectives paid for the table and left the bar. John looked puzzled.

"I hope this conversation will remain between us?" Rick shook John's hand. "I don't want anyone to think I am crazy."

"You're not crazy. This thing will drive anyone crazy. Even the most persistent detectives sometimes get nervous." With these words, he called a taxi and left.

Rick remained standing, pondering the conversation. He did not pay attention to the cold of the night, standing in an unbuttoned coat, exhaling steamy warm air. He wanted to call Stacy. After dialing the number, he began to look at the screen. Three rings later, the call was dropped. Pursing his lips in annoyance, Rick walked along the residential buildings, trying to breathe less in the fumes of the enrichment factories.

He wanted to sleep, but at the thought that he might have a nightmare, he was overcome with confusion. Confusion that in this nightmare Rick will see another murder. He had not yet figured out how to react to such discovery.

When he got home and turned the key in the keyhole, Rick realized that he didn't care. Since it so happened that he was a contemplator of murder, then so be it. He rarely relied on fate, but today was such a case. If he put aside his headache in the morning and terrible visions, then it's really nothing.

Rick took out his phone again to call Stacy, but changed his mind. He lay in bed under the covers and decided to get some sleep. A terrible fatigue set in. Rick realized that he had forgotten the last time he got enough sleep. He missed the moment when he fell asleep. The full moon shone like a bright spotlight in the starless sky.

He opened his eyes when there were ten minutes left until the alarm clock. Rick's head hurt as if he had slept more than usual. He groaned, getting up from the bed.

While he was making coffee, Rick realized that there were no visions before his eyes. It became somehow more fun to brush his teeth. No one called from the station, so there was nothing urgent. Rick was finally starting his day smoothly. He even decided to make himself some toast.

Walking past the mirror, Rick paused for a minute, not recognizing his reflection. His cheeks were sunken even more, his cheekbones became sharper, and there were bluish circles around his eyes. He couldn't understand why he had lost so much weight these days. While washing down his last toast with coffee, Rick decided to increase his diet. More protein foods. His headache went away. It became easier to think.

That day, he even managed to get to work by car. The sound of the powerful Dodge engine has always been music to the ears of car enthusiasts. Rick Castel was one of them.

Everything at the station turned out to be as usual: bustle, noise, unnecessary advice. They forgot to even think about the series of murders, switching to other crimes. After the FBI withdraws cases, the police department investigates others. They search and uncover, periodically handing over especially difficult ones to the feds. He wanted to spit on the floor. Rick walked into his office and finally sat down in his chair. Folders with unsolved cases were already on the table. Robert tried.

Some time later, Rick decided to take a break and go to the lounge to watch TV. No one was sitting on the sofas. The precinct's restroom was rarely used. The police tried to go on a break either at home or to the nearest cafeteria. Rick took pleasure in sitting down in the chair and enjoying the silence.

There was only news on TV. Each channel broadcast material from the previous ones. Taking this opportunity, Rick decided to find a channel where Stacy Richie's reports were broadcast. To his surprise, someone else was reporting on the Jersey murder. The girl was apparently new, because Rick knew the entire cast of the channel. For some reason, he no longer wanted to watch TV. He sat there alone, in silence, when suddenly the phone rang. An unfamiliar number appeared on the screen.

"Detective Castel?" the voice on the phone inquired in a businesslike tone. "I'm Agent Leslie, from the FBI. We need to meet with you. This is about Susan Moon and Jonathan Martello."

"Is my consultation really necessary?" Rick tried not to give himself away, but it's difficult to remove the bile from his voice when talking with the feds.

"We'll send the address to your phone," they said into the phone instead of answering.

Rick walked along the familiar streets of the city, striking in their beauty—shop windows showing everything that was in stock, various songs from speakers, barkers inviting you to visit their particular store. On the other side, there were cafes and restaurants, attracting with their signs and menu prices. The visitors standing at the entrance were happily talking about something.

Rick passed by in a gloomy mood. He knew the area; at the end of the street, there were apartment buildings with exorbitant rents. Stacy Richie's address came through on the phone. He could barely contain his excitement. Trying to walk steadily and confidently, he entered the building.

A couple in black suits, ties, and sunglasses was waiting for him at the elevator exit.

"Detective Castel? Release your documents."

Rick silently handed them his ID. It had always seemed absurd to him that, with access to the database of all precincts, the feds would scrutinize a police ID with the utmost care. Idiots. However, he did not say this out loud but only followed them toward Stacy's apartment.

His heart began to beat wildly when he saw the yellow protective tape on the doors. "This can't be true," Rick said to himself, and he entered the room where another agent was waiting.

"Detective Castel," the caller addressed him, "I'm Agent Leslie."

The man turned out to be quite pleasant-looking, younger than Rick, but taller than him. Long hair slicked back using a large amount of gel. His hooked nose seemed even longer against the backdrop of a thin face with pointed cheekbones. Rick greeted him, looking into his eyes. The federal could not stand the look of the detective's inflamed, half-crazed pupils.

"Your superiors nominated you as a consultant. Therefore, we need your opinion on this murder."

Rick was no longer listening once he was in the bedroom. She was lying on the bed. The burgundy bedspread quietly absorbed her blood. Only a couple of drops that had fallen from her hand were visible on the floor.

Rick's heart sank. Not knowing how to react, he walked closer, examining Stacy. There was complete horror in her gaze, and her mouth was twisted in a silent scream. Her green eyes glazed over and stopped shining with life and mischief. Stacy's hair was crushed by a pillow. Now the black luxurious curls resembled burnt straw. Death is disfiguring. But in Rick's eyes, Stacy Richie remained beautiful.

He didn't want to look, to shift his gaze to the bloody mark on the body that caused the girl's death. Her stomach looked like one continuous laceration. Stacy's entrails were spread out on the bed next to her. What he saw made Rick feel sick.

A piercing headache made him fall to his knees. Concentrating, Rick realized it was a scream. A woman's cry of pain, calling for help. Stacy appeared before his eyes. He felt that she was not alone in the room. Stacy turned toward the window. Noticing movement in the room, she screamed. She spotted her attacker. Her pupils dilated with fear. Before she realized what was happening, she was thrown onto the bed. The next movement shocked her mind. She felt no pain.

Rick saw blood leaking from her stomach, saw organs fall out of her abdomen when Stacy turned on her side. He could smell the stench coming from the intestines. Stacy didn't scream anymore. Her eyes became clouded and glazed over. Suddenly he heard another scream. A howl that made the hair on his head stand on end.

The vision ended as suddenly as it began. Rick didn't know how long he lay on the carpet. When he came to his senses, he saw an agent holding a glass of water. Rick drank it in one gulp.

"Are you okay?" Leslie inquired. "Can I call an ambulance?"

"I'm fine, thank you," he muttered, getting up. "Did any of the neighbors hear the screams?"

"Screams?"

"Her mouth froze in a silent scream."

"Oh yes." Agent Leslie called to his assistant, who handed over the notebook. "Stu Vermont, banker. As soon as he heard the piercing screams, he called your station."

"Having intercepted the call, did you respond to it?"

"No, the duty officer arrived at the crime scene, and then we were called," Leslie answered simply.

"He didn't do anything until the police arrived?"

"He says no. He waited in his apartment until law enforcement arrived."

"Didn't Vermont say anything about the second scream?"

"Second scream?" The agents looked at each other. "I don't understand, Detective, explain."

"Is the witness's apartment opposite?" Rick asked instead of answering, leaving the apartment.

Stu Vermont was in the living room when Rick walked through the unlocked door.

"Who are you?" The banker even jumped out of his chair.

"He's with me, Mr. Vermont. This is the consultant, Detective Castel," Agent Leslie entered after Rick.

Nervously, the witness sat back in his chair. He couldn't find a place for his hands on the armrests.

"The detective claims that there was another scream in the apartment opposite, which you didn't mention." Leslie decided to lead the conversation himself. "We came to see if this is true."

Before looking away, Vermont's eyes widened in horror, and his hands began to shake even more. The agent saw it as clearly as Rick did.

"Mr. Vermont, I'll repeat it again: did the second scream come from Ms. Richie's apartment or not?"

"It was not a scream, but a howl," the witness finally said, stuttering and constantly searching for words. He was now shaking all over. "Not like a human. There is nothing to compare this with. It vibrated throughout the chest, paralyzing the beating of the heart. I remained sitting in the chair after the call."

"Are you a poet or a banker, Mr. Vermont?" Agent Leslie asked skeptically. He didn't believe a single word. Unlike the agent, Rick looked at the frightened banker, and the same scream arose in his ears.

Some time later, they went back to Stacy's room, and Leslie asked Rick a question. "Any guesses who could have done this?"

"I think you have some guesses," Rick began carefully. "I'll only tell you what I saw myself."

Before starting his story, Rick closed his eyes, calming his racing heart.

"The killer entered through the window. According to the concierge, no one entered the lobby between three and four o'clock, and no one had checked in the day before. He met the victim at the mirror, next to the window. After which, he threw Richie onto the bed, and there he began to gut her." His voice trembled on the last word.

The agent listened to the detective's theory without interrupting. After he finished, Leslie began his guess. "First: the victim lives on the fifth floor, and the apartment is not equipped with a balcony, so he could not have entered through the window. Second: your theory does not explain the second scream that occurred in the room, although you claimed, surprising us all, that there was a second scream. Explain yourself, Detective Castel."

Rick already regretted that he was drawn to tell about the scream. "I didn't mention it only because the scream didn't make any sense. That is, the killer is a psychopath. He could be horrified by what he did when he came to his senses. Perhaps during the murders his mind becomes clouded."

Agent Leslie looked at Rick for a long time, trying to determine whether he was telling the truth. Rick held his gaze stoically. He didn't want to tell the agents what he was dreaming about and what was happening to him. Finally the phone rang, defusing the situation. Leslie apologized, picking up the phone.

Rick looked again at the girl's eyes full of horror, and pleas for help sounded in his head.

"Detective Castel!" You could hear from his voice that this was not the first time his name had been called. "Thank you for the consultation. Then we are on our own."

"But you didn't say anything about your version and what kind of evidence you managed to get."

"And this is already beyond your competence." The voice conveyed the pleasure Agent Leslie gave in saying such a phrase.

With a short shrug, the detective silently left the room.

The cats were scratching his soul. Not to say that he was too close to Stacy, but the recent night awakened feelings that had fallen asleep many years ago. It's kind of lousy. He walked down the street without noticing anyone. When he reached his car, he did not start the engine for a long time. He just sat there with his head down. This usually happened when Rick was thinking intensely about something.

Many people wanted Stacy dead. Some even said it out loud. However, talking about murder and committing it are not the same thing. Rick knew Stacy's fellow reporters. Nobody was capable of murder. Turning the ignition key, Rick went to the station. The sun had already been at its zenith for several hours, but gray clouds obscured the sky. Forecasters predicted rain in the evening.

At the station, Rick met John, and both locked themselves in the office.

"The copycat killed Stacy."

"Does the FBI know anything?" Rick realized from the question that John did not mean evidence.

"No, I didn't tell them anything. The visions came already at the crime scene. John, this maniac is a psychopath. I heard him let out an inhuman scream that made my hair stand on end."

"A scream?"

"Yes." Rick thought a little about how to explain. "It seemed to me that he regrets what he did. Like he didn't want to kill Stacy."

"This is some nonsense."

"John, my visions are also nonsense."

Walk had to agree. In his entire working career, he had never seen anything like it. Yes, Rick was considered an excellent investigator who still needed to be found, so he had to believe in all this nonsense about predictions and visions.

"What do we do?" John decided to break the silence first.

"If we can't track down the killer, why not keep an eye on the FBI?" With these words, Rick, putting on his coat, invited his partner to join him.

John Walk also wanted to solve the murder, so they left the station together.

"It's good that they are still here. Otherwise, we don't know where else we would look for them." The detectives sat in the car, watching as FBI agents continued to inspect the area around Stacy's house. "These guys collect evidence carefully."

The promised rain did come. Cafes and restaurants in the area began to fill with wet people looking to relax after a day of work. No one paid attention to the huge black SUV with agents standing on the other side of the street. There is little to surprise people in New York.

After hours of waiting, when the lights on the main street had already come on, when visitors to restaurants and cafes began to disperse, raising their collars higher, Agent Leslie came out of the house. He was showing something on the map to his subordinates. No voices could be heard from such a distance, but Rick caught the essence.

"He tells the agents to split up," Rick said after waiting for John to wake up, pointing to the SUV. "He's sending them somewhere."

Everyone except Leslie picked up their phones and began calling for backup.

They were deciding which of the feds to go after. Rick looked at the full moon peeking out from behind the skyscraper as he walked along the very edge of the street. The stars still did not appear. It suddenly dawned on him. Without saying anything to his companion, Rick took out a map of the city from the glove compartment.

"Where did the first murder take place?" Rick made a mark with a pencil, showing an alley between residential buildings. "And the second?" John caught his partner's train of thought, ahead of his search, showing a point in Central Park on the map. "Stacy is here," he added the final point.

"Rick, but what does this give?" Walk looked with incomprehension at the resulting triangle on the city map. He did not find any connection, except that the search circle was quite small. If desired, they can set up patrols on all streets, watching every gateway.

"Leslie revealed the same card to his subordinates." Rick's eyes burned, but he also did not understand the connection. He just felt like he was on the right track.

He connected the dots, hoping to see what could happen. He even circled them. However, this did not give him anything other than a small search diameter.

"He wants to set up patrols on all the streets," Rick voiced John's guess. "He'll try to get ahead of the murder."

"And if you don't interfere, then I will succeed," a voice sounded near the car, and the detectives jerked in surprise.

Agent Leslie, getting wet in the rain, stood at the open car window. The expression on his face showed how tired he was today.

"Detective Castel, your boss recommended you as the best investigator in the area. That's why I agreed to hire you as a consultant for this matter. Think about the mistake we made in taking a policeman with us to keep an eye on us. While you are thinking, your colleague will come to the station tomorrow to get your things." Agent Leslie, after waiting for the detectives to digest the information, went back to the FBI agents' SUV.

They had no right to object. They were identified, and quite simply. Rick didn't expect this agent to have such a temper.

Streetlights flashed one after another accompanied by the moderate sound of the engine. John looked out the window, watching a random passerby, soaked to the skin, wander home, avoiding deep puddles. Suddenly he was overcome by the desire to drop everything, come home, and not open it to anyone. He was already quite tired of this matter. He had no patience for the federals' tricks. He wanted to get drunk while sitting at home, watching TV.

Rick looked at the road with his eyes, but his head was in complete chaos. He couldn't think about anything but Stacy. Who would wish her death? How could she be connected to the other victims? The killer haunted Rick. *Why did the copycat show up after so many years? Is there really a date that we can only guess about?*

Rick was worried about John, but he understood that the dismissal story was a common threat. *We are all human; we can make concessions.* The agent only confirmed his guess that they were as concerned about the case as Rick. The lanterns began to flicker more slowly.

"I'll talk to Robert about this incident." John was already getting out of the car when Rick turned to him.

"No one will fire you."

"I'm not worried." John smiled tiredly. "I'm already a pensioner."

It seemed to Rick that Walk had aged more in a few days than he had in a year of service at the precinct. Once again assuring him that no one would fire him, Rick pressed the pedal, driving out onto the road.

He wanted to think, so a few minutes later he drove onto the freeway. The headlights on his car flashed across the windshield at breakneck speed.

Two people stood in the darkness. Cold drops of rain, falling to the ground, illuminated the area. The flickering light made it possible to see them in the gateway. The hunter, attacking the victim, did not take into account that she was also a hunter. A shot rang out. Stone chips, breaking off from the wall, fell to the ground. The victim was standing in the middle of the street. There was no fear in his eyes, only surprise. He was not like the previous victims.

The next three shots hit the hunter, stopping the attack. The flickering light turned into a bloody veil, turning pain into rage. The hunter's movements became faster. He wanted to disarm the victim. It only took one swing for someone else's hand to fly. A scream was heard in the alley, giving the hunter pleasure. Finally the victim began to be the victim.

Rivers of blood flowed down the street. The spreading warmth was pleasantly felt by the hunter's feet. For a moment, it seemed as if the rain had become warmer. More affectionate.

When the victim was finished, he drowned in a pool of his own blood. The hunter was hit by splashes that seemed like rain to him. The smell of madness filled the alley.

—◆—

Rick was awakened by a demanding knock on the door. He could barely get out of his soaked blanket. Surprisingly, there was no time; the knocking on the door was already stronger.

He was surprised to see Agent Leslie on his doorstep! In a black suit, with a tie over a starched shirt, the agent looked quite businesslike. The black shoes sparkled clean.

Rick could only imagine his appearance. Standing in front of an FBI agent in a wrinkled T-shirt and pajama pants bought in college was somehow awkward. Leslie didn't even pay attention to the detective's clothes.

"You don't answer your calls, Castel. You're lucky that the murder happened nearby, and I was in the mood to visit you personally." After saying that, the agent bothered to glance at the sleepy Rick. "Can I come in?"

Rick silently let the uninvited guest pass.

Leslie didn't look around the room. He simply smoothed his hair silently, trying not to pay attention to the mess around him. Sitting back in his chair, he turned to the detective.

"We no longer need your advice."

"Is it really because of yesterday?" Thoughts gradually began to come into order, but it was still difficult to think. His head hurt like hell.

Rick sat down in the chair opposite, clasping his palms in front of him. He decided not to continue the proposal. There was no point in objecting to the agent.

"What happened yesterday has long been forgotten." Rick didn't believe the statement based on the cold tone of his voice. "We're on the trail of the killer, so we don't need any more consultation."

"Really?" Rick didn't want to scare the fish away. He needed to carefully find out what this trail was, because the FBI had always kept secrets. His shoulder even itched from excitement. "Are you on the trail of the killer?"

"We have learned that the murders are being carried out by a copycat. A similar series of murders occurred back in 1956. There can be no doubt, there will be three more victims, after which the killer will go to the bottom. The last victim is quite different from the rest. However, it was also not possible to establish connections between the previous ones."

"So you found a copycat?" Rick didn't let up.

Agent Leslie looked at the detective for a long time, apparently choosing his words. "There will be three more murders, after which the maniac will go to the bottom. Three murders," the agent deliberately repeated the phrase, "in the big city of New York."

There was silence in the apartment. You could hear the clock ticking in the next room and cars honking outside the half-open window. Rick's throat was dry, but he dared to ask, "You mean you'll just let the killer . . . kill?"

Silence was his answer.

Rick could not believe that the feds had chosen this solution to the problem. Yes, the analysts were great for finally revealing the similarities to the case many years ago, but to reach such a decision . . . Rick wanted to ask if this maniac had his sights set on high-ranking citizens. How would the FBI react then? They both knew the answer. He saw in Leslie's eyes that the decision was being made consciously. The taste of blood appeared in his mouth.

"That's why your consultation is of no use to us anymore." Agent Leslie stood up toward the exit.

"You said that the last victim was different from the others."

"Yes." He turned around at the exit. "He turned out to have a weapon. We assume this is a mercenary. Such weapons cannot be found in a regular armory. It was made on special order, in a limited batch." Leslie thought for a moment and added, "Although these are my guesses."

The federal left half an hour ago, and Rick was still sitting in the chair. He couldn't believe he could do something like this. Letting innocent people die just because the FBI can't admit its weakness. "A drop in the bucket." Leslie's phrase sounded in his head when he committed such a crime. Rick Castel had no doubt that this was a crime.

For some reason, his shoulder itched. He looked at the source of the itching and froze. At that moment, he forgot about everything. He was overcome by the oppression of growing horror. There were overgrown scars from three gunshots on his shoulder. Simple awareness proved too difficult to understand.

Chapter

8

There was silence in the living room. There were almost no people. Only a few were sitting in guest chairs. The rest were either off on missions or still sleeping in their rooms. The Raven Guild usually went to bed at this time of day. The first rays penetrated the stained glass windows, creating all sorts of glare on the walls, carpet, and fireplace.

Clark walked down the stairs, squinting in the sun. Never before had he felt so content. They talked with Hans until the morning. Although Hans was tired from the road, he did not want to go to bed at night. Hans told Clark his reasons. It turned out they had a lot in common. The tie was squeezing his neck, and he had to let it go by undoing a button on his shirt.

He sat down in a chair by the window. He liked to replay conversations in his head several times. Possessing a phenomenal memory, Clark extracted the most necessary things from stories, remembering even the intonation of the speaker. The sun shone even brighter, warming them more. One thing Clark knew for sure: Hans was a godsend for the Guild. True, he didn't know about it yet.

He heard footsteps behind him. The clicking of heels sounded quite often, and some tension was felt in the gait. Clark knew his subordinates, so he easily identified the newcomer.

"Sylvia, not now. I need some time of silence," he said without turning around.

"But, Master, this is important," said Sylvia, a specialist in the tracking department, hesitantly, like a humble sheep.

Clark dramatically raised his head to the ceiling, turning.

He wanted to say something sharp and caustic, sending her on her way. But when he looked at her alarmed face, he immediately changed his mind.

"Tell me."

"Jorge. His numbers are zero," Sylvia blurted out, adjusting her glasses.

Clark understood what this meant, so he immediately went after the girl. His fatigue vanished as if by hand.

The surveillance department was located on the bottom floor of the building. It consisted of huge system units, the size of a cabinet, and a large number of computers of varying power. A huge number of monitors displayed all the information of the Guild.

Clark rarely came down there, trusting Sylvia to guide him. In truth, the sound of the coolers and the hum of high voltage irritated his head. However, without this department, keeping the Guild under control would be problematic.

They walked past glass boxes in which analysts sat, watching several monitors at once. They reflected information about each member of the Raven Guild. Upon admission, Clark implanted a tracking chip into each person's body to not only know their location, but also monitor their vital signs. And in case of critical moments, send help. Of course, such a system did not allow them to fully determine the degree of difficulty of completing a task. For this, the head of the Guild had his own methods.

Sylvia led Clark into one of the glass boxes, in which several analysts had gathered, noisily arguing about something. He knew that after completing the mission, Jorge went into the city to unwind. He promised to be back by morning.

When the head of the Guild entered, the arguments stopped, and the analysts parted, allowing them to go to the monitor. Clark saw the Guild member's name and vital signs. A steadily blinking dot showed Jorge's location. His heart rate and pulse were at zero.

"Closer to four o'clock in the morning, his heart rate jumped. His nervous system was excited. This lasted several minutes. Afterwards, the pain threshold reached its limit, and the pulse and heartbeat dropped to zero."

"In other words, Jorge stumbled upon someone who killed him," Clark stated, still looking at the monitor.

"We checked the system several times, hoping that there was some kind of glitch," Sylvia began, "but the computer worked without interruption, and the blinking dot shows that Jorge has not moved for several hours."

Clark was no longer listening to Sylvia. He tried to imagine who could kill a storm trooper who shot without missing a beat and did not part with his pistol. Clark looked at the monitor again, memorizing the location of the murder. Thanking Sylvia for the information, he quickly walked out of the surveillance department.

Walking past the rooms, Clark knocked on one. There was absolute silence on the other side of the door. Clark even missed the moment when it opened just enough to see the newcomer.

"Jorge was killed in New York. We need to pick up the body. You have five minutes to get ready."

Avalsa took a few seconds to digest the information. Four minutes later, she left her room. She put on a short jacket over a knitted sweater and pulled a bright-green hat over her head. Avalsa tucked her jeans into beige low shoes. She put the rest of her clothes in her backpack.

The garage was quiet. No one was going to leave this early. He could have sent people to destroy the body along with the chip, avoiding unnecessary trouble, but Clark decided to figure it out himself. Avalsa did not ask unnecessary questions and completed tasks without being noticed. So he decided to take her with him.

"We're unlikely to be invisible at this point." Avalsa watched as Clark, in a red raincoat, mounted a sports motorcycle of the same color. She put up with his flashy clothes, but you definitely can't leave secretly on such transport.

"There are traffic jams in New York in the morning. We'll get there quickly." Clark smiled, starting the engine. The Japanese motorcycle squealed its tires subtly as it pulled out of the garage.

It was worth admitting that they got there really quickly. Avalsa was passionate about speed but had never gotten behind the wheel of a motorcycle. She considered this type of transport suicide. Clark clicked his tongue loudly as they saw the federal cars blocking the alley Jorge was in. Without further ado, Avalsa went on reconnaissance.

She understood the task, so she plunged into the task headlong. It's not every time the head of the Guild accompanied her on business. Even if it was daylight, but in a green hat, Avalsa blended into the crowd. Clark had no choice but to sit down in the cafe across the street and order a cup of coffee. It gave him pleasure to watch his scout at work.

She walked around the block twice, talking to passersby, buying trinkets at newsstands. During lighthearted conversations, she counted how many FBI agents were on the block, how many sentries were posted, who was yawning early in the morning, who was finishing their third coffee to cheer up, who was in charge of everyone. She watched carefully, approaching at a safe distance.

Avalsa was wondering how to get to Jorge's body without being noticed. The Mexican was of little concern to her, considering she didn't even know him. Avalsa kept herself apart from everyone in the Guild; only Chloe was an exception. That's probably why Clark took her on the mission. Having finished counting, she returned to her master.

Clark drank a double espresso, successfully overcoming his drowsiness. He kept wondering who could have killed the Guild fighter. Did this happen by accident, or did someone know about Jorge's occupation? The Raven Guild remained in the shadows, fulfilling various orders. No service knew about its existence. This was something Clark had always tried to ensure. The Raven Guild had different occupations: sabotage, capture, kidnapping, theft, murder. To ensure high-quality work, Clark divided the Guild members into classes. By developing in one direction, you can get good results in a short time. Everyone knew this.

Jorge was one of the best storm troopers. There were rumors about his accuracy. It was said that he prayed to the Mexican gods to bless his precision on every mission. Clark always smiled at this. He knew how hard Jorge trained to achieve results like these.

Clark glanced at the FBI agents cordoning off the alley. He expected that such a murder was an accident. That Jorge was accidentally mistaken for the wrong person and killed by a stray bullet. However, Clark had never seen so many federal officers in any murder. He knew that the station duty officers arrived first, and then three SUVs of FBI agents arrived at once. His thoughts were distracted when Avalsa sat down at the table next to him.

As if on cue the waiter brought breakfast for two.

"There are only twelve federals," she reported after finishing her scrambled eggs, "two at the exits of the alley and two at each corner of the block. Their leader is a thin guy with slicked hair. One of the agents called him Leslie. They said something about a series of murders and that this victim was different from the previous ones. I didn't really delve into it. You can get to the body through the roof of the building located to the left of the alley. There is a closed fire escape there. When climbing, you can remain unnoticed. Exactly what is needed."

Clark listened quite attentively. He liked Avalsa at work. She gave herself completely to her work, sparing no effort. Suddenly her story was interrupted when the waiter brought an ashtray. Clark lit a cigar.

"What are the difficulties?" He knew that there would be no difficulties.

Avalsa was silent for a moment.

"The difficulties lie in the fact that the length of the lane is about twenty meters. I will be able to reach the body unnoticed, but it will take time to dissolve it. You know that the dissolution process is quite noisy, so there is a chance that one of the agents might hear. You can deal with them, but then rumors will appear."

Clark thought for a while, figuring something out in his mind. "Let's do this: get to the body, and I'll distract the feds."

Avalsa did not ask unnecessary questions. She wondered how he would do it, but she was used to trusting her master.

Taking the backpack, she disappeared in the direction of the fire escape of the building opposite.

"Whether you like it or not, you have to." With these words, Clark left a generous tip, leaving the cafe and heading to an FBI agent named Leslie.

The alley was in twilight. High-rise buildings blocked the sun. It was impossible for anyone who came in from the light to even see their hand in the darkness. Avalsa stopped going up the stairs. Having reached the desired ledge, she jumped over the railing, balancing perfectly above the twenty-meter height.

Avalsa managed to shed her regular clothes, leaving her in a tight black Guild suit. The uniform had something in common with a scuba diver's suit, but the similarity was only external. Made of special material, the suit not only protected her from the cold, but also had high strength, providing good mobility.

With short steps, Avalsa reached the other side of the wall, reaching the middle of the alley. After waiting for her eyes to get used to the twilight, she secured one end of the cable in the wall and connected the other, through a bypass mechanism, to her belt. Without the slightest hesitation, Avalsa took a step into the abyss. The rollers rustled quietly. She walked along a sheer wall, supported by a cable.

Avalsa was confident that she had chosen the right place to descend. There weren't any agents around when she touched down. The smell of decomposition filled her nostrils. Trying to breathe every once in a while, Avalsa stopped at the body. Barely holding back a curse in disgust, she came closer, looking at the one who only yesterday had been considered Jorge.

A few meters away was an arm, from the shoulder of which torn pieces of tendons and muscles could be seen. Having gotten used to the poor lighting, Avalsa saw corpse worms clinging to the lacerations on Jorge's collarbone. Several ribs were visible from the chest, white against the background of congealed blood. Avalsa had seen many bodies, but this was the first time she had seen anything like this in New York. It's hard to even imagine who could do this to him.

After standing over Jorge for some time, Avalsa decided to save his body. Using her instincts, she announced through the mini-mic that she was going to pull him out of the alley. Surprisingly, Clark didn't mind. He trusted his scout.

Avalsa took a small ball from her fanny pack. Activating the mechanism, she threw it onto the body. There was a soft bang. The ball turned out to be a weave of steel thread trap, tightly enveloping the body. A couple of seconds later, Jorge's hand along with the rest of his limbs were tightly tied together. The body was ready for transport.

Avalsa raised her head, sizing up the distance. The roof of the building was about a hundred meters away. She put her hand to her ear again.

"I'll use a harpoon. Distract them." After waiting for an affirmative answer, Avalsa took aim with a hand harpoon. She managed to catch the edge the first time. After securing the weapon to Jorge's body, she pressed the rewind button. The body crawled up. When she was sure that it would rise to the top without hindrance, Avalsa went along the same path to the fire escape.

Avalsa had to wait a little on the roof. Clark climbed up the attic stairs when his scout had already dragged in the body.

"I've never seen anything like this before," Avalsa said with hidden alarm. "Do you think it's the work of a man?"

Clark was in no hurry to answer. He carefully examined the wound on the body. He didn't pay attention to the severed hand.

"They say there's a murderous maniac in the city." Clark recalled the information he received from Agent Leslie. "Fortunately, we have a guest who can answer your question."

"Do you want to deliver the body to the Guild?"

Clark didn't answer; he was already calling for reinforcements.

"You've done your job. Meet me at the Guild."

Avalsa decided not to impose her company, so she immediately complied. She didn't like performing such a risky operation, running into the feds and stealing a body from under their noses. So she was more than willing to disappear into the stairwell.

Chapter

9

There was excitement in the Guild. Someone was loudly arguing against the wall with an ancient weapon; some, sitting on the sofa, were quietly grumbling, expressing their dissatisfaction. The storm troopers were eager to fight, demanding reprisals. Respect for the head of the Guild did not allow the maddened crowd to rush into the streets of New York. There were also those who calmly reacted to the death of their comrade. This was less indifference and more a cold confidence that Clark will find the culprit and demand retribution.

Hans went down to the living room, perplexed by what was happening. Having slept off the road, he felt a surge of strength that he had not felt before. He looked at the angry faces of the storm troopers, ready to tear apart the first person they met. Deciding not to provoke them, Hans walked around them along the wall with tapestries, past the calm swordsmen. He felt angry looks, but there was also respect in some of them. Without a mistake, he identified the leader of the squad: tall, aged, with several scars on his face. A memorable feature was the presence of a long mustache hanging like icicles from his chin. Hans greeted him friendly as he passed by. Tom had no choice but to repeat the nod of his head. Already with his back, Hans heard the nickname of the main one—Walrus.

Hans did not find Avalsa in the crowd. She was probably summoned to the head of the Guild. He was warming up after sleeping in his room when a note was thrown under the door—Clark wanted to see him. The note specified: urgently. Since he was interrupted in the middle of his warm-up, Hans went across the entire living room to the master's office.

There were three people in the room. Hans took a quick look at the office. He was prevented from examining the room with many bookcases, antique shelves with strange things, and oak walls with fancy patterns, because a corpse was on the floor. All attention was turned to him.

"This is my fighter." Clark began the conversation as soon as Hans looked at him questioningly. "He was killed tonight. I admit that the killer may not even be human."

Hans looked at Avalsa standing next to the body. She nodded affirmatively to the words of the head of the Guild. Over the past few days, she had to believe in the supernatural. Hans had no choice but to begin the inspection.

For some time, only the ticking of the grandfather clock broke the silence in the room. Clark tried to guess what evidence Hans was looking for, what he was seeing. After hesitating a little, Avalsa shared what she had heard with Hans. She talked about the guesses of FBI agents, about a series of murders that were in no way connected with each other. Only the nature of the wounds.

"I saw something else." Avalsa waited until Hans raised his eyes to her. "A huge pool of blood spread around the body, on which the traces of a man's bare feet were clearly visible. I didn't see any more traces, and that interested me. If you step into blood, there will definitely be traces around. But they were not there. It's as if the one who killed Jorge simply . . . disappeared." Avalsa found it difficult to say the last word.

Hans didn't answer. She noticed that he already knew something; now he was simply weighing in his mind whether to tell it to others.

"The one who killed your fighter, Clark, is very dangerous," he finally began. "To find him in such a big city, I will need the artifact that Avalsa got for you. How many murders are we talking about?"

"The FBI talked about four." The head of the Guild spread out a map of the city, on which there were already four points.

"That means there will be three more murders, after which he will disappear."

"Who is he?" Avalsa asked insistently, but Hans didn't answer, looking at the map. "If you want an artifact, we need to know who we're fighting."

Hans did not want to focus on "we," so after being silent for a while, he began from afar. "Once upon a time, during the Scandinavian war for the lands, there was a powerful army. It was famous for one squad of swordsmen who did not know defeat. They led the army forward, winning battles every time. This detachment was led by Mariusz Castel. The king sent swordsmen to the most difficult battles, to sabotage and to organize sabotage. The squad always emerged victorious. The swordsmen believed in their commander. Among the soldiers, he was nicknamed Cerberus. One day there was an attempt on the king's life in the palace. It was a betrayal; he was killed by his own subjects. Mariusz, suspecting nothing, exposed his back to the royal guard. He was mortally wounded. Before he died, Cerberus took seven with him, tearing armor and skin with a three-fingered claw worn on his hand with a glove."

"This is all quite entertaining," Clark interrupted, "but how does this story explain the murders in New York? Yes, there are coincidences in the form of weapons and seven victims, but are you saying that Mariusz Castel is still alive?"

"I didn't say that," Hans answered patiently and looked at Avalsa, who was completely absorbed in the story. "The restless spirit of Mariusz has been inhabiting people for many centuries. He has only one goal— to kill seven people prone to treason. The spirit then disappears, reappearing in another person decades later."

"Can he possess anyone?" Avalsa was captivated by the story, even though she tried to look bored.

"Only blood allows him to appear." Looking at the perplexed glances, Hans explained, "Relatives."

There was silence in the room. No one paid attention to the smell of a decomposing body; everyone thought about the story. Clark couldn't come up with the phrase about "seven people prone to treason." Apparently, Jorge could betray the Guild. The thought sent an echo of panic through Clark's mind. It appeared and immediately went out.

What was considered a legend was now being realized right before their eyes.

"Okay," Clark concluded, crossing the room with long strides, "I will give you the staff of Anubis, but only with my accompaniment."

Hans looked at the head of the Guild with an unblinking gaze. "I hope you understand what a risk this is? The restless spirit is very strong and dangerous."

"That's why I'll also go with you, in case of danger," Avalsa said suddenly, surprised at her heroism.

Hans understood that he was putting a yoke on his neck in the amount of two people, but they themselves decided to risk their lives. In addition, he had already managed to get to know Clark a little to understand that he would not trust his treasures to anyone. Without the staff of Anubis, there was no hope of finding Mariusz Castel in such a big city.

After weighing all the possible consequences, Hans said, "We need to leave at twelve o'clock."

Clark's eyes lit up like a child. Avalsa just nodded decisively.

—◊◊◊—

There was a bright moon in the sky as the three drove out of the garage in a black car. The weather was calm. Frost sparkled on the traffic light poles, and the streets were covered with moisture, reflecting the lights of the lanterns on both sides of the sidewalk.

Hans held the staff in his hands, carefully peering into the eyes on the pommel.

"Are you sure it works?" Avalsa asked a simple question.

"We need to get to the epicenter of the murders and check," Hans answered patiently.

"We haven't even gotten there yet," Clark supported, slowly driving away at the traffic light.

Avalsa looked at Hans and Clark, wondering why she even volunteered. She knew how to secretly and silently eliminate any target. She could penetrate the most protected object, but not track down the evil spirit. She was driven by one thing—curiosity. Besides, Avalsa did not want to sit idly by in the Guild. Clark announced before leaving that everyone should stay inside until he returned. Of course, the statement caused a lot of discontent, but no one began to argue with the master. Therefore, for her, it was better to be with the two than to watch the slowly boiling storm troopers demanding vengeance.

While she was thinking, Avalsa didn't notice how the car stopped. It was dark all around, and only at the end of the street a lone bus-stop lamp was burning. Clark checked the map. He connected the places where the victims were found, forming a circle. They decided to start from its center, gradually approaching the borders.

"These are residential areas," Avalsa said, recognizing the places. "Mostly factory workers live here. That's why you won't see any light in the windows at this time."

"I have to go back to work in a couple of hours." Clark looked at his watch hidden under the sleeve of his raincoat. He added a hat with a black stripe to his colorful outfit.

"Here, you can check out the staff of Anubis in action."

"How does it work?" Avalsa had no idea when fulfilling the order for the figurine that it might turn out to be part of the artifact.

"It points to otherworldly forces," Hans explained, looking at Avalsa's blank face. "The staff of Anubis points to the location of any spirit nearby."

"By the way, I have a question." Clark turned sharply on his heel, distracted by his surroundings. "How do we know that this is 'our' spirit? I heard that the staff of Anubis locates all evil creatures nearby."

"If we were on the outskirts of the city, then I agree that there would be no benefit from it. But we are in the center of a densely populated city. Entities cannot tolerate large crowds of people. Only a few settle here." Hans gestured around the city with his hand. "Having a sufficiently large force with a dense layer of dark aura that can withstand human emanations." Hans noticed that he was speaking off topic, so he corrected himself. "Here the staff will be able to point out who we need."

Avalsa listened in fascination, while Clark just grinned. Ignoring both of them, Hans moved the top of the staff around its axis. There was a quiet click of operation, and Hans extended his hand forward. For some time, nothing happened.

Avalsa looked at the jackal's head without blinking. She saw a fire begin to ignite in Anubis's golden eyes. Suddenly, a puff of bluish smoke came out of the staff. Instead of dissipating, it stretched into a line and then thinned out into a thread, indicating direction. There was only one thread visible, so all three figured out what it meant.

Clark opened the trunk, taking out an oblong package. He answered the silent questions blithely, "Just in case."

Without saying another word, the trio went deeper into the streets, watching the writhing gray thread.

Avalsa put on her Guild gear while still in the car. Hans managed to wrap a chain around his forearm and tied a curved dagger to his hip. Only Clark did not acquire any weapons. He walked behind the others, holding the bundle under his arm.

"We are too noticeable," she muttered for the head of the Guild to hear.

"Don't worry. I am personally responsible for our invisibility."

Avalsa resisted the question "how?" deciding to silently continue moving.

She was surprised that during their search, they did not meet a single person—in the center of New York! It seemed that this circumstance bothered her more than her companions. Clark just grinned at her, and Hans didn't pay attention at all.

"Keep up," he said, focusing on the thread.

They didn't see it, but heard it. A heartbreaking female scream. Without the slightest hesitation, Hans ran around the corner into the next street. Avalsa turned around, but Clark was no longer behind her. There was no time to think about the reason for his disappearance; she rushed after Hans.

He barely managed to prevent the murder. Throwing a dagger like a boomerang, Hans distracted the creature from the victim. This did not cause much damage, but taking advantage of the time, Hans took off his jacket, leaving only his T-shirt.

During the murders, the essence of Mariusz Castel managed to grow in size. Being three heads taller, the creature advanced on him, armor cast in fluid resin. His hand was one with the legendary weapon—a three-fingered claw. His other hand, like the rest of his body, resembled those of a human. The exception was the horn plates in the shape of the armor of the once-great warrior. His head was also covered with a kind of helmet made of small scaly particles, taking the shape of a grinning dog's mouth.

When Hans appeared, a guttural growl escaped from under the helmet. It seemed to Avalsa that the creature recognized him.

"Help the woman," Hans told her, unwinding the chain.

Mariusz Castel attacked quickly. A person would not be able to dodge. However, Hans managed to place the Grail chain in front of him with outstretched arms. Not expecting such force, he fell to one knee. The creature grabbed him by the neck and lifted him off the ground. Avalsa watched in horror as Mariusz, bringing his toothy mouth closer to the Hans's face, tried to hiss something articulate. She didn't understand a single word. If it was a speech, Avalsa had no idea what it was.

Hans, meanwhile, took out the nail of the Cross of the Savior, driving it into the creature's forearm up to his head. Howling indignantly, Mariusz, also known as Cerberus, unclenched his fingers, trying to reach Hans with his clawed hand. With leaps and somersaults, Hans increased the distance; but without calculating the distance, he hit his back against a trash can. Instinctively jumping to the side, he missed the creature's attack.

The trash can split into two. Covered in its contents, Hans threw the chain. The attack had no result. Mariusz easily dodged the chain, catching it in flight and pulling it strongly toward him. Hans quickly went to meet him, taking the three-fingered claw to the dagger. By inertia, Mariusz's hand was pulled down, but his body still moved forward. Throwing the edge of the chain, Hans used his body weight to drive another nail into the joint of Mariusz's armor. Mariusz roared from the new pain, stronger than the previous one.

It took all of Hans's dexterity to avoid being hit by the erratic swings of Mariusz's claws. With a flowing lunge, he found himself behind the enemy's back and threw the chain around his neck. The links, digging into the creature's skin, glowed. It seemed to Avalsa that at that moment, the creature began to decrease in size. However, it couldn't take a closer look. The entity threw Hans over himself, sending him into a short flight.

Avalsa couldn't understand why Clark disappeared, leaving Hans alone. And why didn't people come running to the sound of battle? They fought on the street, where cars were moving in a three-lane continuous stream. Now she couldn't even see people, except for the victim lying unconscious. Avalsa did not even consider her capacity to help. Even in Norway, she was convinced that in order to hurt such a creature, you need a special weapon and a lack of fear.

Hans quickly rose to his feet, letting the creature's clawed blow pass beneath him. Mariusz missed and made deep furrows in the asphalt. Another nail of the Savior's Cross stuck out in his back.

Avalsa now had no doubt: the creature was really shrinking in size. It was already the same height as Hans. Mariusz spoke again in an incomprehensible language. Avalsa clearly caught only one phrase, which was repeated many times. She did not know its translation, and she was burning with curiosity about what it meant.

The horny plates on the creature's body became wet.

"The ice has broken," Hans said, spitting out blood. Cerberus was still strong enough to make contact. There was another nail left on Hans's belt.

With quick leaps, Mariusz found himself dangerously close, attacking from bottom to top. Hans could not keep up with the speed of the attack; he only managed to deviate his body slightly from the deadly trajectory. The claw cut his side and shoulder. The pain exploded in his head like a bright flash.

During the attack, Hans saw that the person inside the entity was still struggling. Mariusz did not completely take possession of it.

"He's still a man!" yelled Hans at Avalsa. Naturally, this gave her nothing. She just threw up her hands in confusion. "We need to smoke him out," he said under his breath, rushing off into a suitable alley.

It turned out to be a fairly narrow gateway that a car could not enter. Avalsa considered Hans suicidal when he ran into her. Mariusz, blinded by rage, went after him.

It was quite dark in the alley, but both of them could navigate perfectly in the dark. It took Avalsa a while to get used to the darkness. Partly she was offended that the creature did not pay any attention to her. As if he didn't consider her an enemy. However, the truth was hidden much deeper than her wounded pride.

Hans waited until the creature dived into the alley. With quick movements, he drew a rune on his palm and, tightly clasping his fingers in front of him, activated it. After repeating the movement, bricks from the neighboring walls, forming huge palms, closed, trapping Mariusz in a stone trap.

Avalsa couldn't believe her eyes. Two stone palms that grew from the walls held back the rampaging creature.

Hans wiped the sweat from his brow.

"Now the most difficult thing will happen." He turned to the amazed Avalsa. "When I separate him from the human shell, Cerberus will become vulnerable. But this will make him more dangerous."

Hans picked up the Grail chain from the ground and lassoed Mariusz Castel. The creature roared loudly when the links, glowing, began to burn.

Avalsa was horrified by such a roar but continued to monitor Hans's actions. He continued to pull the chain toward him with a determined look. Weakened by the nails of the Savior's Cross, the creature hurled curses in his own tongue.

Avalsa was shocked by what she saw, but what happened next defied any description. At first, barely noticeable, and then more confidently, Mariusz Castel's helmet, along with the horn plates on his body, began to slide off. This was accompanied by hissing and the smell of burning flesh. Like gluten, the entity began to separate, releasing a body that increasingly took on the shape of a human. The lassoed creature gradually released the unfortunate man from his shell. Losing human consciousness, the creature rushed about in shackles.

Hans had a hard time drawing the essence out of a person. It made a disgusting sound. Refusing to give up, Mariusz, already in spirit form, rushed toward Hans with the speed of the wind. Hans barely managed to close himself with the Claw. Mariusz carried him several meters above the ground, slamming him into the wall. The face of the entity, like its entire body, was hidden by a dark haze, as if it were covered with a cloud of darkness.

Hans tried to break free, but Mariusz's grip was strong. Avalsa wanted to help, but a wave of horror and panic paralyzed her body, making it impossible to move.

Cerberus inflicted deep cuts one after another. He enjoyed the sound of flesh being torn. Hans writhed in pain but tried his best to keep a clear mind. Suddenly, Cerberus disappeared into thin air, appearing a few meters away from Hans. In the place where the spirit was a second ago, a blade stuck out, staggering.

The weapon seemed unremarkable in appearance. Narrowed closer to the tip, the had had a double-sided blade. The hilt of the sword consisted of a simple steel V-shaped guard, smoothly turning into a hilt, wrapped simply in a strip of boiled leather. However, it was not the blade itself that scared away the creature, but the inscriptions on the blade. In the presence of the spirit, they glowed with a soft light.

"Just in case." A familiar voice was heard from the roof. Clark deliberately repeated the phrase he had said at the trunk of the car.

Wasting no time, Hans grabbed the sword and pulled it out of the ground. Mariusz attacked decisively, trying to rip open Hans's unprotected throat. With a deft movement of his wrist, Hans deflected the blow, and the runes shone brighter.

Cerberus continued to attack from the depths of his own cloud, appearing unpredictably from different directions. Hans, despite numerous wounds, deftly spun like a top, parrying every blow from the enemy. Avalsa could barely see the blade through the mill of attacks.

Hans's skill was a delight. For the first time in Mariusz's eyes, Hans saw uncertainty about the outcome of the battle. With a deft movement of his hand, he drove in the last nail of the Savior's Cross, threaded into the chain. Cerberus could no longer teleport. Seizing the moment, Hans struck one decisive blow with his sword. The blade passed through Mariusz's collarbone and chest and stopped in his pelvic area. The weapon hissed with dark flesh. Exhausted, Hans fell next to the dissolving Cerberus.

At first, barely noticeable, and then more and more clearly, it disappeared in flakes of ash blowing in the wind. The blade, along with the nails, fell onto the asphalt, ringing loudly.

Avalsa missed the moment when Clark appeared behind her. A question was about to escape her lips, but he interrupted her, "Call the victim an ambulance."

Clark lifted the unconscious Hans onto his shoulders and headed toward their car. Avalsa, having called the rescue service, was convinced that there were still no witnesses around. Then she took the weapon and followed her master.

A few minutes later, sirens were heard. In the alley, except for the damaged brickwork, nothing spoke of what happened to the man lying on the pavement.

Chapter

10

The Raven Guild was empty in a matter of hours. Multicolored tapestries, rhythmically swaying on the walls of the living room, evoked melancholy. There was a ringing silence in the air, arising from a hastily abandoned room.

Clark dismissed all Guild members on assignments. The storm troopers were not entirely satisfied with their vendetta. Some did not believe that Jorge was avenged. However, they did not dare to argue with the tired head of the Guild. Silently gathering their things, they left the residence.

Avalsa looked at the fluttering tapestries, thinking about her own. There were no orders for her. Clark, without saying a word, locked himself in his office along with Hans's unconscious body.

By the evening of the next day, torn by curiosity, she went to Clark for clarification of the situation. The door was locked, but she could hear conversations inside. Quietly sneaking to the door, Avalsa began to eavesdrop.

"You are recovering quickly. I would like such regeneration," she heard Clark's envious voice.

"Believe me, this makes your body hurt no less. I believe that your abilities are much more interesting." The answer was silence. "I revealed myself. Now they will look for me."

"Do you think anyone can bypass the cloak of invisibility?" Clark asked incredulously.

"I used magic. Even if in small quantities, it spread through the air no worse than the smell of rotten cheese. Your cover does not block the emanations of magic. They will run to the smell. Having discovered your traces, they will descend on the Guild with questions. Apparently, you guessed this, since you dismissed your followers."

Clark didn't answer for a long time.

"I'll find something to tell them," the head of the Guild said coldly, clearly planning something.

"They are not to be trifled with, mind you. If they recognize a lie, then you will not escape persecution. I don't think you'll do that."

"For free, no." One could imagine Clark smiling. "Jorge is not the only one who mysteriously disappeared from the Guild."

"Do you want a deal?" Hans grinned.

"I'll send Avalsa with you. She will be very curious about your abilities." Hans wanted to protest, but Clark interrupted, "She knows places where you can wait out the unfolding storm."

"I can be secretive."

"She'll still go after you."

Apparently, this turned out to be the decisive argument, since Hans stopped arguing.

There was silence in the room for some time.

"Where did you get this sword?" Hans asked another interesting question.

"They assured me that this was a sword from the era of Constantine. It was said that its core was forged from the nails on which Jesus Christ was crucified. But when I looked at your weapon, I realized that I had been deceived." Clark didn't seem to be the least bit upset.

"This blade really contains ancient power." Hans took the sword from the table. "Ancient Christian writings are inscribed on the blade."

"I'm not good at this. Since this is not Constantine's sword, I have no use for it anymore." Clark played indifferent.

"If it's a gift, then you could just say so." Now it was Hans's turn to smile.

You could hear papers rustling across the table.

"Here are the places where my students disappeared. I admit that in most cases, they simply died at the hands of man, but anything can happen, right?"

"By all sorts of things you mean spirits, I take it?" Hans took the folder from the table. "I'll leave the Guild tonight. The count will now go to the clock."

"So you will gladly accept another gift."

Avalsa continued to sit in the chair under the wide wrought-iron chandelier, replaying the dialogue she had heard over and over again in her head. She was outraged that they were deciding for her what she wanted. On the other hand, her master's order was not discussed, even if it didn't quite look like an order.

Avalsa carried out Clark's instructions of any complexity, without going into detail. The overheard conversation only added to the confusion in her head. Her curiosity grew more and more intense. Her desire to find out prevailed. Avalsa could hardly suppress such an impulse with common sense.

While she was thinking, she didn't even notice when Clark appeared. His face looked very aged. She had not seen her master since their night outing, but it was impossible to grow old like that in a day and a half. In response to her question, Clark replied that it was temporary.

"You need to gather your strength, and everything will pass." He smiled fleetingly, instantly becoming serious. "I will have a building of a special character for you."

Avalsa had no choice but to pretend that she was hearing about this for the first time.

Her pride was indignant. Her indignation was looking for a way out, but in her heart, Avalsa already agreed with the order. Curiosity once again prevailed.

The gray stretched sky left New Yorkers despondent, leaving not the slightest hint of sunshine. Only the promise of torrential rain, ready to fall from the potbellied clouds at any moment.

Clark looked at the dull city, mired in gray, from the window of a high-rise building. His clean-shaven face expressed a seriousness that was in no way compatible with laughing eyes. He was expecting a guest who should arrive any minute.

Hans was right. What was done that night could not go unnoticed. However, he did not take into account that Clark could prepare for this.

There was a demanding knock on the door. Without waiting for an answer, a man entered the room. In appearance, he looked like Clark's age. The guy had a thin face and short hair. He wore a floor-length coat made of the highest-quality fabric. A person like Clark noticed even such a small thing.

The person who entered turned out to be tall, almost the same height as the head of the Guild. The confidence in his step was marked by shoes with powerful heels. The earring in his ear and eyebrows created the image of a predator. The visitor, coming closer, further confirmed this comparison. His eyes with vertical pupils tenaciously followed every movement, even when he extended his hand in greeting. Clark had already seen eyes like these in Hans. Only they had more warmth and friendliness than the subject standing opposite.

Clark recognized the skilled swordsman by his knobby fingers and firm handshake.

"My name is Kloss," the guest began in a confident tone. "Two days ago, there was an incident in the city involving the use of magic. I'm not talking about the shroud of illusion you applied. I mean a spontaneous spell that was well disguised. I know who he is. The only thing I want to know is where is he?" He said the last phrase with significant emphasis.

Clark noticed that Kloss deliberately switched to "you." He gave out information with pompous confidence, trying to unbalance him. Clark knew that his guest was one of the few followers of a certain clan. In other words, there were very influential people behind him. However, Clark was satisfied that this kind of subject had come. Kloss was ideal for what was planned.

These thoughts raced through his head, and Clark replied, "I have it."

For a second, the guest was taken aback by such an answer; but instantly regaining confidence, he said, "Lead the way."

As he walked down the stairs, Clark could feel how pleased this Kloss was with himself. That his orders were carried out without difficulty, that the mission was successful. Clark caught a glimpse of a weapon behind him, which reeked of elemental power. He was rarely wrong about this. For a moment, it seemed to him that Kloss had something in common with Hans, not just his eyes. Perhaps this was because both were considered swordsmen with a specific gait. They laid out each step, trying to make the transition of the foot as smooth as possible. Few people notice such a small thing.

A couple more seconds and Kloss will be on his hook. He wanted to discourage Clark by declaring that he knew who he was, but Kloss had no idea of his true abilities. When they entered the Guild morgue, he was already at Clark's mercy.

"It is he?" Kloss asked in the same demanding tone, pointing toward the table.

"I couldn't stand the fight with my spirit."

From the expression on his face, Clark could tell that Kloss didn't care much about any spirits. All his attention was occupied by the corpse of Hans, covered up to the neck with a white blanket. Without anyone's permission, Kloss pulled back the covers and examined the body.

He checked the pupils, opening the eyelids one by one. For some reason, he even examined the teeth. Clark could barely contain his smile as Kloss examined the edges of the laceration of a severed limb.

"Apparently he got a strong spirit," Kloss summed up.

"And very dangerous," Clark supported.

Having completed the examination, making sure that it was indeed Hans, Kloss said, "I'm taking the body."

Clark started to object but was interrupted.

"Order of the clan."

Clark dramatically spread his hands, agreeing with this situation. "Anything else?"

"Yes." Kloss clearly did not understand the hint of farewell. "His weapon."

There was a dangerous silence between them.

"The weapon is mine," Clark said quietly and carefully, emphasizing every word.

"You probably don't understand the complexity of the situation." Kloss addressed him like a child. "You're not in a position to argue." As he said this, he dramatically placed a dagger on the table.

The weapon was of a rather strange shape. Clark initially mistook it for a boomerang. Both the handle and the blade were made of the same metal, only at one end there was a fabric band that acted as a handle. The entire boomerang dagger turned out to be dotted with symbols of unknown purpose.

Clark was distracted from contemplating the weapon by a demanding exclamation.

"The dead man's weapon, now!"

The guy was clearly nervous. He couldn't stand prolonged silence. There was spiritual immaturity in this gesture. As if to confirm such thoughts, the dagger on the table vibrated.

"I don't advise starting a fight in a strange place." Clark slowly threw back the tails of his raincoat, removing his revolver from its holster. Placing it next to him, he made sure that Kloss was watching his weapon.

The revolver was an old but well-restored weapon. There could be no doubt that it was in working order.

Kloss at first grinned at such antics, but taking a closer look at the powerful weapon, he stopped smiling. On his face, one after another, were doubt, disbelief, and surprise. Now he no longer stood so confidently in front of Clark.

"Apparently, you know what it is." Clark could not resist and lit a cigar. "So I'll repeat: the dead man's weapon is mine. If you continue to persist, then the body will remain here, and the clan will be left with nothing, thanks to your lack of education. I don't think they'll get a pat on the back for this." Clark switched to his style of communication. "So if there are no more questions"—turning the revolver on his finger a couple of times, putting it in its holster—"all the best."

Kloss, snorting loudly, hid the boomerang behind his back. He placed a small ball on Hans's body and activated the spell, and the body disappeared in a flicker. Grabbing the heavier ball, Kloss headed toward the exit. Already at the door, he stopped.

"I will report what happened."

"I have no doubt about that." Clark unceremoniously closed the door in front of Kloss. Walking steps were heard. Clark continued to stand until the footsteps were barely audible anymore.

The walls of the morgue, like the tables and corpses around them, like peeling paint, began to bubble and dissolve. The room gradually took on its original shape. Clark sat down on the sofa that appeared in the corner and exhaled loudly.

"This guy is strong, I have to admit to myself. I haven't created such an illusion for a long time. The most difficult one went in the transport ball with him."

Clark felt pleasure from the work done. He managed to buy time for Hans, and that's the most important thing. Even if he had to leave the residence in a couple of days, such a scam was worth it. Clark didn't know why he was helping Hans. *Perhaps because when I met him, I realized that I am not alone?*

Clark smiled at the sentimentality.

"You have quite strong enemies, my friend," he said into the void. "I hope you have something else besides my sword."

Clark instinctively patted the holster of his revolver. If it's not for it, he didn't know how such a meeting would have ended. He took a big risk.

Using his regular phone, he dialed the head of the analytical department.

"We're winding down. We have been discovered." These two sentences will entail many preparations and precautions. However, Clark liked the change.

Chapter

11

The sun shone brightly on the horizon, giving an emerald shine to the ocean. With every breath, Avalsa's lungs were filled with sea freshness. Tanned residents, smiling welcomingly, rode bicycles while doing their business, creating their own flavor in the southern country. There were also cars on the streets, but not as often as in frozen New York. Everything around was breathing sun and ocean.

That night, Avalsa and Hans left the city in a hurry. Hiding from an invisible threat, they drove on less congested highways with the fewest surveillance cameras. Avalsa weaved through the city like a fox, aware of her blind spots. Hans followed her silently, completely trusting her. Clark put motorcycles at their disposal, soberly believing that they could escape much faster on two wheels.

At first, Avalsa felt insecure behind the wheel of the Japanese vehicle, which took off with screeching speed. She looked with envy at Hans, who was riding the chopper, as if he were an extension of himself. However, having gotten used to it a little, she began to move forward more and more often, scouting out the situation. The scout liked the high speed.

Spurred on by a hidden threat, they rode in the saddles all night and most of the morning. Out of habit, Avalsa was exhausted by the endless stretch of road. After having breakfast at a roadside cafe, they found an abandoned barn, in which they slept until the first dusk. In the evening, Avalsa got behind the wheel with less excitement.

Surprisingly, Hans was silent the whole way. She noticed how he occasionally looked back, thinking about something. When trying to find out something, Hans always avoided answering. Avalsa's patience was at its limit. She even wanted to bring up that conversation in Clark's office. Professionalism prevented her from doing so; so she, biting her lip, continued to wonder about his thoughts.

Upon arrival in Cuba, the clutches of her thoughts loosened their grip, allowing her to enjoy the local landscape. Avalsa happily exposed her face to the warm sun. After New York, Cuba turned out to be a respite for both. Hans also became cheerful and refreshed.

They left their motorcycles in the suburbs, deciding not to attract too much attention. With Hans's backpack, they looked more like tourists. Avalsa even changed her clothes accordingly.

After receiving approval to go to the beach, Avalsa asked the locals about something suitable, while Hans got a room for two from an old woman. They did not book a hotel room; both knew about the rules of secrecy.

"I didn't think you'd approve of going to the beach," Avalsa said, rolling over. Sunbathing gave her great pleasure.

"We look like albinos now," Hans began, looking at the water. "We stand out too much among the locals."

"That's right, because we are tourists. Or are you no longer satisfied with this legend?"

Without answering, Hans also stretched out on the white sand.

After some time, overcome by the need to share his observations, Hans turned to the scout. "When we were having breakfast in a cafe, I heard a conversation between two frightened women." After waiting for Avalsa to remember them, he continued, "They were talking about a coastal town, a few kilometers to the north, where all the inhabitants disappeared overnight. According to the information, it does not seem that they decided to all leave at once. Things and vehicles remained untouched. In some houses, the beds are not even made."

After listening, Avalsa asked, "Do you want to check?"

Hans nodded immediately. She rolled her eyes to the sky.

"We are wanted. Have you forgotten? Even though I don't even know who, it should be clear to you that the disappearance of residents attracts the authorities. It seems to me that they have already cordoned off that area for kilometers."

Hans was silent, patiently listening to her indignation.

"Clark instructed me to protect you, to make you invisible. Instead, you want to go into the volcano itself and make a statement."

"The local authorities don't care about fishing towns," Hans began, ignoring Avalsa's angry look. "It will even be easier for them if suddenly some village disappears, is washed away by a flood. Depopulation is not such news for the country, especially in the outback. You're right, enough people came there to investigate. Those who were on duty at night also disappeared without a trace that day."

"Who are you really?" Avalsa couldn't stand it, attracting the attention of the beachgoers. "Listening to you, I've been trying for an hour to see at least a hint of a scar from the wounds inflicted by that spirit. I'm not even talking about what happened in the gateway, when the walls moved, repeating the movements of your hands. Clark didn't interact with anyone on equal terms until you came to the Guild. Is it worth raising the question of who is looking for you? And why is Clark risking his people trying to hide you?"

Hans did not answer, waiting for Avalsa to cool down.

"I fight the evil present in the form of spiritual creatures in this world."

"I already know that," she interrupted. "Tell me why there is no trace of wounds on your body."

"I have accelerated regeneration."

"Are you human?"

"Yes, I'm human. There is a lot in the world that a person does not understand, and he tries to reject even more. I can tell you everything that interests you, but hear one thing: you belong to a completely different world. This is how it happened chronologically. To understand, you must give up everything that seems familiar to you. I'm not going to go any further. Just accept what you hear as a forced revelation."

Chewing her lip a little, Avalsa nodded.

"So it's a fishing town."

During their week in Cuba, they managed to get a good tan. The scars on Avalsa's back served as a whitish contrast, but at least the locals stopped pointing their fingers, saying "tourists" behind their backs.

To Avalsa's surprise, the city was empty. Following Hans's instructions, they set out just as the full moon was rising from the sea horizon. She did not approve of his desire to investigate the situation, but she also could not leave him alone. Therefore, armed with Guild equipment, Avalsa began to plot a less visible route. Hans did not object to this.

Most of the way they had to make their way through dense jungle, with spreading vines, ferns, and other wild plants. Thanks to her build, Avalsa warmed up and walked around every bush, going far ahead. Hans had to put his sword to work, cutting off plant leaves in order to keep up with his companion. Avalsa endured the noise of cutting branches for some time but could not bear it anymore and flared up.

"We will be less noticeable if you stop leaving such a clearing."

"But there is no one in the area except insects."

"Believe me, the trap will open suddenly when you least expect it."

They constantly expected an attack, but it never came, so Avalsa led them to the right place in the middle of the night. What a surprise it was not to meet a guarded ring of military or police officers. The silence of the sea bay reigned all around.

The town was located in a hollow, washed on one side by the ocean. Many boats were visible moored at a small shipyard. On the other two sides, the city was surrounded by steep cliffs that formed a bay. The approach to the sea, in addition to the ocean, was provided from the jungle, between the trees of which a road winded.

Avalsa walked out with an uncertain step. She looked around, trying in vain to see anyone. An incomprehensible feeling pressed on her temples. Listening to herself, she felt a fear similar to the one in the mansion with the fiery horse. The buzzing feeling of panic grew as they got closer to the town. It was clear that Hans also felt something, so he unwrapped the bundle with the sword, securing the sheath on his back.

"As soon as you get scared, tell me." There was no mockery in his tone, so Avalsa nodded, letting Hans go ahead.

The town was in ruins. It was as if the sea, having overflowed its banks, licked the roofs of buildings, along with fences and barriers. Shards of stones made it difficult to move along the street. The empty eye sockets of the houses accompanied the uninvited guests with wary glances.

The oppressive silence in the center became unbearable, then Avalsa barely touched Hans on the sleeve. Without saying a word, he drew something on his palm and touched his forehead with his index finger. As in previous times, this technique had a calming effect.

"Is this also magic?"

"More like a natural catalyst. I strengthen your natural resistance."

Avalsa did not bother with questions, as the howling of a hyena was heard in the distance.

"Hyenas don't exist in this area," Avalsa said, not believing her ears. In refutation of the statement, the howl was repeated.

"The howl is coming from somewhere underground," Hans said thoughtfully, already suspecting something.

He headed toward the well in the center of the city, the former size of which was indicated by the piles of stones scattered on the ground. Avalsa stood silently behind him. Before she had time to ask the question, this familiar howl burst out from the well, with numerous echoes.

Hans turned to Avalsa, throwing his backpack. "Will you come with me or stay here?"

"Do you want to go down there?"

Hans just shrugged in response.

Avalsa collected her thoughts. Of course, she didn't want to seem like a coward in front of Hans, but she also didn't want to wait for her return in this terrible city, where all the inhabitants disappeared overnight. She silently took out a cable with small rollers and a claw fastening at the end and handed it to Hans. He watched Avalsa attach the same device to her belt and repeated her actions.

The descent was short-lived, but Avalsa was interested in the claw marks on the brickwork of the well. The furrows were deep enough that she was wary of what awaited them at the end of the descent.

After swimming through a small depression, they found themselves in a small cave created by the endless tides of the ocean. Unlike Hans, Avalsa needed light to see. She crushed the phosphorus stick and threw it on the ground. The wand, flaring up, gave a soft green light of a small radius. It was just long enough to see a dog or something similar to one.

Seeing that Avalsa was trying to examine the creature, Hans explained, "This is a hellhound. She is very weakened, but no less dangerous."

He removed a blade from its sheath behind his back, the runes of which illuminated the space around him with a pulsating light. Sensing the weapon, the dog came out into the light, baring its teeth. Barely smoldering smoke came out of its mouth, also visible on the animal's withers. The elongated, toothy snout had no eyes. Only empty eye sockets with smoldering embers of flame. Avalsa felt an itch in her temples when she looked at the dog.

Suddenly the hound attacked. One movement of his wrist was enough for Hans to cut off the dog's head with his sword. Without having time to get nervous, Avalsa breathed a sigh of relief.

"What was it?" Avalsa felt that the effect of the whiskey she drank had disappeared after the creature was killed, and sober thinking had returned.

"Weakened hellhound," Hans repeated patiently.

"Hellhound?"

Hans thought for a while but still answered, "This name is too artistic, but it can be understood that way."

Avalsa didn't even know how to react. She still had a hard time believing in the existence of dark forces and spirits, but she had already witnessed the appearance of a creature from hell.

Hans began to calm Avalsa in a quiet voice, walking around the cave.

"In this world, their voluntary existence is impossible. In other words, in the normal state of affairs, the appearance of creatures of the underworld is excluded."

Avalsa looked up from her contemplation of the rapidly decomposing body and asked, confidence returning to her voice, "What unusual happened then, since he . . . it . . . appeared?"

"He was called," Hans answered, turning his attention to the floor of the cave.

Due to the meager light of the phosphorus stick, Avalsa did not immediately notice the strip carved into the stone. Taking the wand, she followed the curves of the lines that formed the circle. A square was drawn inside the circle, its vertices touching the edges of the circle. A shiver ran down Avalsa's spine. What adults scared children with, what second-rate vulgar media trumpeted about, was now under her feet.

"Is this a summoning circle?"

Hans nodded curtly. Avalsa wanted to ask something else, but he interrupted. "This circle, as you can see, is two-level, so nothing larger than an underworld hound can be summoned through it. However, the number of hounds made it possible to drag away all the inhabitants of this town with them."

"Drag away? Are you saying that people were taken to hell?"

"Have you met the remains of people on the streets?" Hans answered the question with a question.

She did not question further, trusting his knowledge, but asked, "But who would need such a thing?"

Instead of answering, Hans called her to him, squatting down. "If one of us draws a similar circle, says the necessary words, stamps his foot for greater effect, then we will cause nothing but smiles from those around us. The most important thing is the key." Hans pointed to the indentation in the center of the drawn circle.

Avalsa felt the recess and could not even imagine what could fit there. Even a finger couldn't fit in there.

Without saying another word, Hans headed toward the exit of the cave, making it clear that the revelations were over.

As they were already leaving the city, Hans broke the silence. "We need to know where the next time will be. Now there is no need to ask questions. I will only say that those who are looking for me and those who drew this circle are the same people. If they have what I think they have in mind, there will be more calls. You just need to understand the principle by which places are selected. I repeat: a lot of what I don't tell you is done in order to prevent the world in your head from collapsing. But I can't stop you from trying to understand on your own."

Avalsa did not answer, although many questions were swarming in her head. *The same people? Who are they if they easily open the gates to hell, ruining entire settlements? Why do they need this? How to understand where the next gate opening will be?* These questions were strung around one thing: *Who is Hans?* It seemed to Avalsa that if she knew the answer to at least this, she would already be able to understand a lot.

She just had to rely on all her discipline and be patient. Avalsa knew that if she continued her journey, she would definitely get answers. And even though the story with the hounds from hell scared her more than evil spirits, curiosity prevailed. Avalsa couldn't do anything about it and only responded to Hans's explanations, "Fine."

It's morning in Cuba.

Chapter

12

Chloe looked at the shrinking New York from the porthole window. The pleasant voice of the flight attendant distracted her contemplation. They served coffee, but Chloe decided to refuse. A barely concealed anxiety bubbled inside her.

After Clark dismissed everyone from their assignments, Chloe sensed something was wrong. Her vague suspicion only intensified when Avalsa disappeared. She didn't even say goodbye to her friend. Even if the task was urgent, Avalsa always found time to say goodbye before leaving.

Therefore, Chloe decided to stay in New York to better understand what was happening around her. The development turned out to be terrible. In the morning, she heard a powerful explosion that ran through the walls of the hotel. Chloe jumped out onto the balcony. The room just overlooked the Guild building. She couldn't believe her eyes. Flames were shooting out of the windows of the upper floors of the skyscraper. The wind carried the warmth of the fire to Chloe. Without thinking, she ran down the stairs, skipping three steps at a time, and flew out into the street.

From below, the Raven Guild building resembled a burning torch. A crowd of onlookers had already gathered around. The police had to shout and whistle to clear the way for the firefighters. Chloe knew that there was no point in extinguishing a fire of such intensity now. The temperature was too high. By the time the fire subsided enough for chemical foam to extinguish it, everything inside would have been burned to the ground. She hoped that no one was in the building at the time of the explosion.

Firefighters evacuated work offices on the floors below. From one, Chloe heard that the fire on the upper floors even melted metal beams. The cordoning off of the block began. The onlookers moved very slowly toward the fences. When a hail of fragments fell from the skyscraper, people began to leave the fence on their own and run. Chloe saw the building tilt to the side like a melted candle.

The last worker was evacuated from the office premises. The coordinated work of firefighters from three blocks allowed the top of the skyscraper to fall with minimal losses. There were only wounded. Chloe couldn't understand why there was no smoke coming from the fire during the time it happened. This observation apparently did not bother those around her, as they were busy contemplating the destruction and helping the victims.

Chloe ran her eyes over the faces of the rescued. *Not a single person I know from the Guild.* This observation caused ambivalent feelings.

Some time later, Chloe learned from news reports that "fortunately" there was no one on the fire floors of the skyscraper. The cause of the fire made her laugh nervously—a gas line leak.

Chloe found it hard to believe that there was no one on the floors. Clark may have dismissed all members of the Guild, but the analytical department always remained inside, monitoring the progress of everyone's tasks. Where could they have disappeared to?

Chloe's thoughts stopped at the terrorist attack, even though it made no sense. No one knew about the Raven Guild. The uninitiated believed that the entire skyscraper consisted of working offices of various companies. Therefore, no one could harm the Guild. Then a suspicion crept in that one of their own was to blame.

Her head was spinning from the possible versions. Suddenly a raven cawed overhead. Chloe looked at it with frightened eyes. She was too deep in thought, sitting on a bench in the park. Her phone notification prevented the bird from cawing again. The raven, flapping its wings, took off from the lantern, flying into the sky.

It turned out to be a message. Her equipment had arrived at its destination. Chloe completely forgot that she had a task. She calmed herself with the thought that the message she had received spoke about the work of the analytical department. Then she didn't need to lose heart and would complete the task. After completion, she can start searching for Avalsa. Chloe suspected that her friend was aware of what had happened.

After preparing everything, she went to the airport to take the next flight to the Czech Republic. Chloe saw red rooftops appear through the clouds. She looked with great anticipation at the country of legends and forgotten beliefs, walking along the streets. In addition, it is pleasant for the eye to contemplate bright colors, instead of the glass and concrete of New York.

From the airport, Chloe first went to the nearest coffee shop. She wanted to try Czech breakfast. Chloe was used to trying the breakfasts of famous coffee shops when arriving in any country so that her upcoming task went smoothly.

Chloe was superstitious. Avalsa said it was too much. However, Chloe, as always, took the menu and ordered what the townspeople usually eat for breakfast.

The waiter brought an egg casserole with fried sausages. The smell of food reminded Chloe of her hunger that had developed during the flight. Sweet bagels sprinkled with powdered sugar were served along with the coffee. Chloe fully appreciated the Czech breakfast. On top of that, the coffee turned out to be really tasty.

Breakfast distracted her a little, allowing her to plunge into the charming atmosphere of the city. The street lamps already looked different, shining strange reflections on the wet paving stones. Metal sculptures in the city square evoked increasing respect for centuries of history.

Chloe carefully examined the locals, unmistakably identifying tourists. As soon as she left the cafe, she completely got into character, blending in with the crowd. No one could call Chloe a visiting American anymore. The indigenous inhabitants of the city passing by said to her, "Dobré odpoledne," and she answered them.

In the Guild, no one could compare with her in imitation.

She walked along the paving stones, looking at the city. Prague could be enjoyed. Chloe tried to choose the most picturesque streets along the way. Raising her head all the time, she tried to make out the statues of gargoyles majestically propping up the roof of the council building. Red tiles lined the streets, drawing her back several centuries into the past.

She boarded a bus leaving the city. Huge pastures and lowlands accompanied her almost the entire way. Chloe never felt tired. Only after arriving in Prague in the morning did she again take the several-hour bus to the family estates.

Castles in the Czech Republic were considered a landmark not only of the country, but of the whole world. Tourists came from all over to walk along the walls preserving centuries-old culture. Each had their own legend. Some castles, according to local statements, were cursed, haunting the modern human mind.

Chloe knew a lot about curses, as well as the mysticism that exists throughout the world. But it was not a thirst for clues that brought her to the Czech Republic, but the task she was now facing.

Even in the coffee shop, Chloe heard the indignation of tourists on this topic. One of the ancestral castles, once open to all history seekers, turned out to be closed. A metal fence made of strong rods and with an electronic lock in the center said that outsiders were not allowed to enter.

Chloe positioned herself next to the group photographing the castle at the base of the mountain, taking out her monocle.

In the window loopholes she saw people of a very suspicious appearance. Chloe easily recognized them as mercenaries. The people in the castle strategically occupied the perimeter, as if they were expecting an invasion. Chloe was not particularly interested in mercenaries; through her monocle, she was trying to find the customer. She almost missed the moment when the group moved on behind the guide.

She never managed to identify the main thing. In all likelihood, he was hiding somewhere inside the castle.

The quest said to return the castle to the public. At the end of the sheet, she read the main condition: the castle must be empty. She immediately understood what this meant.

Throughout the week, Chloe worked to collect information about those who had "settled" in the castle. She left the hotel early in the morning, returning late in the evening.

Without attracting too much attention, Chloe dressed differently each time, trying to be remembered by people in this particular image and not in the previous one. She even managed to talk to one of the castle's mercenaries. Chloe was able to find out, hiding behind unnecessary chatter about journalism, that the castle had twenty-four-hour security, including video surveillance. The worst-guarded area was the foot of the mountain, where the castle wall rested. The slope was steep enough for an experienced climber to climb. But she never managed to find out the exact number of mercenaries in the castle. And was there anyone else there besides them?

The guard was talking about some kind of ritual, but this topic seemed ridiculous, so the mercenary did not even take it into account. But Chloe took it. Unfortunately, she was unable to find out anything more, only that they were to be replaced that week. At least that's what management told them. Chloe only frowned at what she heard.

The assignment specified that the castle should be empty. She didn't like to wait. If Chloe completes the task today, the castle will be occupied by new arrivals, and then the questions will begin.

After some thought, Chloe decided to wait for her shift to eliminate two groups in one night. It's a big risk, but she's used to taking risks. Clark paid well for successful ventures. Therefore, Chloe, reluctantly, turned into anticipation, studying all sorts of moves of the castle, the plan of which she got from the library.

When she saw a convoy of SUVs covered with government flags, she quickly realized who it was. After taking a ticket to the castle estates, Chloe boarded the bus.

When she reached the castle, she saw that the SUVs were already parked empty along the road. Chloe picked up her monocle again.

There were people at the main entrance with a wide staircase and double doors. It took her a while to identify who had arrived. The arriving mercenaries wore black uniforms, with full special forces equipment. They did not even hide their weapons, keeping machine guns at hand.

Chloe wondered why their faces were so tense. If the country's authorities were aware of this (otherwise, there would already be an army there), then why did they worry so much? Where can they expect threats?

On the second-floor stone balcony, Chloe noticed another group of arrivals. They dressed in black and gold robes, and high hoods hid their faces.

What she saw alarmed her. What other "adepts" were in the castle? She wanted to call Clark to ask if he knew about such a turn of events. She had no connection with the head of the Guild, so she was left guessing, gritting her teeth in frustration.

Chloe was about to leave her observation post (on a branch, between the pine trees), when she noticed activity in the yard. A man in a raincoat emerged from the folding doors of the entrance. She immediately identified the leader by his gait. Chloe zoomed in, trying to see his face.

Quite young, about thirty, a man with short-cropped blond hair. Chloe looked at his eyes and couldn't believe what she saw. His pupils turned out to be vertical! Of course, it might have seemed to her from a great distance, but she got goose bumps. Chloe had only seen the same eyes on a recent guest of the Guild, Hans. She didn't think it was a coincidence.

Her task became more and more interesting with each discovery. She returned to her hotel and plunged into the bath. Chloe estimated the possible number of mercenaries. It turned out that there were about thirty special forces soldiers in the castle, plus eight people in robes (she decided to take them for civilians for now). The leader, about whose capabilities nothing was known, was considered the last. Chloe plunged headlong underwater, thinking about the details of the mission. She already knew what to do.

Chloe knew how to build a logical chain of possible events, anticipating the occurrence of any situations. She differed from Avalsa in that she built the development of the task in her head. Chloe did not miss anything. She even calculated where the glass of water would fall. Many in the Guild took this as a common trick, as every task was completed with success. Those who knew Chloe argued that this was possible thanks to her developed spatial imagination.

The girl with brown hair was given the nickname Alchemist in the Guild. It had nothing to do with the girl's imagination. Chloe was interested in chemistry—the structure of matter, what is calculated and how, what can precipitate, and what will simply evaporate. She was fascinated by this science.

Some storm troopers were afraid of Chloe's methods of completing her tasks, quietly calling her a witch. She didn't pay attention to them. It was enough for Chloe that Clark willingly sponsored her research, periodically distracting her with personal errands.

Chloe emerged from the cooling water. The task in her head had already been completed; all that remained was to complete it in real life.

The full moon was shining in the sky. Wolves alarmed the area, frightening the villagers with their howls.

Chloe went far from human settlements. Moving through the forest, she navigated by the blinking signal of the GPS receiver. She walked quite slowly. The fir branches tried to scratch her face. Chloe was not afraid of being discovered, because the equipment was located far in the forest, away from human activity. She was just a little nervous about the wolves.

The signal beeped more frequently. Moonlight pierced the forest darkness, giving a tolerable overview. In a clearing, not far from Chloe, there was a matte box on which the light of the moon fell. She breathed a sigh of relief.

Donning her outfit, Chloe transformed herself for the mission. Now this was not a smiling girl enjoying Prague. Now she was a warrior of the Raven Guild, nicknamed the Alchemist.

She attached two identical tubes to her back on top of lightweight alloy plates. Chloe took the last, most important piece of equipment out of the drawer—helmet. After putting it on, she forgot about everything, completely focusing on her task. After waiting for the helmet to launch, Chloe activated her night vision.

After spilling a few drops of the substance from the bottle onto the box, she went north, toward the castle. A hiss behind her made it clear that there would be no trace left of the box.

Chloe ran through the forest at great speed. Every time she put on a costume, the latest achievement of technology, she remembered her past.

Chloe was a model. Even as a teenager, she was considered pretty. Beautiful legs, a small elastic bust, a thin waist—everything she needed for a successful career as a fashion model. Being a leader by nature, Chloe always wanted to be first in everything. To avoid being kicked out of the catwalk, her girlfriends diligently lost weight so that they could easily fit into the latest couture outfits. She was considered thin by nature. However, due to peer pressure, Chloe lost weight along with them. She did not even suspect that such actions were undermining her health.

One day she couldn't get out of bed. Doctors diagnosed paralysis due to nutritional deficiency. Being an educated girl, Chloe did not want to put up with what she heard. A career as a fashion model turned out to be bad for her. Her friends visited her in the hospital for some time, but less and less every day.

Chloe went crazy from the realities of the present. She couldn't cope with her thoughts and succumbed to the oppressive influence, so she was transferred to a psychiatric ward.

To the surprise of many, it was in this hospital that she began to recover. Chloe not only began to walk, exercising muscles that had not worked for months, but also regained her mind.

Plagued by chronic malnutrition, she was still weak and painfully thin, but the doctor did the impossible. As it turned out later, her attending physician was the head of the Raven Guild. Clark recruited a smart girl who was lost in life, and without much thought, he sent her to a squad of spies.

Clark equipped her with this high-tech suit, compensating for the capabilities of a weak body. Over time, Chloe regained her previous shape and muscle strength, but she could not part with the suit, which understood the owner's every movement through nerve impulses.

Bypassing the branches, rushing far ahead, Chloe found herself at the foot of the cliff. After adjusting her equipment, she began to climb, intending to enter the castle from the north.

From a bird's-eye view, the castle seemed deserted, except for the laser pointers that pierced the night for hundreds of meters. Using a voice command, she enlarged the image on the helmet's visor. From the top of the cliff, Chloe could see the mercenaries walking below—clearly.

The approach to the rock from the side of the castle was poorly guarded, since going up and down it seemed impossible.

Using the next helmet function, Chloe marked opponents within range. Now she had targets and meters before her eyes. Of course, such information was distracting, but she was already used to it.

Before descending, Chloe removed the contents of one of the tubes. She retrieved the parts and assembled the composite bow with the methodical precision of a musician. She screwed the last shoulder bolt to the handle and fished out the bowstring from the special case. Unlike bow materials, Chloe tried to select natural ingredients for the bowstring.

Leaning her whole body on her shoulder, she with great effort put on a bowstring made of bull tendons. Satisfied with the result of the stretch, Chloe unscrewed the cap of the second tube. Inside were arrows, designed by Chloe from tip to fletching. Especially the tips. Thanks to them, she got her nickname. Chloe smiled to herself.

Having completed her preparations, she secured the end of the cable in the rock and with one powerful leap flew down toward the castle. The wind in her ears muffled any sounds, but Chloe was sure that no one would be able to detect her. The tension in the cable gradually slowed down the vertical descent.

She stopped when there were two hundred meters left to the first target. Two men at the battlement were combing the area with sniper rifles. They wore full ammunition, but their necks were bare. This strange discovery turned out to be very important for Chloe.

With quick and precise movements, she put an arrow into the necks of the two. They died before they even hit the ground. However, the most interesting thing happened after. The bodies under the clothes began to bulge and . . . dissolve. In a minute, only clothes remained of the two mercenaries.

Chloe was called the Alchemist for a reason. She spent all her time in the Guild laboratory. Using various formulas and compounds, Chloe achieved terrifying results. The created liquid destroyed organic matter. One hit in the blood is enough, and the human body begins to dissolve atom by atom. The discovery is amazing. Clark approved this liquid, so Chloe successfully used it for tasks.

She jumped onto the castle loophole; there were four hundred meters left to the next target.

Risky, she warned herself as she drew the arrow and placed it on the string. The "visor" showed the target and the possible flight path of the arrow. All that was required from Chloe was a steady hand and the right tension.

The bowstring tinkled, sending the arrow flying. Rotating, it went in a gentle arc. Chloe didn't hear it, but she imagined the arrow entering the mercenary's neck. The helmet showed that the enemy had fallen. Considering him no longer a threat, Chloe continued her harvest.

She completely reproduced the scenario from her head. Pulling and releasing the bowstring with crazy speed, Chloe destroyed the enemy, one after another. Attacking from cover, the helmet aimed deadly arrows at the target.

The number of mercenaries was rapidly declining. When people stopped communicating, panic began to be felt. Chloe could see their heart rates rising from the sensors in the helmet.

The number of mercenaries was reduced to ten. Still remaining undetected, she perched herself vertically on the wall, watching the commotion around her. Chloe couldn't understand why the leader, the guy with the strange eyes, hadn't revealed himself yet.

She took advantage of the respite and cleared the castle walls; she needed to "clean up" after herself. Before moving on to clearing the courtyard, Chloe collected the clothes of the killed mercenaries, throwing them into the forest, over the wall. She proceeded with the weapons as follows: she collected them in a general pile, took out the necessary vials from her belt, and poured the contents on the weapons generously, connecting the components. It smelled like sulfur oxide. Metal and plastic dissolved more slowly than human flesh, but after a while, there was no trace left of it.

Carried away by this activity, Chloe missed the signal from the thermal imager in her helmet. The mercenary almost took her by surprise, coming from behind. He was too close to using her bow, so Chloe lunged toward him, the arrowhead clutched in her fist.

The mercenary fired a burst from his machine gun. Luckily for her, the weapon was equipped with a silencer, and no one heard the shots. Chloe planted an arrow in the enemy's eye socket, right down to the middle of the shaft. The man's face instantly, like hot wax, began to dissolve. She barely calmed her heartbeat. She was almost discovered.

Mercenaries were still swarming in the courtyard, guarding the entrance to the castle. It was impossible to eliminate them one by one; they did not let each other out of sight.

Chloe was ready for this. She determined that there were only ten mercenaries left. While still in the shadows, Chloe activated her thermal imager, firing three arrows as quickly as she could. She threw a smoke screen before the shots were fired. Having fallen like a stone on the remaining mercenaries, Chloe pierced the nearby ones with arrow tips and neutralized the distant ones with a bow.

The smoke cleared, and there was no one else in the courtyard except Chloe. Just a pile of clothes and weapons.

"It turned out quite noisy," she commented on her methods.

Chloe wondered why the others didn't come out of the castle. According to estimates, there were still twenty-one left, along with the leader and the guys in robes. She counted the arrows.

The front doors had a high-enough opening to allow entry through the top undetected, which Chloe took advantage of. A deserted corridor, unlit by anything, awaited her inside. Chloe gave the order to the helmet but clicked her tongue in annoyance. The castle walls were too cold and thick for the thermal imager to "see" through them. Determining the whereabouts of the remaining mercenaries was no longer so easy.

Chloe walked along the corridor stealthily. The ceiling was high, even the slightest rustle echoed. This technique from the Middle Ages served as a kind of alarm, making it difficult to silently enter the castle.

Chloe didn't make a sound. She hid in niches set up on both sides of the corridor, holding her weapon at the ready.

She passed the first branch, making sure that there were no stairs inside leading to the lower floors. Chloe's intuition told her that the others might be in the basement.

If it weren't for the task, she might have appreciated the charm of the castle. Everything inside breathed with antiquity. The structure was well preserved; no serious damage was observed. There was dampness inside the castle, spreading like a fungus along the wooden beams. Large drops of it stuck to the walls like transparent blisters.

The branches gave way to doors, powerful doors holding back the uninvited guest. Chloe looked around the throne room out of the corner of her eye, intending to move on. Remembering something, she still turned around, going inside.

The guides decorated this room with restored decorations from the last century.

The throne room was considered a landmark of the castle. The approaches to the throne (there were four of them) were covered with red carpets. The torch stands glittered with gold in the night-vision "visor." Numerous arches, on both sides of the throne, hid doors from which servants or a detachment of guards could emerge, protecting the king. But Chloe was not interested in what chandelier was hanging on the ceiling now; she headed into the niche behind the throne.

Her guess turned out to be correct; Chloe felt with her hand the door leading to the lower floors. The thermal imager was still silent, but Chloe was sure that the "Templars" were somewhere there, in the castle.

The corridor turned out to be dark and damp. In the distance, a monotonous drop of water could be heard as water hit the stone floor. With every step, Chloe felt a growing anxiety, shockingly hitting her nerves. The arrow had long been on the string.

For the first time in a long time of wandering around the castle, the thermal imager worked. Farther down the corridor, a torch was burning. Making sure that there was still no one around, Chloe moved on.

Burning torches became more and more common, and there was no doubt that they had been lit recently. Chloe perked up as she felt a vibration in the ground. Hiding behind a niche, she waited for a while. The castle corridor was straight, without branches or turns. Looking around on both sides, Chloe did not move from her place. No one appeared, but the vibration did not disappear, radiating a monotonous pulsation into her legs. Still not understanding what was happening, Chloe continued moving.

With every step, the vibration became stronger. Chloe turned off the thermal imager. Lighted torches stuck out in the walls every ten meters.

She did not see, but heard the Templars.

At the end of the corridor, where the light was brighter, voices were heard repeating the same words, combining into a monotonous call. Chloe was completely at a loss. There was not even a hint of this in the assignment. The singing made the hair on her head move.

Torn by curiosity, she reached the end of the corridor opening onto a columned gallery. What he saw resembled a picture from the Middle Ages. On the lower floor, eight hooded Templars stood facing each other on top of painted squares framed in a circle. While on the balcony, Chloe watched as, following the singing, the lines of the drawing filled with fire; and its tongues tried to set fire to the robes of the Templars.

In the center of the circle itself, standing on one knee, was the leader of the mercenaries. He took off his cloak and in each hand held a strange weapon, shaped like a boomerang. Perhaps Chloe would have stood spellbound if it had not been for the crack of a broken stone. The fair-haired leader, driving his weapon into the stone, turned it clockwise, as if opening a keyhole.

The shock wave knocked everyone to the floor. Chloe's eyes widened in horror. Through the blazing circle, creatures that looked like dogs began to emerge from that light, their necks blazing with flames. The Templars raised their arms in anticipation. The hounds tore the flesh of the Templars one by one, accepting their victims. No one began to eat the remains. The hounds in the coal mouth carried the bleeding flesh to the center of the circle, to the feet of the next creatures that appeared.

Horned creatures, the size of a man, chained, looked around with hatred. A man with a strange weapon, standing at full height in front of the creature, said something in a guttural language. The chains on their chests broke, freeing their hands along with their axes. With a huge bull's mouth, they chewed the remains of the Templars. The leader of the mercenaries was bypassed, although he was collapsing from fatigue.

The hounds scattered around the castle in search of prey. Horned creatures with axes arrived through the blazing gates one after another. There was agony, hunger, hatred in the air.

Chloe would have stood there, shaking in horror, had she not heard the chatter of teeth very close to her. Without realizing it, she fired three arrows containing alchemical liquid into the dog's gaping mouth. The creature howled. Its head fell into pieces. Other hounds responded to the howl. With great effort, Chloe shook off her stupor, turned around, and quickly rushed down the corridor. "When there is danger behind you, you need to act, and not stand like a pillar." Clark's words sounded in her head.

Chloe ran as fast as she could across the throne room. The growling of hounds was heard from everywhere. She shot her bow backhand without thinking. The alchemical mixture, which corroded a healthy person entirely, affected only small areas on the bodies of creatures from another world. Chloe had to shoot three or even four arrows to destroy the hounds.

The creatures kept coming. The horned men with axes passed through the gates much slower than the hounds. They could barely keep up with them, exhausted in anticipation of the sacrifice.

Chloe didn't immediately realize that she was lost. She turned into the next corridor, hoping to see the exit, but a dead end appeared ahead. Panic began to creep into her consciousness again.

Spurred on by the guttural howl, she feverishly looked around. In the darkness, Chloe saw a narrow window that served as an outlet for the second floor. In terms of size, Chloe could squeeze into it. All that was left was to figure out how to get there.

She regretted that she had left half of her equipment at the entrance to the castle. There was a triumphant roar behind him. Chloe barely turned around on stiff legs. The vise of fear seemed to grab the creature's vertebra-like pincers, sending waves of goose bumps across her skin.

A few steps away from her stood a horned creature, rhythmically exhaling blue smoke from its nostrils. The axes in its humanoid hands shook with anticipation. The hounds crowded behind it, yielding to the stronger creature the right to take the victim.

Somehow, Chloe managed to throw off the shackles of otherworldly fear. With a shaky voice, she activated the X-ray function in her helmet, trying to find out the location of the creature's heart. Confidence, albeit slowly, returned. The horned man's chest turned out to be too thick; an arrow would not pierce it.

While thinking, Chloe almost missed the movement. The horned one decided to attack impudently. Despite feeling some stiffness in her legs, Chloe still dodged. To check, she shot an arrow into the creature's eye. As expected, there was no effect. With the shaft sticking out of its eye socket, the horned one swung his axe with monstrous force. The stone floor crumbled with a crash, showering Chloe with concrete chips.

She couldn't understand why her body was so heavy. It was as if the chains on the creature's chest had fallen onto her shoulders. The arrows ran out, so Chloe had to warm up with a crushing axe again. It felt like the creature was getting faster with every blow.

The stupor was dispelled by the helmet, which showed that the owner's performance was falling. Chloe didn't understand why she was getting slower. She looked out the window hopefully. Her salvation was too high. "A distraction is the key to win a battle." Clark's words sounded in her head again.

Chloe reached into her fanny pack. The creature was approaching quickly. The movement of her hands was as if they were jelly. She barely had time to send a whole bottle of alchemical mixture flying. Having broken on the horned chest, the liquid began its monstrous work. The powerful sternum, at first slowly, and then more rapidly, revealed a coal-scarlet heart, pulsating like magma.

The bull's face roared, stunning Chloe. She roared in pain incessantly. The "visor" of Chloe's left eye burst, letting in a feeling of decline, despondency, and weakness. Chloe and the horned one knelt down. The creature, still conscious, raised its hand with an axe. The victim was very close. With each exhalation, splashes of coal blood, smoking in the air, fell on the helmet.

Chloe was brought out of her stupor by the instinct of self-preservation. The axe began to fall. The creature's movements regained their usual speed. Disregarding her fear, Chloe pulled the arrow out of the creature's eye socket and plunged it into its pulsating heart. Blood poured into her high-tech armor, dissolving like sugar. Chloe screamed in unbearable pain. Losing consciousness, she fell next to the dying creature from hell.

There had been no hounds in the doorway for a long time. They led the rest of the horned beasts to the nearest village to begin their bloody harvest, filling the summoning circle with the power of agony, fear, and boundless pain.

Chapter

13

The huge disk of the scarlet sun rose above the horizon. Its rays, meeting no resistance on the flat wasteland, extended for kilometers. The white sand, which had cooled overnight to subzero temperatures, was rapidly heating up.

The sun was rising higher. Sand dunes gradually emerged from the shadows on the horizon, sparkling with their whitish peaks. The air, heating up, floated between them, creating bizarre mirages for lost travelers.

The African desert was considered a dangerous place. Anyone who wandered here could easily say goodbye to life, regardless of their level of preparation and amount of supplies.

Local residents, having set up villages around small oases, fought among themselves for the only valuable resource in these parts—water.

Avalsa endured the heat stoically. The Cuban tan came in handy for the African sun, which has no equal on the sandy land. Once again, she asked herself why she followed Hans. The stupid desire to know the truth played a cruel joke on her.

Short hair had long turned into straw from the scorching sun and rare showers. The aborigines bathed only in heavy rain, which occurred once every three months.

The inhabitants of the village were different from others seen by Avalsa. Outwardly, they resembled living ghosts, their thinness rivaling the scout's physique. Children generally walked around as skeletons covered with resin skin. The dark-skinned aborigines had little idea of clothing: a loincloth and a torn robe over the shoulder represented their entire wardrobe.

Avalsa had difficulty identifying whether someone he met was a man or a woman. The aborigines had the same facial features and similar physique. They even wore the same short haircuts.

Residents used their time and energy to grow something on the sandy lands. On hot days, the few livestock and living creatures hid in human dwellings—thatched huts with one wide entrance, covered with a blanket.

On cold nights—Avalsa had seen just how cold—the residents slept with their animals, keeping each other warm with their bodies.

Each had their own plot for planting, and each tried to germinate crops on it, providing themselves with food throughout the year.

Avalsa and Hans arrived in the village a week ago, having managed to get acquainted with the local customs. They barely made it, being completely dehydrated. Avalsa experienced incredible relief when, behind another scorched dune, they saw the oasis of the village.

Avalsa liked the collectivism in these people. Despite the morbid thinness of many, the residents smiled. They felt a different idea of time, different values, and different interests. The natives gave them water, food, and housing, without asking anything or setting a price. This cannot be found in the modern world.

Throughout the village, residents dug canals from the reservoir, filling their gardens with water. This was the only way to survive in the desert—by working together.

In the evening, when the rays of the scorching sun waned and night had not yet come, the aborigines lit fires. Around them they sang songs and performed ritual dances. These manipulations were carried out with the aim of calling for a successful harvest, causing rain so that the hunt would be successful, and calling for health in the family. Residents believed that dance was something magical that carried the mind far upward, allowing thoughts to materialize.

Hans, who understood the local language, translated the points of interest to Avalsa and taught her how to compose simple sentences.

From the first day of his arrival, along with other men, Hans laid canals and went hunting. At some points, Avalsa did not understand his excessive rejection.

He didn't sleep at night. As the last one remaining at the fire, Hans peered into the darkness, trying to see a possible threat.

"Do you think this village is in danger?" Sitting down next to him, she wrapped herself in a torn blanket. The question alluded to the hellish creatures that had ravaged a village in Cuba.

"Tomorrow there will be a full moon—"

"We'll check tomorrow," Avalsa finished the sentence for him. "Why this village, Hans? The desert is full of others, but you chose this one." She extended her frozen hands to the fire.

Hans shrugged his shoulders strangely, looking into the fire. "I would choose this one. While talking with a local shaman, I learned that the spirits of our ancestors are worried."

"And you believed him?" Avalsa raised an eyebrow as a sign of sarcasm, but Hans did not pay attention to it, continuing, "This is the most populated village for many kilometers around. This number of people is enough to sacrifice."

"Sacrifices?"

It was clear from Hans's face that he already regretted what he had said.

"Do you remember the village in Cuba?" he finally said.

"Yes. You said that people were dragged to hell, but you didn't say why." Avalsa tried in every possible way to get information about this anomaly, but after his revelation about the difficulties of perception, he didn't say another word.

"In the well, we saw a summoning circle that serves to open the gates of hell. In Cuba, the gates of the first level were opened, releasing hellhounds into the world."

Avalsa was eager to find out what other levels of opening the gates were, but she did not stop Hans's revelation.

"The one who performed the ritual will not stop. He will gradually increase the levels. Various creatures can emerge from the gate, but each requires its own sacrifice to appear. If there is not a sufficient source of blood nearby to fuel it, the ritual will not take place, and the sacrifice will be in vain."

There was silence around the fire. You could hear the crackling of coals and the howling of the wind over the desert horizon. Suspecting that the revelation was over, Avalsa asked, "What will happen if the required number of gates are opened?"

Hans looked at her with snake eyes. For Avalsa, all sounds around her seemed to have died down. For a moment, it seemed that the gold of his iris flickered. The log in the fire cracked loudly. Avalsa, blinking frequently, felt that the stupor was leaving.

"If you don't want to answer, just say so," she said angrily, going into the hut.

"I'll be waiting for you at training in the morning." Hans waved after her, once again being left alone in the night.

—m—

The morning illuminated the surroundings with a crimson haze. Sand, grass, and water were painted the same color—red. Behind the settlement, a little farther from the pond, there was a small area overgrown with coarse steppe grass.

Hans was sitting in the clearing. Embracing the blade of the sword, he waited for his companion to appear.

After Cuba, Avalsa asked Hans to demonstrate some dagger moves that particularly interested her. She refused the words "training," "teach," "lesson," getting irritated if she heard them. Avalsa considered herself a worthy fighter, but the battles would not be with people.

She was accustomed to effectively and silently neutralizing the enemy. Being with Hans, Avalsa became convinced that with such creatures, silent techniques were pointless. A different battle strategy was needed.

She had already mastered the Claw, quickly getting used to the curved blade. All that remained was to hone her attacking movements.

Avalsa did not wait for Hans to rise. With a short movement, she jabbed the dagger from top to bottom. Not really counting on the success of the technique, Avalsa played ahead of the curve, kicking Hans from below and throwing him off balance.

The Claw's next blow was supposed to hit the shoulder. Restoring his balance, Hans parried the blow with his sword, holding the blade with his hands. He never had time to intercept the weapon, continuing to fend off quick attacks with the hilt.

Avalsa knew she had the speed advantage, her dagger shorter than his sword. She weaved deadly patterns, looking for a gap in the defense. Their legs moved to the beat of a dance only they knew. Hans had no particular difficulty in fencing, irritating Avalsa with the confidence of his movements.

With a precise kick, she hit him under the knee, knocking him off balance again. Avalsa immediately threw her hand with the Claw into the gap that had formed, straight to the enemy's throat. The curved blade met the hilt again.

The next move was too fast for Avalsa. Hans twisted the blade, using the cross guard to break the blade out of the hands of the scout, who had no choice but to let go of the hilt. To make the grab, Hans also threw his weapon aside.

As she possessed a small build, Avalsa preferred grappling and power moves to attacking blows.

She ducked under the arm, avoiding the technique, smoothly starting to do her own. Pushing off with one leg, she threw the other over Hans's shoulder, throwing her opponent onto his back with the weight of her body. Avalsa hoped to apply a painful one, but something sharp pierced her chest through her shirt. She lowered her head and saw the Claw in Hans's hands. Out of frustration, Avalsa dropped his hand and rolled to the side. He stood up after her, rubbing his bruised shoulder.

Avalsa saw that Hans wanted to say something, so she beat him to it. "Don't say anything, okay? You played a dirty trick by leaving hand-to-hand sparring."

To her angry look, he replied, "When you get carried away with battle, you forget that many people do not fight like people." She immediately realized that they were talking about creatures of darkness.

"The rules of survival say that you should not bother with your enemy for long. There may be many of them, but you may be alone."

Avalsa, without answering, returned back to the village. Defeated, like the previous times before.

Hans sat by the pond a little longer until he dozed off in the pleasant coolness of the morning before the hot day.

He dreamed of emptiness. Pitch darkness all around, in which a lonely presence was felt. Moans were heard. Endless cries for help, echoing alarmingly in his head.

Somewhere on the horizon, lightning flashed. Its light could not illuminate anything, as if the darkness was woven from something material, oily dense. Hans couldn't tell if anyone was nearby. Where it was and where the edge of this void began also remained beyond understanding. With inexplicable frenzy, the discharge struck only one point, lightning after lightning.

"Help! I'm dying! Stop this pain!" came from everywhere, echoing in his chest.

It was becoming difficult to walk. It was as if his feet were plunging into impenetrable jelly. Feeling the ringing in his ears from the surrounding groans, Hans continued to walk toward the striking lightning.

It seemed like an eternity passed in his struggle with the viscous soil, and the lightning bolts did not come even a meter closer. Suddenly, someone grabbed Hans, lifting him off the ground. There was no point in resisting. The viselike grip squeezed his shoulders tightly. The stench of otherworldly breath hit his face.

"You betrayed us!" the one who grabbed him growled, shaking his body. "You left us! You betrayed us!" Monotonously repeating the same thing, the speaker suddenly lowered Hans to the ground. As if frightened by his accusations, the man who grabbed him began to cry hysterically. Hans fumbled with his hands, trying to find the source of the crying, but in vain. Crying echoed through the thick darkness, appearing from everywhere.

The ground beneath his feet began to move, plunging him into it. Hans tried to break free, looking with his hands for something to grab on to, but the shifting soil continued to suck him in. It became difficult to breathe from the weight that had piled up. His ears were filled with darkness.

"You betrayed us!" It sounded like underwater. "You left us!"

He felt the air fly out of his lungs, accompanied by dark bubbles. Blackness poured into his mouth like a broken dam. Unbearable pain spread throughout his body.

Hans opened his eyes wide. His pupils narrowed to small slits, reacting to the bright sun. It took him several deep breaths to realize that he was no longer asleep. His body began to spasm from his half-sitting position.

Looking around, Hans realized that he had not slept for very long. The sun was not yet at its zenith.

"So many days without sleep will weaken anyone," he briefly summarized his dream.

In the village, everything went as usual. Men brought animals into their houses; women called everyone for dinner. In one of the ditches supplying water to the garden, young girls were rinsing their clothes.

Hans felt a sense of friendliness in the air. There was no trace left of another nightmare. He sat down next to Avalsa, starting to eat.

"Where have you been?" she asked, smiling. The morning grievances were quickly forgotten.

"I was dozing."

"The shaman asked for you. He wanted to tell you something."

"Have you learned to understand the local language?" He was surprised.

"Partially." Avalsa waved it off, flattered by Hans's gaze.

"We'll go searching tonight, so get ready."

"I don't know," she snorted, putting the last spoonful of porridge into her mouth.

The smell of smoldering herbs wafted through the shaman's hut. Hans thought that if he stayed there for a long time, he will begin to rave like a shaman. The shaman turned out to be a skinny old man with a heap of rags wrapped around his thin shoulders.

He stared into space with an unblinking gaze, clearly in a state of meditation. Hans had to cough loudly a couple of times to draw attention to himself.

"Hans, is that you?" The shaman asked the obvious question.

"Yes. You wanted to see me? Did the spirits speak to you again?"

"Perfume? Yes, they did. They came to me in a cloud of smoking smoke. They told about anxiety, experiences playing out in the world of spirits. Our village is protected by the spirits of the ancestors who lived here previously. They are deaf to my requests for protection."

"I'm sure that if you continue your work, sooner or later the spirits will respond."

The old man may have had the gift of a medium in his youth, but senile insanity blocked his talent. He felt the disturbances of the spirits but could not determine the reasons. What Hans heard was enough to begin preparing for what was to come.

Already at the exit, the old shaman told him, "Beware of ghosts. They will appear where you don't expect them at all."

Hans did not work with the other men on the canal today. Pulling the sword out of its sheath, made of thick leather, he began sharpening it. It was incredibly hot outside. Sitting in the shadow of a boulder, Hans gradually moved the sharpening stone along the blade, periodically whetting it.

"It seems you said that this is a charmed blade." Avalsa appeared from behind the boulder unnoticed. "Then why are you sharpening it?"

"A conspiracy does not make a sword sharper." Hans raised his hand above him. "But a whetstone does. Besides, it's just ordinary metal," he said with some strange sadness.

Avalsa pulled out the Claw from behind her back, testing the sharpness of the blade.

"This dagger does not need sharpening."

"Why?"

Hans answered simply, "Blade."

Naturally, this did not satisfy Avalsa, but he did not intend to explain anything.

"We'll set out after sunset today. You still have time to make preparations."

"Will I be of any use?" Avalsa asked a rather unpleasant question for herself.

Hans stopped moving the whetstone and looked at her. "The main power of evil spirits is oppression. By tuning into your background, they awaken fear in your brain, paralyzing it, making it impossible to think. The panic in your head is growing, and you can't do anything about it." Hans paused for a moment, giving her the opportunity to understand what she had heard. Unbeknownst to her, Avalsa nodded. "Once the spirits suppress spiritually, it is not difficult for them to attack your material body." Hans took something out of his pocket. "I borrowed the materials for the bracelet from the shaman. It contains a spell that can protect your mind from the mental attack of evil spirits."

"In other words, will I stop being afraid?"

"Exactly."

Avalsa's face brightened.

Taking the knitted bracelet, she put it on her hand. As expected, Avalsa didn't feel anything, just a little itching at her temple.

Hans waited until the scout had finished admiring the bracelet.

"We will not fight with people, so listen to me during the battle." She heard a commanding tone from him for the first time. "Don't do anything yourself in the battle with evil spirits."

Avalsa did not answer. She stayed to watch Hans sharpen the blade with runic writing it.

For the first time, Avalsa heard someone worry about her.

All her life she considered herself strong. She had no choice. Numerous scars on her body served as a constant reminder of the cost of loneliness. Avalsa performed the most difficult tasks, enduring any pain.

As a child, Avalsa was weak. Her father systematically beat her and humiliated her while in an alcoholic stupor. He took pleasure in beating her mother as well. Avalsa didn't always remember her childhood, but now pictures of the past flooded in.

She watched as her father killed his wife on a cold winter evening. He beat her to death, and little Avalsa stood and watched with tearstained eyes, unable to do anything. She hated herself for it. Therefore, every time Avalsa received a scar on her body, she became stronger.

Clark picked her up as a teenager. He got her out of the penal colony. Avalsa plunged a dagger into her father's neck while he slept.

The corners of her eyes moistened a little from the memories.

"Fine."

Hans did not immediately realize that this was a belated answer to his warning.

—m—

The full moon appeared early on the horizon. With its bloody light, it dispersed the desert shadows, making the night bright, deceptively safe.

Everyone in the village was asleep. No one heard the two leave the village. Leaving the light of the moon behind them, they went deeper into the desert. It was difficult to say what awaited on the horizon. With each dune crossed, the terrain changed.

Hans decided to check the perimeter of the village, spiraling away from it. The height of the sand embankments made it possible not to lose sight of the village. His feet mercilessly sank into the sand. Avalsa did not immediately notice the danger waiting.

A spear approached as if in slow motion. Flying out of the sand dune, it looked with its tip at her chest. Out of the corner of her eye, the scout noticed another movement—a spinning sword. A few centimeters from Avalsa, the two weapons met, shifting each other's flight path. She only managed to duck down. The sword rustled through the ends of her hair.

Her heartbeat quickened, returning time to its real speed. Death again passed Avalsa by. The ambush continued to develop.

Two people who had crawled out of the sand were already pressing on Hans, who was fending off the blows of the spear with the chain of the Grail. Humanoid creatures turned out to be creatures of darkness. The oily black skin shone darkly in the bright moon. They resembled porcupines: each had fragments of spears sticking out of their backs, growing each time after use.

The third sat down on the upper dune, continuously throwing spears at people. It was difficult for Hans to warm up with flying projectiles and fend off the attacks of two at the same time.

Avalsa could not come to Hans's aid. The spears were flying toward her, but the thrower was too far away, so the scout only had time to duck under the flying projectile. She had no intention of hitting the shaft with the dagger. When she saw Hans's sword in the sand, Avalsa tried to get it.

The weapon was close to the spear thrower, but she tried not to think about it. Getting stuck in the sand at every step, Avalsa zigzagged as hard as she could, getting closer to the weapon. The thrower, having guessed her intention, stopped throwing spears at Hans, focusing on her. Avalsa felt the shaft pierce the sand just a step behind her. She understood that if she hesitated for a second, she risked being impaled on a spear. Solutions were racing through her head at breakneck speed.

Suddenly she remembered that Hans had insisted on carrying a pair of nails of the Savior's Cross with her. Avalsa did not understand how such a weapon could be useful to her, but now it came in handy. "Holy weapons require faith, not skill."

Avalsa took one nail from her belt, weighing it in her hand. The target was about seven meters away. To throw a peg of this weight, you need to use the inertia of your entire body. Stopping abruptly, Avalsa discouraged the thrower. The enemy's hesitation was enough to throw a roundhouse nail. The enemy was lucky; instead of its head, the nail of the Savior's Cross hit its chest. However, Avalsa wasn't looking. Throwing spears from the flank was interrupted.

When she reached the sword, she called out to Hans, throwing him the weapon. The scout needed to deal with the wounded thrower to the end. The oily shell on the its began to drain, turning into thick resin. She had observed Hans's past battles, aware that the creature's armor had been compromised.

With wide swings of her Claw, Avalsa struck the wet areas of the shell. The eyeless creature screamed in pain in a raspy voice that made its jaws close. However, the creature was not going to give up. Lunging with a spear, it tried to impale Avalsa on the shaft. But she was no longer afraid.

Although the disgusting scream ran through her ears like an unpleasant wave, the paralyzing fear was no longer felt. Avalsa seized the moment, plunging the second nail into the creature's hand. But she only slid along the armor, flying out of her hands. In surprise, she almost missed the fatal blow, instinctively turning around. Finishing the turn, Avalsa threw out her hand with a dagger and hit her opponent right in the ear. The creature of darkness fell like a heavy bag onto the sand. It died while still in flight.

Not having time to rejoice over the first killed creature of darkness, Avalsa hastened to help Hans. It turned out that help was no longer needed. As soon as he got the blade in his hands, he turned into a deadly mill. The enchanted blade sliced through limbs like melted butter. The creatures didn't stand a chance.

Having dealt with the last one, he looked at Avalsa with eyes fierce from the battle. He came to his senses and said the only thing he considered important at that moment. "Thank you."

Avalsa smiled with difficulty. In the short period she spent in the battle, she was more tired than in a whole day of training in the Guild. She found nothing better than to collapse on the cold sand.

"You're the one who saved me, so there's no need to thank me. I was just returning the favor." Avalsa felt awkward being thanked. "What were they?"

"They once served in the legion's army. These are spearmen. In one of the battles, several warriors were left to guard the observation tower. Located in the rear of the main army, the tower served as an important strategic object."

"Did they tell you that?" Avalsa stood up, wrapping herself back in her poncho, protecting herself from the flying sand.

"I'm just familiar with the history of some battles," Hans lied without blinking an eye. "After all, many spirits remain restless on the battlefield. Through time, this place can become anything: a football field, a supermarket, a garden, a desert, in the end. The earth remains the earth. It doesn't matter what is built on it. What matters is what its history is."

Avalsa did not immediately catch this turn.

"By the way, about history." Hans began to look around. "Since we've dealt with the guards, maybe we'll look for the tower itself?"

"What about the gates of hell, the defense of the village?" She ironically repeated Hans's words.

"They won't open them here."

"Why?" Avalsa was taken aback by what she heard.

"The world of spirits is like a world of predators: the strong feed on the weak." Hans began to move away from the battlefield. "If the gates opened somewhere here, the spirits would scatter for many kilometers. These spearmen"—Hans pointed a finger behind him—"were an hour's walk from the village. Therefore," he decided to finish his thought, "if the spirits have not disappeared, then the call will not be here. The village is not in danger."

Avalsa was annoyed by Hans's excessive detail. It was reminiscent of some kind of moral teaching. It felt like she was at a lecture. But still Avalsa overcame her irritation, saying, "I have another question."

Hans was just choosing a direction in the desert, picking up a handful of sand, scattering it through the air. Avalsa could not find her way in the endless sands. There was nothing to be attached to here, but Hans thought otherwise.

"Ask." Hans felt that the tower was somewhere nearby. The emanations of the slain spearmen led to her, but he patiently answered questions.

"Why didn't the second nail go into the creature? It simply slid across the armor without even scratching it."

"What happened to the first one?"

"The first one pierced the shell when I threw it."

Hans thought about it. He was pleasantly surprised that such a heavy nail could be thrown.

"Remember what I said about this weapon: to use it, you need faith, not skills." Over time, Hans learned that faith is also a skill, but he said the following out loud: "Without strong faith, this weapon turns into an ordinary piece of metal."

"Then why did you come in first?"

"Think and you will answer yourself."

Avalsa almost boiled at this answer. She bit her lip hard, calming herself down.

The sand rustled underfoot, slowing down their pace. It had become quite windless in the desert; there was no need to cover their face from the cutting grains of sand. The answer came so suddenly that she said it out loud.

"I was sure that I would hit the target when I threw the nail. The second time I thought that it would enter the creature itself."

"Exactly." Hans smiled. "Thoughts strike like weapons. Therefore, be careful when using them."

"Can we do it without unnecessary philosophy?" Avalsa couldn't stand it. "I myself understood why this happened. And your explanations are useless."

Having cooled down a little, Avalsa agreed that Hans had led her to understand the problem. She didn't say anything out loud, of course.

A crash was heard underfoot, but Avalsa managed to roll over her shoulder, holding the Claw in her hand. In the place where the crash was heard, sand was drawn into the funnel.

"It doesn't look like quicksand," Hans remarked when the sand stopped flowing away, revealing the opening. There was a whiff of musty air coming from the entrance. Without saying anything, Hans dived into the darkness of the resulting opening. Avalsa followed.

The floorboards creaked underfoot, but the scout walked silently. It took a while for her eyes to adjust to the twilight. The light of the moon penetrated through the cracks in the stone walls, piercing the room with whitish rays. Instinctively, Hans walked around them, trying not to cross the moonlight. Avalsa followed suit from the shadows of the room.

"It turns out that the tower is covered with sand from the outside," she whispered.

"You're right," he answered, looking into the doorway.

From the inside, the tower seemed quite strong. In one of the rooms—Hans assumed it was the dining room—wooden benches were preserved along with a long table. He did not check whether the bench would support him as he carefully walked past.

Without much difficulty, they explored floor after floor, descending down the spiral staircase and raising columns of dust. Avalsa was overcome by an inexplicable feeling associated with this tower. With each room she examined, she became more and more convinced of its relationship with the building, which could not be considered true. Hans seemed tense, expecting some kind of danger. However, he had a similar feeling.

Inspecting each room, Avalsa did not notice that Hans was walking along the tower with a confident step, unerringly choosing the direction.

He was the first to notice the first oddity, as he was better able to navigate in the dark. The walls on the lower floors no longer let in light from the street.

"What's happened?" Avalsa asked as Hans abruptly stopped in the middle of the room. Instead of answering, he took her hand and brought her to the wall. Her palm felt the power supply wire. In the darkness, Avalsa did not immediately identify it, but the discovery was very surprising.

"You can see from the markings that the wire is this year." Hans shook his head, noticing more and more signs of habitable premises. The first were the numerous footprints on the dusty floor. Several gas lamps were visible on the ceiling; the wiring to them had been hastily constructed. It was amazing to see a structure of antiquity equipped with the amenities of the modern world.

"Do you think there's someone here?"

"Let's check." Hans nodded to Avalsa, who was kneading a phosphorus stick that dimly lit the room. He himself went forward.

After passing through two rooms through a corridor, Hans quickly turned around, covering the light in the scout's hands with his jacket.

"I can hear movement on the landing." Hans moved so close that Avalsa could hear his breathing. He quickly untied the scabbard behind his back, handing her the sword. "These are people. I can't say how many, but footsteps are carried along the lower floor."

"Do you want me to wait here for you?" Pride began to be indignant, but Avalsa quickly extinguished it with common sense. She was no help to Hans in the dark.

"As soon as the lights come on, be prepared for a commotion."

Hans let go of her hands, leaving her alone in the room. To be sure, Avalsa took up the Claw.

Hans heard two people on the stairs joking with each other. Little red cigarette lights illuminated their faces. A window was visible on the landing, but the moon no longer sent out rays to illuminate the room. Each of them had swords hanging from their belts, raising even more questions in Hans's mind.

Without thinking twice, in two steps he found himself in front of the discouraged faces, his eyes sparkling in the darkness. They didn't have time to make a sound. Two precise blows from the sinker of the Grail chain sent the smokers into unconsciousness.

There was a commotion on the landing below. People wanted to take Hans by surprise, without turning on the light, wielding a sword in the dark. Having dodged two attacks, Hans looked at his attacker. The attacker was blindfolded. He attacked based on hearing. Unfolding the chain, Hans took the blade into its links.

Someone in the room shouted for the lights to be turned on, but Hans paid no attention. They failed to take him by surprise. In the darkness, no one could attack a stranger except a blind man.

There was a feeling of skill in the man's hands. He used lunges and feints similar to Hans's. His speed was sufficient for Hans to parry the blows in time. Hans seized the moment when the blind man attacked with a diagonal swing to wrap a chain around his blade at the lowest point. As Hans expected, the attacker tried to kick. Stepping over the sword, using the chain as leverage, Hans threw the man over himself, sending him into a short flight. He never dropped the weapon from his hands.

Before Hans could move on to another opponent, the lights came on. It happened so unexpectedly that he went blind for a few seconds. When his vision was restored, Hans saw that those present in the room did not think of attacking, taking advantage of the moment. At the other end of the room, an arrow was aimed in his direction.

The bowstring tinkled quietly. The shooter fired the arrow decisively, without missing. The sudden light was supposed to disorient the enemy. He didn't stand a chance.

Hans felt a jolt. Looking down, he saw an arrow sticking out of his shoulder. His hand went numb in a matter of seconds. Avalsa's scream prevented the shooter from firing another shot.

She ran into the room as soon as the lights came on. Avalsa looked around the people, assessing the enemy, accidentally bumping into a familiar face. A beautiful girl with green eyes and thick brown hair was no less surprised than she was.

Chloe couldn't believe her eyes.

"Avalsa?" Chloe looked from Hans to her and back, wondering, "Is he with you?"

"It's a long story that Clark is involved in," Avalsa answered briefly, calming down. The arrow was without the deadly mixture that the Alchemist loves to use.

"Didn't you recognize him?"

"I did," Chloe said coldly, "so I shot him in the shoulder."

Hans hissed in pain as he tried to pull the arrow out.

"You don't have to try. The tip is serrated on both sides."

Avalsa was slightly surprised by her friend's cold tone but decided to wait with her questions.

"How did you end up here?"

"Out of necessity. I'll tell you the rest in my room. Let's go." Already at the very exit, Chloe turned around, turning to one. "Jerome, help him with the arrow."

Avalsa silently followed her friend, hiding her surprise and expecting quick answers to her questions.

"The wound will need to be cut," Jerome said some time later, when there were three left in the room. The others left the room, going to catch up on sleep in the predawn hours. They didn't care about the stranger.

Jerome was considered the squad's healer. The tall dark-skinned aborigine knew a lot about herbs and poultices, and his surgical education allowed him to competently use a scalpel.

The detachment consisted of eleven people. Hans was amazed at the coincidence when he heard that they came from the Raven Guild. The detachment wandered around the lands for several years, without any assignment. Many of their hair was covered with thick gray hair.

Several years ago, they tried to find a connection with Clark by visiting Guild residences in European countries. But every time, crossing the threshold of the branch, the detachment saw an empty, dusty room, where for several years, it seemed, no one had lived. On the notice board hung the same order, given by him before all this cyclical mysticism arose: "Protect Africa from poachers."

Hans made friends with the captain of the squad, who turned out to be that blind swordsman. His name was Seraph.

"Is Seraph short for Seraphim?" Hans asked while Jerome pored over his wound.

The tart smell of herbs was in the air. It was necessary to give credit to the doctor: Hans felt almost no pain when the scalpel cut the flesh around the arrow shaft with pinpoint precision.

"Yes," Seraph answered briefly and smiled. "A warrior of light who from birth sees only darkness."

Hans appreciated the irony but reminded the captain of the history of the detachment's wanderings.

"At first, we took the task seriously," Seraph began, adjusting the blindfold over his eyes. "We killed poachers, human traffickers, and other carrion unworthy of being called human. Bringing evidence to the Guild residence, we again met an empty hall and this task on the order board." Seraph was silent for a while, remembering something. The deep furrows on his forehead showed that he often thought.

The captain's head may have been covered with thick gray hair, but it did not interfere with the precision and balance in the swordsman's movements.

"We carried out the same order about a dozen times," Jerome interjected in the conversation, his nostrils flaring angrily, "but we could not meet either Clark or the other members of the Guild. It was as if he was mocking us. Only this stupid task made it possible to think that the Guild still existed."

"What about New York?" Hans asked, hinting at the main branch.

"We didn't find him," Seraph answered briefly, surprising Hans. "Knowing the address and location, we didn't find the Raven Guild.

"Since then, we have been wandering as an abandoned detachment. There was no doubt that Clark wanted to forget about us. We don't know any other weapon than the sword, so we try to visit less developed cities without attracting much attention."

Jerome grabbed the arrowhead with tongs and pulled it out in one sharp movement, applying a compress. Hans didn't even have time to shout.

"Thank you," he said, rubbing the patch on his shoulder. "Let me ask: how long ago did you receive this strange task?"

"Twelve years ago. I still remember. I turned fifty then, and instead of celebrating, we went on this mission."

"It would be better if we celebrated your anniversary," Jerome said angrily, but Seraph did not support him.

"We were the best squad of swordsmen only because we completed all the tasks that Clark gave us."

Hans suspected why Clark did this to them. In the short time that he got acquainted with Clark, he saw that the head of the Guild was sentimental. He had only young fighters subordinate to him, approximately the same age. There were no gray-haired people in the Guild. Perhaps Clark simply sent the squad into "retirement" without telling them about it.

"Did you meet Chloe in Africa?" Hans decided to change the subject.

"We found her in the Czech Republic," Jerome said, his face noticeably darkening.

Before he said anything more, Seraph put his hand on his shoulder and continued, "Chloe had one foot in the grave when we stumbled upon her."

"When we saw her along the road, not far from the castle, we realized that something terrible had happened. Chloe's whole body was covered in burns." Jerome picked up, not focusing on the incident in the Czech castle. "Her high-tech suit melted in many places, exposing the affected skin."

They fell silent for a while, giving Hans the opportunity to imagine the degree of pain the unfortunate girl had endured.

"We had to do a difficult operation: cut off the charred suit centimeter by centimeter, freeing the charred flesh. Many of our guys thought that the girl would not survive. There were too many burns on her body. Being delirious, Chloe called Clark, wanted to warn him about something." Jerome deliberately did not say what exactly the warning was. Hans had no doubt that those present knew more than they were telling.

"She was unconscious for a month. Chloe didn't come to her senses even when I changed the bandage. Nevertheless, the girl's young body did its job: the burns gradually healed. The wounds no longer looked so painful."

"We suspect that her unconscious state is somehow connected to the shock she suffered in the castle." Seraph decided to intervene in the conversation. Hans had a rough idea of what kind of shock they were talking about and what these two were not saying. However, he continued to listen without asking questions.

"Having come to her senses, Chloe said that she was from the Raven Guild. We already knew this after examining her equipment. And in her delirium, she often mentioned the name of the head of the Guild.

"As soon as she got back on her feet, she immediately decided to go to Africa, greatly surprising us."

"Why did she need Africa?" inquired Hans.

"She said that in order to complete the order, she must go after the victim. Since we were from the same Guild, we offered our help by going with her."

"The girl was too weak to travel alone," Jerome said in a deep voice. "Even though we didn't want to return to the desert, we were interested in the girl's desire."

"Who exactly was Chloe going to track down?"

"I don't know for sure," Seraph once again lied straight to his face, "but Chloe didn't get off the Internet for weeks, taking notes. Chloe didn't share much of her thoughts with us. She was grateful that Jerome saved her, but the psychological trauma still affected her behavior. It was felt. We may not have known each other before, but it seems to me that Chloe is a very open girl."

There was silence in the room for some time. They could hear the measured hum of a gas lamp under the ceiling, the dry sound of rosary beads being fingered, and muffled voices in the next room.

Hans understood why they were hiding certain aspects of the story. The truth seemed so fantastic that the squad was afraid that Hans simply wouldn't believe it. He understood them.

Hans was distracted from his thoughts by Seraph's voice.

"Thanks to blindness, I understand people better than sighted people. I heard you put your sword down before you came down towards us. By the way, this is also a merit of blindness—good hearing. You knew that there were people in the tower, but you didn't intend to kill anyone. Don't deny it. You are a good person." It was time for Hans to be surprised by such statement. "That's why Chloe shot you in the shoulder, although she could have killed you."

"The fact is that we know her." Hans told Seraph about visiting the Raven's main residence.

"Business," Jerome said after thinking a little. "Then it's unclear why Chloe shot at you, knowing that she recognized your face."

Hans didn't answer. He just looked through the doorway where Chloe and Avalsa had disappeared some time ago.

Chapter

14

From the first few minutes of their conversation, Avalsa noticed that Chloe was nervous. This was not evident in her voice, but her gestures looked intermittent and too abrupt. As Chloe closed the door, Avalsa could see her bandaged hands.

"Before, I didn't notice your love for so many bandages, friend," Avalsa joked to relieve the tension. Without answering, looking straight into her eyes, Chloe undressed. Avalsa's face fell in surprise. "God, what happened to you?" Continuing to remain silent, her friend removed the bandages from one hand.

"And this is all over my body." Chloe extended her hand with scarred skin. Avalsa looked from the burn to the bandages along her friend's chest and stomach.

She brushed aside the thought of a failed experiment with substances. Chloe was a fairly good specialist; she would never allow negligence in the preparation of chemical mixtures. Scrupulousness was in her blood.

Having finished examining the wounds, Avalsa decided not to guess, but to ask directly. "Why are you like this?"

Chloe's face twitched at the memory. Exhaling deeply, she recounted her experience to her sympathetic friend.

Avalsa listened to the story and could not believe what she heard. Hans's words were true again. They deliberately searched for the summoning site to prevent the threat, but Chloe was "lucky" to stumble upon the opening of the gate first. Although one can speculate about the latter, because it was Clark who issued the task to clear the castle in the Czech Republic. To avoid getting lost in her thoughts, Avalsa continued to listen.

"The blood of that monster was so hot that it melted the armor. I lost consciousness from the pain. I didn't think it was possible to survive something like this." Chloe was silent for a second, suppressing her tears. Avalsa, supporting her friend, took her hand. She continued more calmly. "While I was unconscious, I had visions of dozens of horned creatures with axes following fire dogs to the nearest town. I saw how they kill everyone indiscriminately: women and children, old people and cripples, young boys and girls. I could feel the taste of blood in my mouth, settling like a mist on my skin. It fell into my lungs in small drops with every breath. Avalsa, I saw how the creatures, having had their fill, returned back to the castle, leaving the city without a single living soul. Overnight it became deserted. Only traces of blood on the pavement, the walls of the house, on the carpet of the apartment showed that something terrible, irreparable had happened. Unable to restrain myself from what I saw, I began to cry. I cried and woke up. Tears were streaming down my cheeks when Seraphim's people found me.

"To this day, I don't know how I was able to get out of the castle on my own." Chloe was distracted for a while, making coffee. She handed the second mug to her friend. Avalsa could now clearly see how the movements caused discomfort.

"I spent about two weeks in delirium. Quite a clinical coma. Mostly I had nightmares filled with fire, agony, fear, pain. It even happened in different sequences." Chloe grinned. "But I couldn't get out of my head the man with snake eyes who appeared in the Czech Republic at that time. He opened the gates of hell, Avalsa. Yes, he was helped by fanatical Templars singing ritual songs, but it was his movements that opened this fiery gap. I saw it with my own eyes." Chloe looked at Avalsa carefully, fearing that she wouldn't believe her. But her friend nodded confidently, signaling her to continue. Avalsa was engrossed in the story.

"When I came to my senses, I rejoiced at my saviors. By an amazing coincidence, I was saved by a squad of swordsmen from our Guild. Without thinking, I laid out the details of my assignment and what happened to me. They believed me. Unlike our swordsmen, Seraph was kind to me. It later turned out that they had not been in contact with the Guild for more than ten years. Can you imagine something like this?"

"I can," Avalsa answered gloomily. She remembered the blind captain of the squad.

As Clark's student, she admired the blindfolded swordsman who was superior to sighted swordsmen. Avalsa also wanted to learn how to fight blindly, so she asked Seraph for a couple of lessons. Clark prohibited it, arguing that for the speed of Avalsa's attacks, she needed a younger teacher. And then Seraph disappeared along with the entire squad.

Avalsa thought that the swordsmen in the Guild had been disbanded, but after a while, Clark recruited new ones. She was unable to find out about Seraphim's fate. Avalsa was loaded with training by Clark from morning to night. Over time, such curiosity dulled and then was completely forgotten. Then Chloe appeared, and the head of the Guild decided to create a squad of spies. Chloe's voice did not allow Avalsa's memories to play out further.

"The experience made it impossible for me to remember where else I had seen eyes like those. The answer did not come immediately. It wandered in the back of my mind, which was focused on restoring my body. And when Hans appeared on the steps of this tower, it struck me like thunder. Without thinking, I shot at him. At that moment, I wanted to interrogate him, to find out about his involvement in all this." Chloe pointed to her bandages. "But when you appeared, enlightenment was covered with clouds of misunderstanding."

"Chloe," Avalsa began, not even knowing what to say to her friend, "to tell you, at least approximately, what is happening and what we got ourselves into, we need to talk to Hans. I can only say that it was Clark who entrusted me with keeping an eye on him."

Chloe's face froze in surprise. Such a coincidence simply could not be accidental. Avalsa promised to question Clark carefully about his plans. She had no doubt that Chloe's meeting with her took place with the assistance of the head of the Guild.

"Let's go. They've already waited for us."

When the door opened, everyone except Seraph turned around. Chloe quickly ran her eyes over those present, asking Jerome where Hans had gone.

He went to wander around the tower and promised to be back by breakfast. "Are you hungry too?" Jerome looked at Avalsa, expecting her to introduce herself. Her stomach was truly empty. She did not want to eat at the village, because supplies in the desert were very limited.

"I won't refuse."

"Great." Jerome clapped his hands. "Then help the guys set the table while I do the bandage."

Chloe wanted to object, but the dark-skinned giant left her no choice, luring her into another room with a huge hand.

For some time there was silence at the table. Seraph was the first to break it.

"You're from the Guild too, aren't you?"

Avalsa nodded, then remembered that there was a blind man in front of her and answered out loud, "Yes, from a squad of spies."

Seraph smiled at her confusion. "Then to avoid wasting time, I suggest that you start setting the table while continuing our conversation."

The members of the squad, previously bored, perked up, introducing themselves and extending their hand to the small, fragile girl. Seraph only smiled once again at the childish behavior of adult men.

—⟋⟋⟍—

Hans walked up the stairs, crossing the next floor. He was heading back to where he and Avalsa had come from. Checking room after room, Hans noticed a chest standing in a dark corner of a room with many rotting beds. The tower's warriors spent the night there. They left personal belongings in the chest, which were locked with the commander's key.

He returned to this room and stood over the chest. It turned out to be quite massive. Nearly half Hans's height, the chest was lined with layers of leather and metal at the joints, protecting the wooden sides. Thanks to the dry climate, the metal was well preserved and did not succumb to rust.

Hans took the lock in his hands, weighing the complexity of the mechanism. It turned out to be heavy and ancient. Not knowing where the commander's key was, Hans decided to use other methods. He smoothly ran his fingers along the curves, searching for secrets. Having found nothing, Hans took out the master keys from his belt and slowly, one by one, launched them into the keyhole, raising the flags.

It was unknown how long Hans sat for opening the lock. He enjoyed the process, so he didn't keep track of time. When the lock quietly clicked, he even felt a slight sadness but immediately brushed it aside, lifting the lid of the chest.

Much of the fighters' personal belongings were inside. It was difficult to say how long all these things had been stored; everything seemed untouched by time. Hans felt that his find reeked of antiquity.

The chest contained breastplates made of boiled leather and capes made from the skins of killed animals. Hans found several helmets, which he identified as trophies. He also found numerous trinkets: rings, bracelets, necklaces. The soldiers of the tower put into the chest not only their personal belongings, but also what they had gained in battle.

But that was not what Hans was interested in. Through the pile of things, he pulled out a stack of papers, yellowed with age. These were soldiers' letters received from relatives. The addressee was barely indicated in faded ink on the title page.

Letters from family unusually boosted the morale of a warrior serving far from home. Hans peered at the old squiggles, sorting out the words in them and putting them into sentences.

He took the top letter from the stack. It turned out to be unsent; no wax seal was visible on the paper. Hans peered at the pages, analyzing what was written.

> Dear Heinrich! I received your letter and I want to say that I am proud of you! It is a great honor to march in the front ranks of the Lord's army! You can probably watch the Lord from behind every day. Not every warrior is given this opportunity.

Even though I have the fate of being a watchman on this damned tower, I can also boast of something. The other day the Lord visited us. Personally. Alone. Because of the unexpected visit, our commander even forgot what orders to give while standing face to face with Him. The soldiers could hardly contain their laughter.

The reason of his visit, of course, is unknown. The Lord was interested in everything: whether we sleep well, whether we eat enough, how often the changing of the guard occurs. He asked me how accurately I throw a spear. I didn't know what to answer, so I just nodded. So ashamed. Such power emanated from the Lord that it was difficult to stand next to him without bending. He offered to compete. Heinrich, I threw a spear together with the Lord, can you imagine?

The whole tower gathered to watch the competition. In the first ten meters I was not inferior to him, but when the target was set at fifty, I still had to give up. But the Lord still gave me a souvenir. Said it would give my hand better accuracy. I could barely utter words of gratitude.

Deep at night, the guys and I snuck into the commander's quarters to eavesdrop on the conversation between the Lord and the commander. He told him about a rift north of the tower and advised him to increase vigilance in this direction. The commander assured that not a single viper of the usurper would capture the tower. Apparently satisfied with the answer, he disappeared as suddenly as he had appeared. It seemed to us that for this he used . . .

The letter stopped midsentence. Hans sat with his back to the chest for a long time, looking at the letter with an unblinking gaze. The sun's rays pierced the holey walls more and more, making the room brighter.

He closed his eyes. The thoughts in his head became louder. The muted feeling of guilt returned with renewed vigor. Hanging his hands from his knees, he did not let go of the letter, looking at it as if it was the last survivor on earth.

Hans involuntarily clenched his teeth in anger. The voices from the vision became even louder. "You left us! You betrayed us!" There was no end to the repetition. Somewhere from the depths, Hans heard Avalsa's voice. This was not the first time she addressed him.

"Breakfast is ready. You didn't respond when I called you. Are you okay?"

In defense, Hans held out the letter. "I found history. A letter from a fighter of this tower. It is even possible that the author was one of the three spearmen who ambushed us."

Avalsa took the letter with interest to read but returned it, annoyed. "It is in an incomprehensible language. For me, these are just squiggles."

"His name was Vilis, the guard of the siege tower. He wrote to his brother, Heinrich, who was serving on the front line. For some reason, Vilis did not have time to send it. The letter was not completed."

"That's why you're so upset?" Avalsa didn't understand why he should be so sad about an unsent letter written many years ago.

"Vilis mentioned a place where the opening of the gate could possibly take place," said Hans, standing up.

"So we were guarding the wrong village?" Hans nodded gloomily to the question. She exhaled noisily. "So what will we do?"

Without rushing to answer, he looked at Avalsa. It was hard to tell from her face whether she was angry or just didn't care. Suddenly, a thought came to him. "Let's have breakfast first."

There was a fairly friendly atmosphere at the table. The squad quickly accepted Avalsa as one of their own. She was forced to listen to the adventures of each of the swordsmen. Seraph was silent, enjoying the voices of others. Hans was also silent for his own reasons. He felt Chloe's searching gaze on him.

Before sitting down at the table, they had a conversation where Hans convinced her that he was not a traitor. However, he was very interested in the guy performing the ritual. To Chloe's surprise, Hans did not ask about the creatures that had escaped from hell. He only asked to describe in as much detail as possible the fair-haired man with snake eyes. This news shocked him, but he did not intend to share his thoughts with anyone. Avalsa had gotten used to the thoughtful silence of her new partner, and Chloe was still trying to get Hans to talk. She didn't trust him, that's obvious.

Hans waited until everyone had eaten to start talking.

"Due to the news that has emerged, it turns out that we have a common goal. I know this is unusual to hear, much less realize, but someone is opening the gates of hell, releasing creatures that destroy villages in one night. Each time, creatures emerge from hell stronger than the previous ones. Their hunger is also greater."

"Hans, we are a squad of the Raven Guild, not schoolchildren listening to fairy tales," interrupted Lloyd, a red-haired Scandinavian with a huge beard. "Seraph gives us a task, and we carry it out. No unnecessary questions or clarifications. This way your conscience is clearer." The red-bearded grinned. "So stop talking about your hell and tell me what to do."

"Fight," Hans answered briefly.

"With these creatures, or what?" Lucas clarified, burring a little. He constantly adjusted his glasses, betraying his nervousness.

"With those who call these creatures. Chloe told you"—Hans looked in her direction—"that challengers are just people."

"But still, we will have to fight the creatures of hell if the gates are opened earlier," Seraph remarked thoughtfully, and everyone fell silent.

"I'll teach you," said Hans, looking toward Avalsa.

There was an uproar at the table. Many of the detachment did not believe what they heard. They tried to laugh it off, causing everyone to doubt it. Someone insisted, backed by the experience of gray hair, that this could not happen in real life. That Hans was trying to push the squad into an unknown adventure.

From the confusion, Hans concluded that not everyone believed Chloe when she explained the nature of her burns. Only the squad captain was silent at the table. He turned his blind gaze to each of the new arrivals in the tower, unmistakably determining who was sitting where. Seraph settled on Hans. As if trying to see something, he knitted his eyebrows in concentration.

When the captain spoke, everyone fell silent.

"We will move to the indicated place today. It's good that we managed to get to know Africa. We've been sitting idle in this tower for too long. Now I ask everyone to disperse. We're heading out in the evening, so it's time for operational preparations."

The squad dispersed without a single objection; only Jerome looked questioningly at Seraph.

When the latter closed the door behind him, the captain of the squad turned to Hans. "You shouldn't have said openly what awaits them there."

"I had to tell the truth."

"They don't need it at all," Seraph interrupted. "Our squad carries out the assigned task, coordinating on the spot."

"Maybe improvising?" Avalsa decided to clarify.

"Coordinating." Seraph did not yield. "We are no longer young. Everyone has a gray head. To be honest, we are tired of tracking down poachers alone. My guys are used to obeying and trusting their captain in everything." He paused to address himself. "Hans, you convinced me that the African village needs protection. Nothing more is needed. The squad told you so. We have been in this tower since we delivered Chloe from the Czech Republic."

"A month and a half," Chloe interjected in the conversation.

"The squad needs to warm up. To prove that swords are still worth something."

Hans exhaled noisily at what he heard. Hans was not satisfied with sending people straight into the creatures' mouths without preparation. So he came up with a compromise.

"Okay, but on the road, I would like to practice fencing with each of your people."

"Oh, that's as much as you want." Seraph smiled, ending the conversation.

Hans managed to understand that the captain was a tough man and would not yield to any persuasion. Hans could not use force against these people. He needed brave warriors, not embittered puppets.

Chapter

15

The night turned out to be cold, and since there weren't enough blankets for everyone, it was even too cold. The bright moon had already begun to diminish its rounded silver outline. At high speed, nothing could be heard except the roar of the engine and the noise of the wind.

The three buggies left the tower as the sun dropped below the horizon. They had discussed the route in advance, so they drove in a line, not really talking to each other. And there was no one to talk to. An hour later, the members of the squad, wrapped in blankets, dozed to the rhythmic rocking of the shock absorbers.

Hans did not sleep. Ghosts of the past appeared in the darkness. He shook his head, regaining clarity of mind.

"Are you trying to drive bad thoughts out of your head?" Without getting out from under the blanket, Avalsa moved closer to make Hans feel warmer. "I do that too. I shake my head. Sometimes it helps. Sometimes it doesn't."

"I suppose the latter is more common than the former," Hans remarked, and they both smiled.

Also in the buggy were Lucas, George, and Jerome, who was driving. The squad doctor drove the car with concentration, so he didn't delve too deeply into the conversation. In the desert, it is very important to maintain a semblance of a road so as not to accidentally drive into a cactus or get stuck in quicksand.

"Chloe, of course, got it." Avalsa recalled her friend's story. "I didn't think that anyone else besides us would encounter this mysticism."

"Believe me, I didn't expect this either. It was a miracle that Chloe survived being so close to the gate."

Avalsa silently agreed. During the journey, they began to understand each other much better. She felt that Hans was gnawing on something, but could not understand the reason. In response to sympathetic questions, he only smiled bitterly and said that she wouldn't understand.

Hans looked at the car next to him, in which Chloe was driving. She did not sleep, peering into the dark horizon.

"She's an archer, isn't she?"

"Yes, and quite accurate. Of course, many explained that such accuracy was due to her helmet, but I don't agree with them. The helmet does not guide the hands." Avalsa highlighted each word for greater persuasiveness.

Hans said nothing, continuing to look at Chloe. Suddenly Hans shouted to Jerome, "Look out!"

The driver turned the steering wheel at the last moment, miraculously missing the rising sand. The car following was less fortunate. The buggy hit an obstacle on one side and flipped over in the air, scattering people and things across the sand. Somewhere nearby there was a nasty grinding sound.

When the sand settled, a shocking picture was revealed to their eyes. Something that looked like a huge worm was chewing the car's bumper. The metal crunched disgustingly. Swearing could be heard all around. Seraph gave the order to the group, and groaning people were pulled out of the overturned car.

Meanwhile, the worm spat out the dented bumper and went underground again. Panic caused disorder. Only Avalsa and the squad captain kept their cool.

"Hans, what the hell was that!" the captain shouted.

Hans did not have time to answer. Sand kicked up next to another buggy.

"Stay away from cars!" He pulled the sword out of its sheath. The runes glowed brightly in the night.

The creature emerged from the sand, stretching to its full height. It looked disgusting. Its body consisted of half-decomposed human limbs, covered with flowing resin. The worm turned out to be about twenty meters long. Its limbs moved in time with its pulsating body.

The creature tried to attack Lucas, who was lying unconscious, but Lloyd stepped between them. Roaring loudly, he swung his two-handed axe, bringing the blade down on the creature's head. The axe passed through the armor with a nasty clang, leaving no scratches. The worm tried to crush Lloyd with its body. The lasso from the Grail chain prevented it from moving. The creature roared. Twisting its body, the creature sent Hans into a short flight. Dodging in time, Hans managed to slash with his sword, cutting off one of the creature's many limbs.

While he distracted the worm toward, Chloe fired two arrows in a row at the target. The ampoules in the tips burst, covering the disgusting ring-shaped body with the alchemical composition. The mixture, which saved the castle from the creatures from hell, flowed down the body onto the sand without causing any harm. Chloe didn't believe what she saw.

"First, you need to weaken the armor." Avalsa ran up to her friend, taking out the nails of the Savior's Cross.

There was chaos all around. The worm, contracting its entire body, tried to get to the people. It felt the fear emanating from the combatants who were in a wave of panic. The creature grabbed the gaping Jerome by the throat with its numerous appendage hands, slowly squeezing its palms. The huge aborigine was almost no longer visible; the body of the worm was slowly being pulled Jerome inside. Hans, without hesitation, cut off its limbs one by one, trying not to lose sight of Jerome. The creature wriggled, so it was necessary to use all of Hans's dexterity in wielding a sword.

Ishmael, a short Arab, arrived in time with twin swords at the moment when Jerome collapsed unconscious into the sand. Miraculously, without being crushed, the worm moved after Hans, forgetting about its prey.

Chloe fired the arrows one by one, changing the mixtures in the tips. She couldn't understand why this creature wasn't affected by anything. Only its armlike appendages dissolved, revealing the tarry areas of its body. The worm's armor could not be penetrated by anything.

"It's an evil spirit!" Avalsa shouted. "A big evil spirit!"

"But he's physically real?"

Avalsa just nodded sullenly.

The girls were protected by three members of the squad. As soon as the creature disappeared underground, they began to fuss. Avalsa ran to Hans. Judging by his breathing, the role of bait was difficult for him. Halfway there, he had to make a sharp turn toward a heartbreaking scream. The worm emerged with its mouth upward, in the place where the archer's guards were. The cries of pain and calls for help were drowned out by the crunch of grinding bones. Avalsa rushed back, cutting nails with her sword as she went. But they did not reach their goal; the worm disappeared underground. Seeing nothing because of her tears, Avalsa fumbled with her hands in the sand. Having stumbled upon someone's body, she began to dig. As if emerging from the water, Chloe took a deep breath of air, spitting out the sand. Avalsa was relieved. Her friend was saved by Seraph, who at the last moment heard the creature approaching. Avalsa turned around. Hans also saw how those unfortunates died, unable to do anything.

"Hans, it's huge." Avalsa didn't even know what to say. They had no weapons to fight this kind of thing. She was overcome with despair. It seemed to Avalsa that the worm, underground, could feel fear; so it was in no hurry to show itself, enjoying the situation.

"Stay away from each other! Together we are vulnerable to the big mouth!"

Hans saw that the squad needed to say at least something. The soldiers felt a significant loss of strength. Ishmael, on his knees, tried to revive Jerome. Lloyd shook his head uselessly, trying to stop the ringing in his ears. It hit him hard on the hood of the car. Ludwig clutched the handle of his two-handed weapon with his white knuckles, looking around madly. Lucas was lying under the car, not showing any signs of life.

Hans turned his gaze to his sword, as if asking the weapon for reassurance.

It dawned on him so unexpectedly, as if the sword really spoke to him. For what he had planned, he did not need a charmed weapon; an ordinary blade was enough. Throwing Clark's gift aside, he shouted to Ishmael, "Give me your sword."

The Arab didn't hear him. The worm moved toward them, raising columns of sand. Hans rushed to the overturned buggy, taking the sword from the dead man.

The members of the squad, dispersed, watched Hans with interest. There was nothing else left. He understood that they could not defeat such a huge worm. Hans was also sure that if nothing was done, the campaign would end before it even began.

He knelt down. With a subtle movement, Hans took a nail out of his bag and pressed it between his palms. His lips were already whispering the necessary words.

"What is he doing?" Chloe didn't understand the meaning of his actions. The danger was too close to sit quietly on your knees like that.

No one heard what Hans said, and even if they did, they couldn't understand a single word. The next movement made Avalsa cry out. Holding the nail in one hand, he hit it hard with the other. The point entered his flesh entirely. Hans drove the nail of the Savior's Cross into himself. His unconscious body fell onto the sand.

The worm was approaching Chloe. Avalsa tried to distract it, screaming and throwing pieces of the car, but to no avail. Her friend had not fully recovered from her wounds, so she could not run quickly, getting stuck in the sand.

Suddenly a flash pierced the sandy night, a streak of light in the darkness. Avalsa couldn't believe her eyes. The arrow of light repeated again, passing through the worm. The creature slowed down, stopping in front of the uncomprehending squad. Without making a single sound, it fell into pieces, and the resin armor hissed and bubbled as it dissolved.

Avalsa saw Hans standing with his back next to the creature. The molten stump of a sword taken from the deceased was smoking in his hands. It seemed to her that the worm's body was emitting a glow against the background of darkness. This simply could not have happened, but what she saw was amazing.

Avalsa called out to Hans, but to no avail. She ran up worriedly and touched his shoulder. He turned around. For a moment, Avalsa was overcome with horror, but she forced herself to act. She was not a helpless girl, but an infiltrator of the Raven Guild.

Black blood poured from Hans's mouth. Darkening circles under his eyes created a death mask on his face. He tried to say something, but blood bubbled on his lips, swallowing his words. Avalsa threw the charred blade aside, placing Hans on the sand, which was instantly stained with blood.

Avalsa tried to find the wound to stop the bleeding. Her fingers felt a familiar object in his chest area. She tore his T-shirt and was horrified.

"What is this?" Avalsa didn't notice that Chloe had approached, sitting down next to her.

The nail stuck out in Hans's body, spreading black threads around it. Avalsa went into a stupor. She didn't know what to do; her hands were shaking treacherously. "He drove this nail into himself." An afterthought came to her tired head. Avalsa touched the nail. Hans groaned, spitting out more blood. She pulled away in fright, but he took her hand and returned it to its place.

"He wants you to pull it out." Chloe was no less worried than her friend. She saw that Hans had lost a lot of blood, and if nothing was done, he was unlikely to last long. Taking a more comfortable grip on the nail, Avalsa told her friend to keep the bandages ready. Once Chloe had brought what she needed, she pulled out the nail with one effort. Avalsa was surprised at the ease with which this was accomplished. She did not immediately notice that the bleeding had stopped. The walls of the wound were charred.

"What the hell is this?" Chloe instinctively covered her mouth with her hand. Avalsa didn't know the answer to the question. The nail in his hand rusted in seconds and scattered into ash in the wind.

One surprise gave way to another. The black cobwebs on his chest began to disappear, as did the circles under his eyes. Now Hans's face had taken on a deathly pale hue. This was not surprising, because he lost too much blood.

Avalsa continued to hold Hans's hand, afraid of losing his pulse. She didn't know what would happen next, but now she just wanted to sit and catch the ragged breathing of the man who saved them all from the evil spirit.

Not long ago, she considered him a burden when Clark assigned her this task. Now Avalsa really believed the words that humanity was in danger. And the one who can stop her was unconscious in her arms.

Avalsa still could not understand how Hans managed to cope with such a huge creature of darkness. She had no doubt that it was him.

The sun rose again over the desert.

"Looks like it's all over now?" Seraph uttered a rhetorical question, coming closer. He had already managed to assess the damage, issue orders to collect things in the surviving car, and dig graves.

"This is just the beginning," Avalsa whispered, but Seraphim heard her. He chuckled to himself and went back to check on Jerome. The squad needed a doctor.

Chapter

16

The corridor seemed dark and unwelcoming. Footsteps echoed menacingly off the granite walls, carrying the sound far ahead. You won't meet anyone in the castle at this time. The day's training was in full swing. At the end of the day, there will be one less in the castle. Not everyone could stand it; not many survived the training process. These words, like a hated motto from the past, rang in Kloss's ears. Nevertheless, knowing what reward awaited them, many strove for it and killed for it.

However, this was not what Kloss was thinking about now. The owner called him for a personal meeting, so he had to leave his preparations for the trip.

Orienting himself perfectly in the dark, Kloss climbed the spiral staircase to the top. The owner deliberately kept the castle in twilight. Recruits thus got used to the darkness faster and saw better in it.

Kloss did not understand this method, nor did he understand the dependence of lighting on a person's inner world. However, the boss understood this; Kloss was only able to carry out orders.

The master's chambers were located in the upper turret of the castle. Daylight came in through an oblong window. Only in his chambers there was natural light. Kloss walked to the door and knocked hesitantly. Through the lower slit, the sun's rays stretched like light lines. He experienced such uncertainty only in the presence of the master.

Kloss entered when he heard permission. As soon as he crossed the threshold, he dropped to one knee and bowed his head in submission.

"Master, did you call?" He appeared as quickly as the wind brought him.

There was no answer, and after a while, Kloss dared to raise his head. The owner was looking for something to read, sorting through the spines of books on the shelf.

He was dressed in all snow-white. Against the background of the window, the master seemed covered in light. Every detail of the man's clothes shone with immaculate whiteness. Before Kloss stood a true aristocrat, fully aware of his position. His white hair, carefully combed, was gathered into a low ponytail. Thin light eyebrows, barely noticeable on a pale face, emphasized the predatory gaze of a man accustomed to command.

Kloss felt his strength; he physically could not get closer than three steps to the master. The silence unnerved Kloss, but deciding to break it, the boss raised his hand in a warning gesture.

"Not a word. Did you find it?"

"Master, my people continue to search, but after New York, there have been no outbreaks of magic," Kloss stammered, trying to speak more confidently.

"Did you find him?" he repeated the question, looking at Kloss point-blank.

"Master! The gate is in the final stages of opening. At all stages of the ritual, a sufficient number of people were sacrificed. I have found the place where the last rites will be performed. Then the demon will show itself." Such news clearly satisfied the master. He paused to explain the change of topic.

A century had passed since the previous demon was summoned. The owner now needed a new fighter to carry out his plan.

Kloss watched for a while as the boss drummed his fingers on the table, thinking.

After the false body was brought, Kloss thought that he would no longer live. However, he was given another chance to track down and bring the deceiver, the head of the Raven Guild, to talk with the master. But here too he failed. Kloss understood that he would already be dead if it were not for the ritual. He was not flattered by the thought that there were only four people like him in the castle; the master's mercilessness was unpredictable.

"There is a fighter in the clan whose strength needs to be tested," the master finally said. "Go to the training ground and check if he is worthy of being another owner."

"What is his element?" Kloss was happy, because the boss decided not to touch on past failures. He's giving him a chance again. In addition, Kloss had long wanted to warm up, and these calls only drained his strength.

"Wind," said the boss, and Kloss saw a glint in his eyes.

He was about to leave, but suddenly stopped. The boss raised an eyebrow in confusion.

"That's not why you called from Africa."

"You were the closest."

Kloss strongly doubted it.

Larisa, the master's favorite, spent her free time in the master's chambers. Even now he could smell the foul smell of cinnamon.

"I know that after one more ritual, the demon will appear. Therefore, I must be confident in the candidate. And besides," he said, turning to the window, "you are in my debt. Go."

Kloss came to his senses when he closed the door behind him. He knew that the other three were engaged in selecting candidates, training them, and mastering the elements. Kloss was perplexed, because anyone could check the candidate, without necessarily calling him. There was only one explanation, said by the master: "You are in my debt." Kloss didn't dare disappoint him anymore. Therefore, with hidden determination, he went to the training ground.

The weather outside was sunny and frosty. Kloss had to squint at the white snow, reflecting the bright rays of the sun. The mountainous terrain made the frosty air thin, as was usually the case at altitude.

Kloss meandered along the serpentine path, rising higher into the mountains. With every step, he heard more clearly the familiar voice slaughtering the recruits.

"Where are you looking? And who will think about protection? Why are you pouring so much into weaving? Do you want to be torn to pieces? What a clumsy attack! You will not defeat your opponent this way, even if he has just learned to walk."

Good old Bison. He was called that name already during Kloss's training. Nobody knew his real name. It seemed that the tyrant mentor did not have one. Broad shoulders hid Bison's massive neck. Huge in height, almost two meters, with ropes of muscles rolling under his skin, he turned into a merciless training machine.

Kloss did not know his real age. When he joined the clan as a boy, one hundred and twenty years ago, Bison's head was already covered with gray hair. By soaking in magic and manipulating it, they can change the structure of their body, and the effect of age on their health became less and less noticeable.

The buffalo had another distinctive feature: he never wore outerwear, not even a T-shirt. Natural hairiness warmed him in the fierce winter, causing incredible discomfort in the summer. The recruits initially mistook him for a yeti. Kloss smiled at such memories, because he once thought the same.

For some time he just stood there, watching the training process. At the training ground, the stone parade ground was divided into several zones. When he was in bad mood, Bison forced everyone to go through four circles, while the norm was always one. The recruits were afraid of the hairy giant.

Kloss had always paid attention to the elemental control zone. At the top of a triangle drawn on the ground were three barrels. A fire was constantly maintained in one of them, sand was poured into the second, and water occupied the third. In this triangle, for the first time, he felt special. He felt power and control over himself. After discovering the elements, his training became even tougher, reminiscent of survival.

The tyrant's shout brought him out of his thoughts.

"Kloss! My boy! You arrived!"

Kloss did not believe a single amiable note from the hairy giant. It may have happened a long time ago, but he remembered how Bison treated them. "Thanks" to him, of all the students, only Kloss survived. Therefore, he reacted coldly to the teacher's warm words.

"The owner said to check the training of one fighter," he said briefly, looking into Bison's dark eyes.

"It's about time," he grunted in a bass voice.

Bison was prohibited from sparring with recruits. During the battle, he entered into a battle frenzy and did not see any other outcome other than the death of the enemy. Kloss heard about it. This hairy creature had killed more than a dozen talented students. The owner introduced a strict ban on fighting with students.

Otherwise, Bison possessed irreplaceable qualities as a teacher. He could teach everything: from fencing and silent combat to mastery of the elements and the creation of elemental weaves. Kloss was perplexed at how much knowledge could fit in one head.

"Tiara, come!" Bison barked, bringing Kloss out of his thoughts for the second time.

Sweating and breathing heavily, a young girl, above average height, with short-cropped hair, approached them. No one was allowed to wear their hair up, so everyone cut their hair the same way.

However, the primitive haircut could not affect the girl's pleasant facial features. A pointed chin and a thin nose with neat petals spoke of the girl's unbending will. This was also indicated by the scars on her back. The buffalo whip did not tolerate disobedience.

The plump lip, bloody, did not seem to bother Tiara much. The girl just wanted to take a breath so she could stretch to her full height to greet. Dark skin and black eyebrows were reminiscent of the natives of the western lands of the Atlantic Ocean.

Kloss felt a slight sympathy for the girl. Her eyes hadn't changed yet, but it's just a matter of time. Once you touch the demonic force, changes will not take long.

The girl looked at Kloss with curiosity. When joining the clan, all free time was spent studying textbooks in the castle or at the training ground in the mountains. Every day: Bison, basics of weaving, Bison, rules of the elements. At one time, Kloss thought it would never end. Therefore, he understood this questioning look. She mentally asked Kloss, "How much more training? When will I be able to walk around the castle as freely as possible?" He could not answer the questions, since it depended on the master how long her training could continue.

173

"Tiara, right?" The girl nodded excitedly. "I'll do some training sparring with you."

"Try not to give in to me." Tiara smiled tightly.

"Clear the parade ground!" Bison roared right above his ear, and the students were blown away like the wind.

Kloss took off his raincoat—a layer of snow had already stuck to the hem—and rolled up the sleeves of his shirt. In one motion, he took the boomerangs out of their sheaths and sent them into a short flight. The weapon was stuck in a training post next to Bison.

At this time, Tiara tightened the bandages on her hands and checked the lacing of her boots. There was excitement in her movements.

The rest, taking advantage of the respite, sat around, some on the snow, some on the stones. Kloss was surprised that the students were not chilled by the cold and strong wind. Tiara worked out in a T-shirt and compression pants. It was chilling for him to look at her. Tiara's body was shiny with sweat, and the snow falling from the sky instantly melted on her skin, turning into drops.

"Try to reach the body." Kloss stood up, making an inviting gesture with his hand.

Exhaling briefly, Tiara drove away her uncertainty, and her body breathed with determination.

Having reached her goal in three leaps, she tried to knock Kloss off his feet with a low tackle. Snow splashed into Kloss's eyes. Raising his leg in time, he missed the blow, but Tiara had already managed to release two weaves. Transparent crescent moons were released from her palms, capable of cutting an opponent in half. With short strokes, Kloss broke the cutting crescents with his bare hands. But Tiara did not watch. She knew how speed rather than strength could be an advantage. Going behind him, she took him in a death grip, squeezing his neck. Two blows to the legs should have knocked Kloss down, but they never happened. Rolling over his shoulder, he threw her off, sending the weave after her. The compressed air, crushing bones, was directed at Tiara's feet. However, there was no sound of a fracture. During the flight, she released the element, throwing herself into the air. Knowing that she was vulnerable in the sky, Tiara put up an air shield in front of her, heading into the gorge in long leaps. Appreciating her ingenuity, Kloss followed her.

Like a caress, Tiara twisted and wriggled, amazing with her dexterity and speed of thought. Kloss didn't give her a break. With currents of air, he threw boulders at the foot in her direction. The stones flew slowly enough that Tiara managed to complete the complex weaving before dodging.

Kloss saw small ripples running through the air over the edge of the gorge. It suddenly became quiet around, as if all sounds had stopped at once. The silence was oppressive, and his ears were ringing disgustingly. Kloss's breathing, like a clap of thunder, disturbed the silence of the gorge. He felt a blow. There's another one behind him. There was a taste of iron in his mouth. Spitting blood, Kloss tried to determine where the blows were coming from. He didn't hear anything.

Tiara struck one after another, hitting the nerve endings, intending to immobilize the enemy. Before he saw Tiara, whose transparent silhouette was refracted in the sun, his whole body ached in pain. Ignoring the paralysis in his arm, Kloss grabbed the girl by the neck when she got too close. Twisting like a cat, Tiara bit his hand, escaping his grip. The sounds hit Kloss's head again, like the ringing of a church bell.

The flickering stopped. The girl became visible again and stood on all fours, gasping for air.

"I believe this is your best attack," Kloss stated, allowing her to come to her senses. "I remember it was called Canopy of Silence. This weaving is effective for a group of opponents, but not for a single target. You need to save energy during the battle, and you unleashed a breakthrough on only me, who is still standing on my feet."

Without responding to his lecture, Tiara again stood at the ready. Using the wind, she moved as close to Kloss as possible, again attacking from below. He dodged the blow without much difficulty. Kloss was already convinced of the student's abilities, so the fight should have ended.

He couldn't stand contact combat and didn't even develop in that direction. Tiara struck quickly, so it was necessary to increase the distance. This was difficult, since Tiara noticed Kloss's weakness and fearlessly advanced. He released two "air sledgehammers" again, but they crashed against the shield Tiara put up. When the shield burst, Kloss took a kick to the body, pinning the girl in a hold. Having activated the weave, which had been created for a long time, Kloss kissed the girl.

She pulled away, unable to say anything. All her efforts were spent on breathing air into her lungs. Tiara couldn't breathe. Kloss watched as the blood vessels gradually burst in her frightened eyes, as the veins in her temples and neck swelled. Tiara opened her mouth in vain, trying to take a saving breath. Her vision was slowly getting dark.

At the last moment, Kloss broke the weave. Tiara, with the greed of a drowned man, gasped for air, standing on all fours. Kloss stood nearby for a while, looking at the girl. Making sure she would come to her senses, he turned around without saying a word and walked back.

The buffalo stared at him with black button eyes, sparkling with indignation. He saw the battle to the end, so Bison didn't like that the student almost died. The hairy giant liked to drive his students into unconsciousness himself. Without saying a word, Kloss walked past his former teacher and took his weapons and clothes, leaving the hated training ground.

—◊◊◊—

"Allow me to take Tiara as a student," Kloss asked, once again in the chambers.

"She is that good?" A slight smile touched the master's lips.

"The buffalo will kill her. The girl has a clear predisposition to weaving. Contact combat only slows down her learning. Some of her fingers are already knocked out, and one hand is completely broken! Tiara quite competently and quickly summons the elements, using energy almost sparingly."

"Almost?" The owner highlighted the word for a reason. He saw the fight but wanted to hear a remark about the mistake made.

"She used Canopy of Silence, knowing that the enemy was only one person. I won't lie, luring me into a gorge is a pretty smart trick, because if there are walls, then all that remains is to close the 'roof,' but this is still not reasonable."

The master mentally assessed his remark but said the following out loud: "Tiara is quite a young fighter. Recruits, going through the training process, come up with everything themselves. They are not condemned for experiments, an excessive thirst for knowledge, or the desire for something new. There is only one requirement—to survive. You should know this. When you achieve results on your own, experience becomes invaluable. The one in your sheath"—Kloss instinctively put his hand on the boomerang—"has no mercy. The weapon will eat you if you are not prepared."

Kloss listened to the boss in fascination. There was magic in his words. Each revelation was stored in his memory, from the first word to the last letter. Kloss knew that he owed everything to the master: position, long life, forbidden power. The master accepted only one thing in exchange: devotion. Devotion to his ideas, vision of a new life. Kloss had little idea of the end result of the clan's efforts. However, the scope with which his plans were accomplished was enormous.

He did not take his eyes off the master as he sat down in the chair. Kloss did not break the silence, waiting for what else the master would say.

"Tiara is an outcast student. Canopy of Silence is a high-level weaving that requires large amounts of energy. The answer to what happened in Prague determines whether you can take her on as a student."

"Someone already told him", The idea flashed through his head with annoyance. The tension in his voice betrayed his excitement, but Kloss had no choice but to tell the truth.

"Someone killed all the mercenaries guarding the castle during the call."

"Two groups, forty people. All that was left of the people was their uniform and weapons," the boss interrupted, and Kloss saw an angry spark in his eyes.

He lowered his head and continued guiltily, "We managed to find out that this is the work of a human." It seemed to him that a shadow of relief ran across the master's face.

When the incident was reported to the clan, the master thought that it was a demon that had escaped control and had broken the summoning circle. Naturally, this news promised big problems. There was a huge difference between controlling a demon and pacifying an enraged one. The latter was beyond the power of any of the four close associates of the master. Matters would have to be taken into their own hands. And this meant exposing themselves, and therefore the clan, to a big blow. However, he was distracted, listening to Kloss's arguments.

"I found human blood in the castle, next to a dead minotaur." The owner didn't have time to object before Kloss anticipated his thoughts. "The sample was immediately sent for examination. The analysis showed that this—"

"Hans," the boss blurted out.

Kloss had no idea that Hans was the only threat to the clan's plans. After all, only this person forced the master to take precautions.

"The analysis showed that the blood belonged to the girl. My guess is that the girl may be from the Raven Guild," Kloss completed his interrupted sentence and bit his tongue. He didn't want to be reminded of his failure.

The head of the Guild misled him by passing off another as the dead Hans. However, the master did not react at all, thoughtfully drumming his fingers on the table.

"After combing the entire castle, we couldn't find her anywhere. Having followed the bloody trail, I concluded that she was not a survivor, since she had lost so much blood."

"However, there is no body," the boss noted calmly, and Kloss had to agree.

"The ritual took place. The sacrifice was sufficient," Kloss mentioned in order to somehow make up for another mistake.

However, the master didn't listen to him anymore.

After thinking for a while, he said, "On the way to Africa, prepare an apprentice to do everything on the spot." Kloss understood what the master meant, so his eyes widened in surprise. "We need a new fighter. We'll deal with the Guild later."

Enlightened, he headed toward the door, but the master called on his way out, "No one has canceled the search for Hans." Kloss nodded, leaving his idol to think.

Chapter

17

It was difficult to open his dry lips, taking a deep breath. It was not so easy to tear apart the dried flesh. He was very thirsty. He had difficulty understanding what was happening around him. Like a crimson haze, retreating, showed several pictures of reality. Voices from the receding nightmare mixed with the surrounding sounds.

He opened his eyes. His vertical pupil narrowed to a thin slit, focusing on the bright light. Being in the shade, you could feel the hot sand through the blanket, burning your back. Avalsa sat nearby, nodding off, leaning on a stone. Fatigue plunged the girl into a doze. Feeling his eyes on her, she opened her eyes and saw Hans looking at her. He heard her calling to Jerome. Their movements seemed slow, as if Hans were watching a recording. He tried to say something, but he only produced an incoherent grunt. Approaching, Avalsa held out a fairly empty flask. Hans felt the saving moisture slowly spreading through his insides, quenching his thirst.

"How are you?" You could feel the worry in her tired female voice.

Hans didn't have time to answer. Jerome approached and began to examine him. He belatedly noticed the bandage on his chest. Unwinding the bandages, the doctor exclaimed, "I don't understand anything! I have never seen such regeneration. The deep wound healed in less than a week. I didn't even dare to put stitches. Amazingly simple." Unraveling the bandages, Jerome showed Avalsa. "Here you go."

The girl looked at Hans's chest, on which a small scar was already turning pink. The terrible wound, with charred edges, healed. Avalsa lowered her eyes, hiding her smile. She had seen this more than once, which could not be said about the stunned doctor.

"Who is he anyway?" the dark-skinned man continued to ask in a loud voice, having finished with the bandage. "Fight a terrible monster of enormous size and stay alive! We owe him our lives, but I still don't understand what it was and how it's even possible. During my years of service in the Guild, I have never seen anything like this, but in recent days, I have begun to believe in my grandmother's horror stories about spirits and evil forces."

Avalsa could not explain anything to the dark-skinned aborigine, because she too had to face misunderstanding once. At Jerome's voice, the rest of the squad pulled up. The doctor fell silent when Seraph was behind him.

Hans stood up, fighting off the dizziness. There was still pain in his stomach, but it was already bearable. He counted those present with his eyes. Only seven of the squad survived. Each looked at Hans differently: Ishmael with interest, Lloyd with respect, and Jerome still could not believe in the healing. Ludwig maintained his British arrogance, eyeing the survivor warily. There was blood on his bandaged head. Seraph broke the silence, voicing a general demand. "Tell me."

Hans guessed that the captain was interested in the worm and where it came from.

"Somewhere in the sands there is a mass grave of warriors from the era of the Crusades. Having died not by natural causes, the fighters refused to accept oblivion, deciding to take revenge on the world of the living."

"Are you saying," Ishmael interrupted, "that that twenty-meter-long 'thing' is a mass grave?"

Hans nodded slowly, and the party became thoughtful.

There was doubt on their faces, so Avalsa decided to interject. "When I was fulfilling an order from the Guild, I encountered something similar. At first, I didn't believe what I saw, even when Hans dealt with a similar creature. It was difficult for me to understand what I heard, because he was also trying to explain. During our journey with Hans, we met more creatures, but they had the same nature of origin—war. Dying an unnatural death, a person refuses to leave the world of the living. His spirit wanders, accumulating agony, thirst for life, pain, hatred. The sum of these feelings, multiplied by centuries, is the very dark energy that Hans is talking about. This force maintains life in such beings appearing in the present."

Avalsa said her guesses out loud for the first time, thereby surprising Hans. There was a thoughtfulness on his face that defied explanation. Hans was always difficult to understand.

Now the members of the squad looked in shock, first at Avalsa, then at Hans. Chloe couldn't think of anything else to do except nod as a sign of trust.

"You want us to fight . . . this?" Seraph turned out to be inexorable.

"No. I want you to fight the creatures of hell." Hans decided that there was no point in hiding anymore.

Jerome's eyebrows rose again.

"So what we encountered in the desert was not a 'generation'?" Ludwig also decided to insert himself into the conversation by asking a rhetorical question.

"The creatures of hell are made of flesh and blood and have their own weaknesses, which cannot be said about the creatures of darkness. I can teach you how to fight them, but I really hope it doesn't come to that. The most important task is to prevent the ritual."

Ishmael opened his mouth at what he heard. A heavy silence reigned, which was again dispelled by the captain of the detachment.

"We'll have to think about that later. We have a priority task that needs to be completed." Seraph made it clear to everyone that the discussions were over; it was time to plan the further route to the gorge.

During the time that Hans was unconscious, a lot had changed. Of the three cars, only one survived. Being exhausted, the members of the detachment were barely able to collect the surviving bales of food and equipment. The plastic canisters with water were full of holes in places, so not all of the precious moisture was saved. As soon as the preparations were completed, Seraph decided to immediately set off, taking turns changing the helmsman. There were no objections—no one wanted to be near the decaying worm.

Hans was placed in the back seat, and the rest were placed wherever they could in the cabin. The detachment set out when the sun had already lit up the sand. People toiled in the heat, fidgeting on the heated seats, stoically enduring difficulties, encouraging each other with strained smiles.

Seraph knew the direction, navigating the terrain, so panic was avoided. To prevent the car engine from boiling, they stopped every half hour in places that more or less resembled shadows.

Avalsa was constantly next to Hans, wetting his body with water. He was feverish. Jerome was surprised that Hans was not burned from the inside in the scorching sun.

Nights, especially cold ones in the desert, were spent together, clinging to each other, keeping warm. The tent was lost somewhere among the rubble on the battlefield. There was nothing to start a fire with—the surroundings were deserted, not a single tree or twig.

Those who died that day were buried in the sand; no one objected. Jerome read a prayer for each member of the squad, who continued their journey in another world. The rest listened silently, grieving in their own way. Chloe clenched and unclenched her fists in impotent anger. No one was ready to lose friends. You can't prepare for something like this.

On the third day, the car began to boil and did not want to go anywhere else. By order of Seraph, they took the most necessary things and simply left the rest in the car. A stretcher was built from the seats, and a canopy was made from a piece of canvas, protecting Hans from direct sunlight.

People moved through the flickering mirages only thanks to their unbending will and unconditional faith in their captain.

Avalsa encouraged herself with other thoughts. She was focused on Hans's recovery, so she reacted weakly to what was happening around her. He didn't regain consciousness, and that was worrying. Avalsa saw how he dealt with the creature, but she could not imagine that such a thing was possible. They talked to Chloe about it, but no one ever understood what happened.

"It seems to me that he is not human," Chloe said, but Avalsa remained silent. She wasn't entirely sure whether she felt the same way. She gave Hans something to drink and continued to wet his body in the hope that he would eventually regain consciousness.

One day Ludwig suggested leaving him so as not to slow down the movement of the detachment. Water supplies were running low, and only bread was left to eat, so the squad was nervous. Before anyone could respond, Avalsa knocked him to the ground with one punch to the face. There was no need to say anything; the others did not argue.

When Hans came to his senses, Seraph said that they were one night's march from the oasis. As proof, he pointed to a subtle path among the dunes.

"This oasis is often used by nomads, making a stop on their way to the southern lands. Very few people were able to find out about his whereabouts."

They ate the last of their provisions. Hans got a dried apple. They set off as soon as the sun hid behind the horizon. There was a feeling of encouragement in the squad. Perhaps this was because the nightmare will soon end or because Hans was already moving on his own legs, or maybe all of the above.

Avalsa seized the moment, left alone with Hans. He peered into the quickly fading horizon and did not immediately notice her presence. Hans lost a lot of weight; recovery took a lot of energy.

"You didn't tell Seraph, but your reticence about that night didn't escape me." Avalsa's gaze was demanding. "What force did you use when you killed the worm? I saw how you drove one of the nails into yourself, and just try to deny something and refer to my misunderstanding."

He didn't even turn in her direction. He just stood and continued to peer into the horizon.

When Avalsa's patience was about to burst, Hans spoke. "History claims that when Jesus Christ was crucified, they used four nails, nailing hands and feet alternately to the wooden cross. Whether they left the nails on the cross when it was removed or took it with them is unknown. The next mention of nails appears during the reign of Constantine, the founder of Constantinople. He ordered the found four nails of Jesus Christ, which by that time had become a sacred relic, to be melted down and forged into a sword, a helmet, and a bridle for the royal horse. Constantine believed, owning such artifacts, that the Lord would always be with him."

Hans fell silent, giving Avalsa the opportunity to compare the information with what was in her hand.

"But it turned out to be not true," Avalsa whispered in shock, squeezing the tetrahedral nail of the Savior's Cross tighter.

"No one forged any weapons," Hans confirmed, "and there were not four nails, but six." The sacred relic was in the possession of the church for a long time.

"Until darkness appeared in the world and the artifact became a weapon," Avalsa suggested; and Hans, to her surprise, nodded.

"Drive a nail into the darkness, and it dissipates, making the creature weaker. But if you use the relic on yourself, the opposite reaction will occur. A crushing force arises within."

"The power of Christ?"

Hans smiled bitterly at the assumption.

Avalsa stood for some time in tense thought. The more she learned about her companion, the more she realized that the world is not as simple as it seems. In the Raven Guild, her worldview narrowed to the point that there are only vile and corrupt people who deserve death at the hands of the scout. Such blinders of thinking fell away when traveling with Hans.

"Wait, you say that there were six nails in total, but there are only four here." Avalsa remembered how one nail crumbled in her palms and corrected herself, "Three. Where did the rest go?"

Hans didn't want to answer. She felt that he was going to close again. "Do not be silent. Tell me why there are only four left."

"I used them." The revelation turned out to be simple and at the same time stunning. "In the world, there are not only such entities as in the desert. There is something more serious and global than a mass grave."

"And you fought with them?" She couldn't imagine that this wasn't the first time Hans had used such power. To voluntarily take such a step, knowing the consequences . . . He spent five days in an unconscious state, being in Avalsa's arms. She was unfamiliar with such rejection.

"This relic has some limitations." Hans no longer saw the point in hiding the rest. "After using a nail, the internal resources of the body are depleted, so it is necessary to wait a certain period of time before using the next one."

"How long?" Avalsa wanted to know everything to the end.

Hans looked into her eyes carefully and said slowly, "Thirty-three years."

She blinked, looking into his eyes and processing what she heard. Stupefaction came with the next thought. After all, if Hans used three nails of the Cross of the Savior, then how old was he really? Avalsa looked at her companion in a new light.

"You can't be that old." She refused to believe, shaking her head negatively.

It was impossible to read anything but pain on Hans's face. "I wasn't going to tell you this," he reminded her.

Hearing footsteps, they both turned around.

"We're moving out. The captain told me to find you." Ishmael found it difficult to speak generally.

With her glance, Avalsa made it clear that the conversation was not over yet, setting off to get ready for the road.

The detachment set out around twelve. It was pitch black all around. The cold stars gave almost no light; they had to use flashlights. They moved through the desert in a chain. Seraph found the path in the afternoon, so the members of the squad walked confidently, almost without getting bogged down in the sand.

Hans walked far away so that the irritating light of the lantern would not blind his eyes. Now he tried not to part with his backpack. Hans thanked Seraph for saving his things, because some were taken from the tower chest.

Walking with a brisk step, Hans felt a bottomless emptiness inside. The nail sucked out all the energy that had accumulated for so long in secret from his pursuers. He did not regret using the relic, because the people for whom he was responsible were saved. They followed Hans and trusted him. He had no right to fail. The thoughts that popped up in his mouth made him feel the long-forgotten taste of bile. *This time everything will be different.* Hans gripped the strap of his backpack tighter, peering into the darkness.

"What were you talking about there?" Chloe asked her friend again. Being the rear of the detachment, they walked shoulder to shoulder.

"I asked how he killed the worm." Avalsa frowned, but Chloe didn't notice, continuing to ask, "I'm interested too. I then saw an incomprehensible light, then wide strokes, and the next moment the creature was falling apart like shredded sausage." Avalsa smiled at the comparison. "Then I saw Hans with a red-hot sword in his hands, the blade of which, like wax, spread in large hot drops on sand."

"It was magic," Avalsa replied.

"I knew it! However, I don't understand one thing: why Hans hesitated, allowing several members of the detachment to die."

Ludwig, who was walking ahead, heard the question and answered without turning around, "Because he doesn't care about us. He used what you call 'magic' to save his own skin. Hans defended himself, but it just so happened that we were nearby."

Avalsa wanted to throw the daring Briton to the ground again, but Seraph intervened, "If it weren't for him, everyone would have ended up in the sand. That's a fact."

Ludwig breathed angrily but remained silent.

"I don't know who Hans is, but I'm sure we're fighting on the right side."

There were no more such conversations in the detachment.

—⟋⟋⟍—

Morning came suddenly. At first, a grayish haze covered the horizon, revealing in some places the dull blue of the sky. At one moment it flashed crimson, revealing to the detachment the pinkish top of the heavenly disk in the east. The sun rose, illuminating the tops of the sand ridges, one by one tearing them out of the gray haze of the night.

The air began to heat up rapidly. The squad undressed one by one, trying to cover their heads with a light piece of fabric. Seraph claimed that another two or three hours of walking and the oasis would reveal itself; but Hans, who returned from long-distance reconnaissance, told a different story.

"There are only dunes in the distance. Perhaps there is an oasis somewhere among them, but the path does not lead to it."

"You're right, it doesn't lead to an oasis." Jerome approached him. "But there is a landmark on the path."

"I only saw the stone, but I didn't find any inscriptions on it."

Jerome, exchanging glances with a smiling Lloyd, asked, "Did you turn it over?"

Hans quickly led the detachment to the indicated place. There were dunes on both sides of the trail, so most of the route was in relative shade. A little to the left of the path the mentioned stone was visible, half covered with sand. It could easily be missed as part of the landscape, but in this area, there was nothing but sand that stretched for kilometers around.

The path led farther, between high sandy mounds, reliably hiding from the afternoon sun. Hans had already made sure that there were no signs of moisture in that direction. Meanwhile, Jerome and Lloyd dug up the block and with their joint efforts turned it over. Hans thought they were joking about turning over the stone, but something appeared under it.

"Inscription." Avalsa squatted down, sorting out the squiggles.

"The oasis is there." Jerome indicated the direction, checking what was written. Lloyd smiled from ear to ear with his gap-toothed mouth and was the first to begin climbing onto the sand dune.

"Did you turn over the stone?"

"Do you think it's inhumane?" Ludwig asked a frowning Chloe, deliberately emphasizing the last word.

"Lost travelers following this path could save their lives if there was a sign in front of their eyes."

"There is no place for 'lost travelers' in the desert," Ishmael retorted, adding, "Here moisture is more valuable than gold. They even kill for it."

No one else objected, concentrating on breathing. Walking up into the open sun turned out to be a serious challenge for tired people. The sand became so hot that it burned through the soles of their shoes.

The line of eight men rose and fell over the sand dunes like fleas on the back of a camel. Everyone hoped, ascending the next hill, to see the desired greenery of plants. However, the hills gave way to hills, and on the horizon, only a floating haze of alluring mirages was visible.

Avalsa's lips were chapped; sweat ran in streams, flooding her eyes. The growing thirst hit her head like a ringing bell. No one had even a drop of water; everything turned out to be drunk in the morning. Avalsa felt the general tension. For fear of losing their course, people walked strictly in the indicated direction. It was very easy to get lost in the unpredictable sands.

"I see something." Hans made a visor with his hands, peering into the distance. Surprisingly, he was the most cheerful of all, considering his recent injury.

Ludwig nervously licked his dry lips as he looked at Hans.

"Perhaps this is it." Jerome stood nearby, feeling the subtle smell of moisture.

"Captain, are we there?" People looked at Seraph with hope.

"I think I can feel the taste of water in my mouth." The squad gained new strength from what they heard.

Indeed, with each dune passed, the air became more humid, and it became easier to breathe. The landscape had also changed. The smooth sands ended, and there were bushes of green grass on the soil. The greenery became more and more dense. Chloe could hardly stop herself from running.

It appeared as if by magic. Such beauty can only be seen in the desert. In the midst of dead sands, lizards, and scorpions, there was a green area with meadow grass, green trees, and singing birds. A river flowed between the trees. Several springs merged together to form a crystal-clear pond.

Lloyd and Ishmael, screaming wildly, rushed toward the river, plunging headlong into the water. Jerome, shedding his clothes as he walked, followed them. Ludwig moved farther downstream, walking waist-deep, cooling his hot body. People were filled with energy in a matter of minutes. They wanted to live again.

The girls, moving farther up the river, where the bank was hidden behind tall bushes, pressed their burnt lips to the surface of the water, gradually quenching their thirst. Hans couldn't take his eyes off the catlike arch of Avalsa and Chloe, who were on all fours at the edge of the river.

"You saved them." Seraph found himself next to Hans, drinking from a flask.

"It was you who led people to the oasis. You knew the way, not me. The riddle with the stone was not for me."

"I'm not talking about an oasis," Seraph said, and Hans fell silent. "I don't know how you managed it, but I'm not interested in the details. I suspect that at a high price. They may not admit it, but my guys owe it to you."

Hans remained silent. He did not know how to react to the words of gratitude from the blind captain.

"I promise you," Seraph continued, "they will follow you."

"Are your people ready to learn?"

"They are all old wolves, Hans. It is unlikely that they will be given any science."

"Then let's quench our thirst and rest, because everyone needs this now. We can stop here for a while."

Hans left Seraph, climbing higher along the riverbed, going around the girls, climbing higher up the hill. He felt the source; he called to it as soon as the squad approached the oasis. Hans climbed higher and higher, losing sight of people, hiding behind dense trees. The oasis turned out to be huge. There were even a few fruit trees growing wild among the deciduous trees. Hans found ripe fruits that looked edible. But now he walked past them, driven by another need.

He found what he was looking for, at the very edge of the spring. There was an unbearable ringing in his ears. Hans sat down on the ground, leaning on a small tree. *Take a deep breath. Close your eyes.* He hadn't done something like this for a long time, but he knew it was no longer time to hide. For some time Hans sat motionless, concentrating. Opening his eyes wide, he saw the source. A clot of pure energy emanated from the ground.

The source resembled a spectrum shimmering with all the colors of the rainbow. Without thinking, Hans dived into it, opening his mouth wide to exhale. Pure energy bypassed him for a while, but the deeper

Hans sank, the stronger the pressure built up. Finally, the barrier could not stand it and burst, and the source sent streams through his body.

Hans continued to listen to the ringing in his ears, but the sound no longer seemed so deafening. He even forgot how to breathe. Energy filled his muscles and passed through him, washing away fatigue. Feeling his fingers begin to tingle, he emerged from the source, gasping widely for air. If he stayed inside the spectrum longer than usual, the energy would simply tear his body apart, dissolving his remains.

"It's like you crawled out of the ground." Avalsa caught the moment when Hans emerged from the spring, sliding his hands through the mud.

"I quenched my thirst. My clothes and whole body were stained with clay. Is Seraph downstairs?"

She watched with suspicion for a while, still waiting for the continuation. As always, without waiting for an answer, Avalsa nodded.

"Hans, I know what you want to talk to him about." She watched as he shook himself down the slope. "They are quite old warriors. You cannot force them to learn anything."

Hans turned around, smiling slyly. "The trouble with age is that with old age comes excessive pride, especially among warriors. They won't need to be forced."

Avalsa didn't really understand what he meant, but she trusted his confident voice.

The semirelaxed state of those around Hans was in no way conducive to a serious conversation. Someone was lying on the shore; someone was swimming. Jerome went to collect edible fruits. Seraph sat in the distance, listening with pleasure to the high spirits of the fighters.

"We'll stay here for the night," he said, hearing Hans's footsteps behind him. "The guys need a break."

"We all need a break. One night won't be enough."

Seraph turned his blind eyes to Hans.

"You need to prepare your fighters for what's coming. There is still a month until the new moon, maybe a little less. It's about a three-day journey to the canyon."

"Have you also been to Africa?" Seraph was surprised.

"Once upon a time," Hans answered evasively, "but I don't remember this oasis."

"My guys found it by accident. Judging by the wildness of the place, it does not seem that anyone other than poachers knew about the source." The captain of the detachment caught the thoughts of his interlocutor who wanted to take cover.

"I hope that is so." Hans still foolishly hoped that he would remain unnoticed until the last moment.

"I know I already asked, but do you really think that my guys can fight otherworldly creatures?" Seraph's eyebrows knitted under the bandage.

Hans understood that the captain of the squad also meant Chloe and Avalsa.

"The devil is not as terrible as they paint him." Hans smiled at the old saying. "With sufficient training, a person can cope with the creation of hell of the third level."

"Are these creatures even divided by levels?" Seraphim scratched his head, again trying to accept fantastic information as reliable.

"Yes, but it's quite difficult to understand, much less explain. I'll just repeat what I said before—your guys can do this if you prepare them."

Seraph looked at him for some more time and then turned toward the water, where his faithful fighters continued to bask in the sun.

"We'll start tomorrow," said Hans, taking his silence as agreement.

He went to the watering hole. He was terribly thirsty.

Chapter

18

The monotonous sound of the hammer was absorbed by the rolling of water over the stones of the riverbed. The party set up camp near the pond, chatting cheerfully around the fire and sharing the news of the past day.

At first, many were indignant, refusing to accept any teachings or training. Hans responded to such protests with a trick.

"Try to reach my body," he then said to the arrogant Ludwig. There was no need to ask twice; the Briton impudently attacked the enemy. Naturally, nothing came of this; Hans reached his neck with two false attacks, ending the fight.

Everyone tried to deal with Hans. Captivated by the excitement of fencing, the squad trained for days on end, improving their skills. As planned, the "old people" managed to get interested by personal example. In wielding a sword, Hans had no equal, with the exception of the captain of the detachment. Seraphim excelled in feints and powerful attacks, combining them with body movements.

Hans achieved his goal. The pride of the veterans was wounded. In the following days, the detachment trained with increasing eagerness. Driven by each other's aspirations, they trusted him. Hans appreciated this.

—◊—

His fire burned much higher than the main camp. Having asked not to be disturbed, Hans collected the fighters' weapons, placing them next to him. The diamond chisel made intricate squiggles under the blows of the hammer.

Hans obtained the engraving tools in a box from the tower. Having replenished his strength from the source, he generously poured energy into the writing applied to the blades. The sweat that appeared stung his eyes, but Hans continued to work without distraction. Engraving required special care.

—☲—

Surrounded by a brightly burning fire, the squad discussed their latest training. Ishmael then opened up, risking being pierced; but with an absurd somersault, he missed the fatal thrust. Lloyd was just trying to reproduce—to the general laughter—the Arab's somersault when Hans walked into the light of the fire. The squad stopped laughing and looked at him carefully and respectfully.

"The applied runes will make your weapon effective against the creatures of hell."

They silently dismantled their weapons, admiring Hans's work. Matte runes reflected the flames, intricately playing with the light.

"They will shine as the creature approaches." Hans watched as Lloyd looked at his axe in admiration.

"I'll say thank you when I check it out." Ishmael voiced the general mood.

"Where is Chloe?" when the distribution of weapons was finished, Hans asked.

Slowly chewing an apple, Avalsa replied, "By the pond. She decided to take a swim for the night.

"Then we'll wait here." Avalsa thought Hans was embarrassed, sitting down next to him. However, he was the first to break the silence. "You're making great progress with the Claw."

Avalsa automatically looked at the weapon donated from Cuba. It took her a long time to get used to the curved blade with a reverse sharpening, practicing every morning.

"It looks like you handed out weapons to everyone." Avalsa conveyed Hans's uncertainty. "You look tired."

He only nodded to the remark, fingering a black glove made of an unknown material in his hands.

"Listen, do you really think they can fight? They won't be afraid, they won't run, but they will take the enchanted swords in their hands and attack the toothed creature?"

Hans, as always, hesitated to answer, looking at her. "No, I do not think so."

"What?" The girl was taken aback. Making sure that no one was listening to them, Avalsa switched to a whisper. "So you don't think so? Why then did you start these trainings?"

"Avalsa, don't get me wrong. I don't want it to come to the point of performing a ritual. Too many creatures will appear from there. The squad will not be able to cope with them. They will be swept away by numbers."

"Then why was—" she began again, but Hans interrupted, "Dangerous people are engaged in conscription. A certain skill in battle is also required against them. You heard Chloe's story about how a man opened the gate alone."

For some time there was silence between them.

"When we find ourselves in the gorge, my task will be to prevent the call. Once we stop these people, the mission can be considered successful and the innocent people saved." Avalsa felt bitterness in Hans's last words. "Seraph's people will have to cover and hold the borders, neutralizing the ritual being carried out."

"Well, what about me?" Avalsa had not yet realized her participation in Hans's plans. She saw how her interlocutor's face changed and flared up. "Don't tell me you're going to leave me here."

Hans didn't answer, but he didn't deny it.

"Well, I will not! I've come too far with you to sit in hiding. My task was to look after you, and so far no one has canceled it."

Avalsa continued to breathe angrily as Chloe came out to the fire, drying her hair with a towel. Noticing them in the distance, she headed toward them. Avalsa leaned over and whispered in Hans's ear, "If you don't want to take me with you, that's your business. But don't forget that I am a scout of the Raven Guild and can follow any squad unnoticed."

Avalsa straightened up abruptly, walking away with a firm gait.

"There's no doubt about it," Hans whispered after her.

—∿—

"Are you alone? I think I saw Avalsa with you." Chloe sat down on the ground next to her, continuing to dry her hair.

Hans looked at her for some time until he realized that he was involuntarily making a comparison. Chloe's facial features, like her habits, were feminine and sophisticated. You can't imagine her in a fistfight. Of course, it cannot be said about Avalsa that she had brute strength, but her movements were much more aggressive. She fought like a cat, always landing on all fours. Avalsa planned every step, without making a single unnecessary movement. The longer he thought about the scout, the wider he smiled, not hiding his emotions.

Finally, returning to reality, Hans answered belatedly, "She went into the forest, wanting to check the surroundings."

"Do you think anyone else might be in the oasis? Do you need to post sentries?" Chloe was seriously worried. Hans could hardly contain his smile.

"The territory is huge. The oasis is impressive. I think as soon as Avalsa returns from reconnaissance, she will tell us everything. I have a request."

"What is it?" Chloe easily switched to another topic. She didn't tend to worry for long.

During the training, the girl also gained trust and admiration for Hans. Suspicions remained far in the past against the backdrop of their experience. She was ashamed to remember the incident in the tower, how she shot him.

Hans stopped twirling the glove in his hands, handing it to Chloe. "Giving weapons to others, I thought it would be bad to deprive the only archer among us. Take this glove. Put it on before bed so we can start training tomorrow. I don't doubt your skill. On the contrary, I want to make it more useful." He caught Chloe's interested glance. "This glove used to belong to the spearman from the tower. I found it in a chest of personal belongings."

Chloe accepted the gift, surprised. She didn't know what to say. Surprisingly, the glove was heavy. The matte fingertips were made in the shape of claws, and instead of a fabric base, there were small scales of chain mail cells. Chloe doubted that the shapeless glove would be able to stay on her miniature palm, but she put it on anyway. Before she could get scared, the links tightened around her wrist, taking on a new shape. The jet-black scales flickered red, like the embers of a fire. The links crawled along her forearm, stopping at her elbow. She looked at Hans, who remained calm. Chloe took a deep breath, forcing herself not to panic. The flickering ceased to be chaotic; the scales pulsated rhythmically, all together.

"The glove has tuned in to you." Hans looked carefully at Chloe's hand. "Now it reflects your heartbeat."

"What if I want to take it off?" she asked a simple question. Chloe touched the glove in several places, making sure that it was now like a second skin, tightly enveloping her hand.

"It's enough just to give an order," Hans answered but hastened to add, "There's no point in doing that now until nothing works out. We'll take it off tomorrow, but for now you should spend the night with it."

Chloe looked at Hans suspiciously but didn't answer. She moved her fingers, admiring the shine of the matte claws, without feeling any discomfort. It seemed that the glove no longer had weight, although it was made entirely of metal. With a sad sigh, Chloe headed back to camp, wondering if her claws would break the string as she pulled.

The night was dark and cold. In the desert, nights could be chilling. The cold crept through the trees and grass with cold tentacles, paralyzing the living. The trees in the night emitted the ringing sound of a frozen trunk. The stream was not frozen only thanks to the rapid current originating on a high hill. Hans had to wrap himself tightly in a bag and sit closer to the fire in order to fall asleep without chattering his teeth. Steam was coming from his mouth. However, as soon as the dawn sun appeared on the horizon, the shackles of cold and tentacles of ice were destroyed and retreated into the shadows, patiently awaiting their hour of the night.

The morning turned out to be gloomy. The dawn sun illuminated the pinkish clouds on the horizon, warming the exposed land. The trees of the oasis, as if animated, bent under the bright rays of the desert sun. It seemed to Hans that such a battle between living nature and the dead desert had been going on for a long time, and not in favor of nature.

Avalsa was still angry with him; so instead of a fencing lesson, she went to the other side of the pond, causing questioning looks from the squad.

Fencing passion no longer helped. People gave up exhausting training.

"Hans, we are no longer at that age to swing iron every morning," Ishmael said frankly to the general agreement of those around him.

Hans had to give the squad a day off to boost their morale. This was not part of Hans's plans, since the white crescent moon had already appeared in the daytime sky. Time was running out.

"Are you also not at the 'right age' for training?" The mood soured, so the question came out rather rudely.

Chloe stayed behind when people scattered along the pond, where everyone found something to do to their liking.

"I wonder what else this glove can do besides nightmares."

Hans looked at her more carefully, clarifying, "Why do you think it was the glove that caused the nightmares?"

"I dreamed of battles. Pain, pleas for help, blood, fear. I saw torn flesh. I saw the likeness of people capable of tearing the muscles of the enemy with their bare hands. You said that the glove was from that chest, so don't ask such questions." She returned the rude tone to Hans.

A smile touched his lips. "Let's go." He turned around, heading toward the lonely trees on the hill. For the girl's peace of mind, he did not mention that she might not wake up from nightmare visions.

Climbing the hill, Chloe saw two targets made of boards. "Are we going to compete?" She looked at the drawn red and white circles with disbelief.

Hans silently took one of the targets and carried it to the nearest tree. "You are superior to me in shooting, and no competition will prove otherwise." He approached the girl, taking another target. Having installed it in the right place, Hans began to count the steps.

Chloe opened the case and collected the bow, watching with interest what was happening. Stopping, Hans turned to the girl. "Here."

The target was fifty meters away. Chloe clicked her tongue in disappointment.

"Are you serious? Do I need to hit the bull's eye from a child's distance? Without a helmet, my record is one hundred and eighty. So tell me you're joking, and we'll move away and recalculate the footage."

However, Hans was not joking. He continued to stare at Chloe, irritating the girl. Finally, unable to bear it anymore, she sent the arrow home in one swift motion. Hans appreciated the beautiful shot and said the following out loud, "Your goal is the second target, immediately after the first."

He set up targets on trees growing one after another.

"But the first target blocks the view," Chloe objected. "I can't go around the tree from where you are. The arrow will not change its horizontal trajectory, even if you shout after it."

"But you still try," Hans said convincingly, causing the girl's internal indignation.

Chloe did not consider him crazy, but at that moment she decided to reconsider her conclusions. She forgot about the glove, pulsating in time with her rapid heartbeat. Having calmed down, Chloe took the arrow and put it back on the string. Holding the feathers with her clawed fingers, she took aim. Still confused about how to get around the tree, Chloe fired, presenting a second target. No miracle happened. The arrow pierced the target next to the first one in a straight path.

"Can you tell me about the properties of the glove? What should I do with it?"

Hans saw how the girl was tormented in search of an answer. She fired arrows one after another, but the second target remained untouched. He wanted the girl to understand for herself, to instill confidence that it was not the glove that mattered. But the full moon would rise very soon, and Hans had no time left for such tricks. The squad needed a good archer.

"When shooting, try to swing your hand before the arrow reaches the target."

Chloe did not ask, "What will this do? What is the point of this?" but simply did as this distraught man asked. She was dumbfounded by the result. The arrow did not reach its target. Chloe found it a few meters away, just in the direction where she waved her hand.

"You can change the trajectory of the arrow if you want." Hans's words no longer seemed so crazy to the girl.

Filled with excitement, Chloe raised her bow to fire again. Noticing where the arrow was flying, the girl realized something: control requires speed and dexterity of the hand. Lost in her thoughts, Chloe stopped noticing anyone, so Hans decided to leave her. He didn't mention that there were consequences to using the artifact. Chloe should learn this on her own.

She shot with a bow until the evening. Feeling Hans's presence in the distance, she focused on the target. Stopping only to drink water, Chloe shot arrows one after another, like someone possessed. Already at dusk, her shoulder became completely numb and refused to pull the bowstring. Chloe consciously worked herself out, sensing Hans's hurry.

—⟋⟍—

In the desert, Chloe spent a long time talking with Avalsa. In every conversation, one topic came up: "Who is Hans?" She listened to her friend's travels, gradually becoming convinced that the stories about the other world were far from fiction.

"We visited different places on the mainland, trying to determine where the next ritual would be performed," Avalsa said one evening when Hans lay unconscious. "Spending nights in libraries, I learned a lot of new things about a seemingly fictional world. We saw the consequences of opening the gate, so we tried to find these people as quickly as possible. Try to interfere. But the case turned out differently."

"I found them instead of you," Chloe voiced her friend's thoughts, "not realizing the power of these fanatics."

After being silent for a while, Chloe decided to voice an assumption that she had been harboring for a long time.

"You know, for some reason it seems to me that Clark knew he would be in the castle."

"So he sent you to death?"

"But I survived."

"But you could have stayed there." Avalsa did not concede. She had no doubt about the involvement of the head of the Guild in what was happening, but she could not believe that he could set Chloe up like that. After the incident, she believed in the importance of preventing the ritual. Therefore, the Alchemist worked until exhaustion. It reminded her of her first archery lessons. Then Chloe trained just as hard, aiming at the target. Having torn her fingers bloody, she could not bend them for a week. Thanks to the black glove, her fingers, covered with matte scales, did not know fatigue. When the claws frayed the bowstring, a new one had to be pulled.

—◊◊—

Chloe arrived at camp in the evening. Jerome was just poring over the pot, securing it over the fire. Today it was his turn to cook dinner.

"There will be vegetable stew," he answered the unasked question, handing Chloe a half-empty mug of cocoa.

She nodded gratefully and took a hard sip, clutching the mug with shaking hands.

"Hard day?" Jerome glanced sideways at her tired face, smiling.

Chloe couldn't answer. It was as if needles had been stabbed into her temples, and a flash of pain clouded her mind. Instinctively, she clenched her teeth and dropped to one knee. Cocoa spilled onto the ground from the released mug.

Chloe no longer heard Jerome's words. Due to dryness in the mouth, her tongue became rough, as if cracked. Feeling the moisture on her lips, Chloe licked it off, the taste of iron filling her mouth. She ran her hand over her face and saw blood. Chloe pressed her sleeve to her nose, but a scarlet stream had already crossed her chin, and large drops were falling to the ground by the fire.

Completely confused, Jerome laid her on the blankets and looked for Hans. When he arrived, the glove on her hand was pulsating with the frequency of a moth. Without explaining anything to anyone, he took the brew from the fire and opened his bag, finding the necessary herbs. After kneading them on a nearby stone, Hans poured the crumbs into the fire. Roughly lifting Chloe, he dangled her over the fire, ordering her to inhale the swirling smoke. She inhaled as drops of blood fell onto the hot coals.

The rest of the squad members had already gathered around the fire. Not understanding what was happening, they asked questions, but Hans did not explain anything. He intently observed Chloe's condition, as well as the pulsation of the glove. The blood stopped, her eyes rolled back, and her consciousness became foggy. Her heartbeat gradually leveled out.

As Hans put Chloe back on the blankets, Avalsa walked up and slapped him loudly. Nobody expected this.

"It's you! It's all your fault! She trusted you to bleed like this now!"

"Will someone explain to me what happened?" Seraphim closed everyone's mouths with one exclamation and stopped the angry lamentations.

"A side effect of the artifact," Hans answered dully, but what was said did not make it any clearer. "A glove. It meets a new host. Today Chloe discovered her abilities but overused them. The side effect hit her brain like a sledgehammer."

"But why didn't you warn her?" Avalsa calmed down a little, watching her friend's even breathing.

"She had to feel it herself. You cannot explain in words what needs to be felt. The artifact takes root only through pain. By morning, she will feel better and regain consciousness."

"I'll stay with her until the morning," Avalsa said in a tone that could not be discussed.

The rest, on Seraph's orders, scattered back to their sunbeds; but Hans noticed that they began to look warily at the writing on their weapons.

The fire burned, cheerfully crackling dry branches. The scarlet light of the fire partially snatched out of the darkness the sleeping members of the squad, their backs pressed to the warmth. In the night sky, the light-bellied moon had already passed halfway, gradually eclipsing the sun in the morning.

Hans threw branches on the fire, and the sparks that flew illuminated his tortured face. The sharpening stone moved steadily along the edge of the sword, calming the owner and putting those around him to sleep. Chloe, covering her head, was breathing evenly; and by the middle of the night, she had stopped talking in her sleep. There was no longer any need to knead the herbs every hour and let her inhale, calming her agitated mind.

Avalsa was awakened by the quiet sound of a grindstone. She climbed out of her sleeping bag and quietly sat down next to Hans.

"Is she all right?" That was the first thing that came to mind.

"Her consciousness has calmed down. Her breathing has evened out. In the morning, he will wake up along with everyone else." Hans's voice showed weariness.

They just sat in silence for a while. Avalsa didn't know how to start a conversation. She wanted to say a lot. Her thoughts were intertwined into one lump. Pulling on one thread meant unwinding it, and she did not know how it could end.

The fire was enticing with its patterns and shimmers of light, like an unknown dance of a living creature flowing from one bizarre silhouette to another. The flame gave courage, calmed, and made it possible to put raging thoughts in order.

"You don't sleep well at night." It came out of her mouth. "I haven't seen you fall asleep with everyone else. In the short hours of daytime naps, you fall asleep like a knocked-out one and wake up with anxiety or with an expression of complete horror."

Hans paused his hand for a second but continued to work with the whetstone, continuing to listen to Avalsa.

"A similar facial expression after sleep lasts only a moment, but after seeing it once, I began to notice it constantly. What are you so afraid of, Hans? Why don't you sleep at night? Is it because of the upcoming mission? Do you think nothing will work out for us?"

"I haven't slept at night for quite some time," Hans answered dully. "In the past, the distant past, I did something terrible. It haunts me, punishes me, without giving me redemption." Avalsa felt that it was painful for Hans to speak, but he continued under the sympathetic gaze of the girl. "Every time I come into conflict with evil, I try to atone for my guilt, hoping that this creature is the last. The past keeps me up at night. You can consider it a curse, if that makes sense. What I have done cannot be redeemed, much less forgotten, even if I desperately hope so. Those people performing the summoning ritual themselves do not understand how it will turn out for them in the end. Or they simply weren't told. The balance of the world has long been disrupted. By their actions, the callers only increase the scale of destruction."

When Hans tried to explain the reason for his nightmares, Avalsa understood something, but when the conversation touched on the imbalance in the world, she gave up.

"Can you say something directly? No riddles, no branches, just the way it is. I guess that in the past, the 'distant past,' you had a high rank. I can assume that you were betrayed. That's why you made such a mess that you are raking to this day." When Avalsa was nervous, she spoke rudely and harshly. "But there is no need to compare your past with the creatures of darkness against which you are fighting. This makes my head spin."

"You wanted to know why I don't sleep at night." Hans smiled bitterly.

"I think if you just said who you are, a lot could become clearer."

Hans flashed his eyes in the darkness, thinking about something. "I'll repeat now what I said in Cuba: I can't tell you a lot, but I can't forbid you to find out on your own. The time will come, and you will understand. I really appreciate your concern. Monitor me to find out when I sleep. Bravo, you did a great job. But don't try to squeeze a confession out of me. This is punishment." Hans spread his arms to the sides.

Avalsa had no choice but to raise her eyes to the starless sky, exhaling noisily.

For a long time, Avalsa continued to lie in the bag, unable to sleep after her conversation with Hans. It remained a mystery to her: why was a man who bravely fought the creatures of darkness, calmly talking about creatures from hell, so afraid of his past? She was aware that thoughts about Hans occupied her more than what would happen next with the Guild, where Clark had gone and what awaited them in the gorge of Africa. Avalsa refused to accept that this was a manifestation of feelings. "It's just morbid curiosity," she said to herself, wrapping her head in a bag.

Hans saw in the darkness how Avalsa was tossing and turning, unable to find a place for herself. He didn't give the answer she wanted. Hans couldn't tell her the truth. Not all at once. If she knew now who he was, she would hate him. It's his fault that he let Avalsa get so close to his thoughts. Just think about it! The scout was watching him, but he did not notice. Hans turned his gaze to Chloe, checking her condition again. However, that wasn't what he needed to worry about right now. The meeting that Hans had been avoiding for so long was coming. Perhaps even too long.

"The balance is doomed to be upset," he said into the darkness, resuming his sharpening work.

Chapter

19

Time flies inexorably fast, especially when you are in a hurry. Trying to keep up, you can lose even more than you had before.

Kloss looked up at the night sky, exhaling clouds of steam. In a week, the moon will reach its full strength. He turned his gaze to Tiara, sleeping among the camels in a deep sleep. Kloss once again wondered, was he going too far in training with his student? Time was running out. The girl must be ready, but at what cost? Pushing the itching thoughts away, he decided to go around the camp.

Hearing Kloss approach, the mercenaries perked up, throwing playing cards into the fire.

"Everything is quiet?" He pretended not to notice the trick.

"It's dark as if you poke your eyes out, Commander. If it weren't for the hollow, our fires might have been noticed. Desert, you understand."

"Have the posts in the west and north reported for a long time?"

"They also confirmed the calm situation. With a night-vision device, you can only see jackals scurrying around and a couple of hyenas in the surrounding area."

Kloss knew that the camp was not in danger. He was just trying to keep himself busy.

Kloss again hired mercenaries for the campaign. He did not want to be distracted by all sorts of little things while traveling, leaving the guard to trained people. To gain time to train with Tiara, Kloss decided to walk to his destination. The decrepit priests of the challenge resisted and wanted to complain to the master, but Kloss found a way out of the situation by buying camels in Ethiopia. A chain of fourteen camels walked along the hot sands of Africa. Each priest received a camel.

Kloss hated old men in robes. Possessing grains of demonic power, they imagined themselves as demigods, obeying only the master. The work of a nanny tired Kloss, but he did not show it. He patiently endured their antics and consoled himself with the thought that he would not have to endure it for long. Once the last gate is opened, everything will end.

Because of the camels, the camp grew to the size of a caravan. It was necessary to stock up on animal feed and water. Things for mercenaries and priests took up a fair amount of space on the backs of the "desert horses." Kloss knew nothing about camels, so he had to hire an aboriginal camel keeper in the nearest village. He spoke the common language poorly but handled camels masterfully.

Kloss looked at the bright dark-blue tent in the center of the camp where the priests were located. He wanted to take a torch and burn it along with the sleeping old people. His fingers clenched into a fist, and he unclenched them again. Kloss tried not to show emotions outwardly, suppressing them within himself.

The only relaxation and island of calm for him was his student. For her sake, Kloss started the trek on foot. Instead of SUVs, he bought camels, guides, everyone. Tiara, of course, had no idea about this; but she felt the pressure.

For training, they left the camp at dawn, returning to the wandering caravan only at dusk. Kloss entrusted the care of the priests to mercenaries. The nasty old men, fortunately, were not against it. They didn't care who worshipped them. People were paid generously for this, plus bonuses for not asking questions. Kloss liked corrupt people who served whoever had the most money.

In the east, the sky and the dunes began to turn pink along with it. Far, far from the hollow, the sand dunes filled with crimson light one by one, illuminating the horizon more and more brightly. Kloss stood on the hill for a while, enjoying the morning scenery. Having descended back to the camp, he gave instructions to watch the driver more closely (there was a suspicion that the aborigine was guessing about his fate after completing the hike) and returned to the extinguished fire.

Kloss leaned over his student, whispering in her ear, "Get up."

Tiara instantly opened her eyes, rising from the blanket. During training, her hair grew long, almost touching her sharp shoulders. She twirled them on top of her head, piercing the bun with two sticks.

Even in the evening, Kloss chose a place among the sands for the upcoming training. The area resembled a hollow; they set up camp in a similar one, which once served as the bed of a dried-up river. Now there was only a small puddle at the bottom, reeking of the stench of animal corpses hundreds of meters from the gorge.

"The water is poisoned." Tiara stood on the edge of the gorge, covering her nose with her elbow.

"But there will be shadow here all day long." Kloss quickly connected several weaves using the elements and threw them onto the gorge. The smell of rotting ceased to reach both of them. Without waiting for his student, Kloss dived into the gorge, descending through the air, as if on steps. Tiara had to cling to the petrified sand, gradually sinking to the bottom.

"I'm already tired of waiting for you. Where are you going?" Kloss liked to tease his student, watching how her oriental features took on a stern look.

"I don't yet have enough elemental control to walk on air."

"It's good that you said bye. Otherwise, I would have doubted that I took you on as a student."

Not knowing how to react to such a remark, Tiara remained silent.

"By the way, it's good that you mentioned control of the elements, since today we have to learn exactly this." Without saying another word, Kloss again created a weave and walked along the surface of the water, as if weightless.

Tiara watched in delight as he crossed a ten-meter puddle. Stepping onto the ground, Kloss turned around. "I'll give you a hint: don't complete the weaving of the elements. Leave a loophole to add energy."

The student digested what she heard for some time. While studying a new weave, she imagined it in her head several times as accurately as possible. Tiara memorized the passes with Kloss's hands, breaking his movements into fragments in her memory.

Approaching the shore, she took the first step. The water began to swirl underfoot, and the splashes reached the shore. It seemed to Tiara that she was walking along a thin pole with an unsteady step. Stumbling, she nevertheless plunged waist-deep into the water, bringing a smile to Kloss's face. Trying to get out, Tiara soon realized that she was stuck in the mud. The surface of the water concealed a clay bottom in which her feet were deeply embedded.

"I'll help you the first time, but then get out yourself." Kloss approached her, pulling her out of the mud in one motion.

Kloss hated Bison for not developing the girl's talent. The hairy creature had noticed Tiara's affinity for weaving; he had no doubt about that. Bison deliberately trained her along with everyone else, forcing her to learn martial arts. Tiara, at night, risking the wrath of the clan mentor, sneaked into the archives, studying energy flows and their relationships by candlelight. Without explanations, such books were quite difficult to understand, almost impossible. There was no doubt that the master knew about this. No one entered the archive without his knowledge. Perhaps that's why he gave permission to take Tiara as a student?

During the month spent in the desert, the girl with oriental appearance achieved great results. She was glad that finally her desires were supported and developed. True, joy did not manifest itself outwardly—training took all her strength.

Sometimes it happened that Kloss carried her to the camp on his shoulders. She had no strength left even to go back. But Tiara didn't complain. Every time she challenged herself, she succeeded. Now, plunging waist-deep into the mud, with incredible efforts, she broke out of it in order to again stand on the shore, trying to recreate Kloss's weaving.

The dirt made her hair roll into icicles. All covered with brown slurry, hindering movement, Tiara returned to her original position; and the water bubbled under her first steps.

Kloss watched her with admiring pleasure. He didn't fight. At first, the absence of a fight was unusual for Tiara; in the Bison Clan, every day there was a struggle for survival. Kloss developed hidden talents in his students by focusing on weaving. He talked about energy that he knew himself, which the master had once shared with him.

"The element can only be used where it is in abundance. If there is no element, then trying to recreate it, you will waste time and energy. There are five elements in nature: fire, water, earth, air, and lightning. The last element is a very rare phenomenon in nature."

"We are very lucky, since there is air everywhere." Tiara nodded happily, but Kloss corrected, "Our element is wind, not air. Wind is power. The stronger the wind, the greater the power."

Kloss noticed that Tiara could not even take a step on the water; she immediately fell through.

"I'm empty," she said, annoyed.

"It's time to climb out of the gorge and remember the last lesson about storing energy."

Approaching the edge, the girl began to climb up. Being in the dried mud, Tiara looked like an earthen titan climbing Mount Olympus.

Kloss closed his eyes, drowsy. Not a single hour will pass before Tiara replenishes her reserves. Passing wind currents through her, she caught elemental veins with channels of energy.

The sun was at its zenith, heating the sand white. There was a heady haze in the air, giving the exhausted travelers empty hope. The sand around the depression was different from the virgin dunes of the desert. Small weeds spread out in small carpets, throwing protective thorns to the sides. A reminder of the once-full-flowing river was the yellow grass, a broken line stretching over the horizon. It was getting stuffy in the hollow. Above, beyond the edges of the dry riverbed, the blue sky stretched.

Kloss opened his eyes as Tiara came back down. The dried mud protected her skin from the sun, but her face was burned, and the scorching sun made her hair look like straw. Tiara cared little about appearance. She turned her attention back to her weaving.

"You should get rid of the dirt first." Kloss stretched his stiff body. The girl irritably shook herself off the clay in order to quickly resume the interrupted activity. "Do you remember the structure?" Tiara nodded, taking the first step into the water. The muddy surface began to bubble underfoot. On the fourth step, Tiara overdid her energy and would have dived into the mud again if Kloss had not caught him in time.

"You're pouring in energy too quickly. Take your time. Increase your strength gradually by interacting with another element."

"First, you talk about control." Now that she needed to interact with another element, Tiara was irritated about failures quite violently, but the girl could quickly pacify the oriental temperament, which Kloss liked.

"Interaction is control. You must create a spell within the boundaries of your element, sensing where the other is. The more you control the wind, the closer you will get to the edge of interaction."

Confirming his words, Kloss blew up a wall of sand with the wind, forming it into a pattern.

Observations of sand in the wind dawned on Tiara. She believed that it was necessary to adhere to the framework, separating one from the other. In fact, she needed to see the end result and not be afraid to experiment.

With a subtle movement of her hands, Tiara created a weave of elements. She closed her eyes. There was no need to watch where her foot was stepping. Tiara tuned to the threads inside. She held one of them in her hand, guided by her.

The student opened her eyes when she had walked halfway through the riverbed. With trembling legs, she stepped onto the ground.

"It doesn't look so difficult now, does it?" Tiara smiled triumphantly. "Always remember control. Don't let go of the elements." Kloss spoke seriously, not allowing her to rejoice at the results. "Now do the same with the wall."

"Do you want me to climb it?"

"'Rise' would be the right word." Kloss smiled with his eyes.

The training continued until sunset. After completing one task, Kloss gave the next one, and it seemed to Tiara that this could go on forever. When the dunes turned crimson, he announced the end of classes.

Having emerged from the hollow, Kloss destroyed the weaving with a snap, and Tiara heard that she "stank" of corpse dirt. She wanted to complain, but her teacher interrupted, "I don't smell any better."

A few kilometers before the camp, they found an artesian well. Some time passed before Tiara and Kloss washed themselves in the cool water. He saw the scars on the girl's back. Bison beat his students for disobedience. A fit of impotent rage again blurred his eyes.

"You look better." Tiara's face, washed from dirt, turned purple. The sun burned her skin.

"At least I don't stink." She took a few breaths, sniffing.

They entered the camp in deep twilight. Kloss did not tell anyone about the apprenticeship. After dinner, Tiara fell asleep with a mug of tea in her hands. He was taking a risk by exposing her to the elements every day. Time was running out. The moon was already filled with its magical light; the full moon will come in a week. He really hoped that Tiara would hold up and not break.

The camp lured Kloss into routine care as soon as he tucked his student into her sleeping bag. Listening to the mercenaries' reports on the costs of provisions, water, and animal feed, Kloss checked what was said himself. He was not surprised to realize that supplies were running low. Camels consume too much food. However, the summoning priests were much more of a nuisance than the starving beasts.

"What's wrong with the driver?" Kloss reminded them about the morning request to follow the aborigine.

"You turned out to be right. Our company does not attract him, so he tried to escape. However, my guys discouraged him from such a desire."

Kloss saw that the native's eye was swollen shut, and his lip was cut. Without answering, he patted the mercenary on the shoulder as a sign of approval.

"You're going to kill me," the aborigine muttered as soon as Kloss bent over him.

"You wanted to escape, but we have a contract with you. Once we reach the gorge, you and the camels can be free."

211

"Kill me," repeated the dark-skinned man.

Kloss looked at him carefully. Without dissuading him otherwise, he went to the priests, leaving the native with gloomy thoughts.

Kloss entered the tent after being invited. The priests' dwelling was as richly decorated from the inside as from the outside. Bronze goblets, encrusted with jewels, filled with wine, stood on tables with curved legs. Animal skins were spread across the floor.

Kloss was indignant, looking at the luxury goods around him. The luggage of the animals could have been much lighter if not for the bronze candlesticks placed at the corners of the tent. Metal, silk, in the desert, you can do without all this. But the priests didn't care. They wanted to live according to their usual way, ignoring other people's opinions.

The priests huddled over a massive brazier in which coals crackled. Handfuls of unknown herbs were thrown, and sheaves of sparks rose into the air. Kloss rolled his eyes, again trying on the hated deference.

"You've returned." One of the priests looked him up and down.

"Yes, I'm done with business." Kloss walked closer to the brazier, peering into the coals. The old men, as one, turned around, blocking the flames. Kloss barely managed to hide his irritation.

"The coals show visions only to the priests."

One of the wine drinkers asked, "How is your student?"

"Okay, thank you for asking." Kloss did not want to talk about Tiara's success. The priests did not react in any way to the tense silence.

"The coals showed that the demon at the gate is already waiting for the opening." Kloss didn't really believe in fortune telling by coals, but he managed to make sure that sometimes their predictions came true.

"Oh yes, the demon is very strong. Hungry and fierce." The second priest picked up. "Your student needs to be ready to meet him. Otherwise, the master will be unhappy."

"The owner believed in her, allowing her to perform the ritual next to the gate."

The priests began to whisper among themselves. No one dared to contradict the master or disobey his will.

"The demon is very strong. She can't do it alone," the priest began to babble, but Kloss interrupted, "I'll help her. If you open the gate, the rest will be up to me and the student."

"When we open the gates," the priest corrected, making it clear that the conversation was over.

Kloss greedily inhaled the cold night air after the stuffy tent of the priests. The demon was already on the threshold; all that remained was to carry out the ritual. He closed his eyes, remembering the map. The ritual will be held in the canyon, where a mighty deep river once ran. Ancient villages live in communities along the canyon. Kloss hoped that several such communities would be enough for the demon to enter this world.

Everyone in the camp was asleep. You could hear camels chewing cud nearby as they digested their late dinner. Kloss pulled a weapon from his belt. The smoky steel gleamed dully in the light of the fire. He looked at the weapon seriously. Blade of deamon. Kloss hadn't used his boomerangs for a long time. One hundred and twenty-one years had passed since the last call. Then Larisa, the master's favorite, got the blade. Kloss didn't want to remember it. He then saved Larisa from death. She considered the victory over the demon a personal achievement.

Thinking about the past made him sad. Having sheathed the boomerangs, Kloss remained by the fire, watching as the last living log, engulfed in fire, turned into ashes scattered in the wind.

Chapter
20

The canyon turned out to be securely hidden among the sand dunes. Without knowing its exact location, you can wander through the desert for a long time until you accidentally fall down while crossing another dune.

The depth of the canyon reached sixty meters. The walls consisted of sand and rocks of varying densities. A layer cake made of earth and sand kept lifesaving coolness at the bottom. Here and there small springs were observed, unfenced by anything, gushing out in cold springs into the blackening mud.

As soon as the caravan reached the canyon, Kloss felt the approach of a force hiding its tentacles somewhere at the bottom. He walked to the edge, trying to determine the width. It turned out to be at least a hundred meters in that place. Kloss tried to imagine the power of the river that flowed along this bed many centuries ago.

About half of the mercenaries remained at the entrance; the rest went on reconnaissance. The latter turned out to be superfluous, since no human had ever set foot on the dry riverbed.

The priests gradually descended lower along the canyon, looking around enthusiastically. They too felt the power spilling around them, waiting for centuries for release.

Tiara shared the delight of the priests. At this point, the shortage of provisions, the minimum supply of water, and the growing needs of camels faded into the background.

Kloss chose a suitable place for the ritual. Thanks to the wide riverbed, it was possible not to crowd, but to walk freely, even with camels. Kloss ordered the animals tied next to the wall. The priests agreed with the decision.

Tiara considered herself sufficiently prepared for what was to come. Even though she didn't really understand what was required of her, obeying her teacher was considered a priority for her. Kloss was just explaining to her that during the ritual, she should hold on to him, under no circumstances letting him out of sight, when the body fell from above. The mercenary lay with an arrow in his temple, blankly looking at the evening sky with dead eyes.

Without thinking, Kloss put up an air shield to protect the priests. Tiara followed suit, looking out for their opponent. The last to react was the mercenary commander, and twelve M16s rushed with their muzzles upward.

"Above, answer!" They sought from people, but there was no answer.

Tension spread across the canyon floor. The minutes slowed to hours. Kloss was the first to shake off his stupor.

"Get busy drawing." He handed the priests one of the boomerangs. "Tiara, stay on guard. If something happens, call on the radio."

Before Kloss created the weave, rising into the air, arrows rained down from above. There were bursts of machine guns behind them. He did not see the enemy. Arrows fell as if from the sky. Three more mercenaries died when Tiara put up a shield where the remaining ones huddled.

The priests stopped with the drawing, but Kloss barked, losing patience, "Continue! You are protected."

The answer to the careless statement was an arrow that changed direction, piercing the priest's throat. Kloss couldn't believe his eyes. He felt a slight breeze of magic too late to stop the arrow. Without hesitation, Kloss lowered a cube of dense air onto the priests, standing out against the general background. Not paying attention to the murdered man, the priests accelerated the drawing of geometric lines, imbuing them with the power of the demonic blade.

Meanwhile, the arrows continued to change trajectories, killing two more mercenaries.

215

"Tiara, come to me!" Kloss shouted, noticing movement behind the stone, two hundred meters away from them.

His vision did not fail him; he saw where the arrows were flying from. Compressing the wind into a thin needle, he threw a spear, intending to pierce the shooter hiding behind a stone. A powerful monolith rose from the sand, taking on the elemental attack. The spear burst with a loud ringing sound, crashing into a boulder.

Kloss stared in shock at the darkening monolith in the distance.

"It can't be." Kloss was filled with anger. He was angry with himself for not taking Hans's appearance into account. It was too careless to believe that the final opening of the gate will take place without his intervention.

He walked toward him with a confident step. Hans was wearing rags of worn-out clothes, and the hilt of a sword was visible behind his back, which he did not even bother to draw. The arrows continued their murderous harvest, sending two more mercenaries to the next world. The remaining five opened fire on the stranger. One movement of the hand was enough for the rising sand to absorb the bullets. The mercenaries released all their horns, refusing to accept what they saw.

"Tiara, remember joint weaving?" Kloss didn't care about people with guns. That's why he hired them, letting them be the first to go. He asked the question to his student so that only she could hear. "Don't yawn." After waiting for Tiara's affirmative answer, Kloss rushed to the attack.

As he ran, he noticed slight vibrations in the ground, so he had to act quickly.

"Up!" Kloss shouted to his student, rising higher above the ground with each step. An impassable swamp formed under them. The training was not in vain; Tiara trotted after the teacher, not lagging behind.

Hans continued to create weaves without moving. From the walls of the canyon, huge earthen palms rushed toward the fleeing opponents. Not expecting such a scale, Kloss and Tiara went down, barely touching the creeping surface with their feet. Huge hands closed behind their backs, separating Kloss from the priests.

Time had compressed. Kloss managed to stretch the thread that fed the protective weave around the ritual design. Now the creation of serious elemental spells turned out to be unavailable, so they had to limit themselves.

A sand hammer fell on Tiara's head, and a column of sand was advancing toward Kloss. His eyes began to blur, and he concentrated on his defense. Kloss released several air cutters blindly, calming the sand. Hans had to dissipate the weave to dodge the compressed air.

Kloss found Tiara and worried about her. The girl coped with the attacks of the elements but could not go on the attack. The next moment something happened that none of them expected. Defending herself from another hammer, Tiara put up an air shield in the shape of a curved lens in front of her. With one movement of his fingers, Hans set it on fire; and Tiara, engulfed in flames, screamed wildly. Before Kloss dispelled the weave, the girl's hair was singed, and burn blisters bloomed on her arm. He stood over the girl in complete disbelief. Tiara was conscious, hissing in pain, trying to calm her burning skin with the wind.

Hans commanded two elements! The chances of defeating him in a spontaneous duel were zero. However, it took time to go on the attack with other weapons. He could not leave the weave that protected the priests.

Kloss, having calmed down, began to think logically. It's not like Hans wanted to kill them. Otherwise, he would have done it long ago while he was bent over his student.

"You don't need to open the gate." Hans's voice sounded calm, decisive. "You don't understand what you're doing."

"I thought besides the master, no one else can command the two elements." Kloss was stalling for time.

"You don't even suspect that by your actions you are leading the world to destruction."

Kloss honestly didn't know what he was talking about. He didn't even understand the meaning of the words. He had no doubt that Hans was considered one of them. The snake-shaped pupil can only be possessed by owners of the demon blade.

"Why did you give up your weapon?" Kloss continued to stall for time, feeling vibrations in the ground. Hans, feeling the same, did not answer but began to weave again.

Kloss released his air spears one by one, piercing the rocks falling from above. He felt that his legs had sunk knee-deep into quicksand, which hardened in an instant. He tried to crush the earth around him with air axes. The air sparkled, once again engulfing the aircraft in flames. Instinctively saving his life, Kloss put his boomerang forward, and the elements dissipated. Beside himself with anger, he attacked the enemy with a demon blade. Hans managed to draw his sword and meet the weapon with a block.

"No elemental technique can interfere with the demon's blade." Kloss triumphed, launching the boomerang into flight again and again, moving away from the enemy. In the heat of battle, he forgot to think about a crushing weapon, trying to surpass Hans in weaving. Now Kloss had compensated for this omission.

The magical duel exhausted Hans; he barely missed the flying weapon. Blocking blows with his sword, he winced in pain every time. The steel gave way to the smoky alloy of the boomerang. With each parry, Kloss left a deep notch in Hans's blade. Hans needed to get closer to Kloss.

"Without the elements, you are nothing." Kloss reveled in superiority. "I don't understand why the master has been looking for you all these years."

Hans did not listen to his chatter. Due to the numerous jagged edges, the blade could burst at any minute.

Kloss hardly noticed that the thread feeding the protective weave around the design had broken when he used the demon blade. This satisfied Hans's plan. The rest was now up to Chloe and Avalsa. Hans felt Seraph behind him, waiting for the signal to attack along with his squad. If Avalsa managed to neutralize the priests, then the squad's help will not be needed.

Hans continued to fight off the attacks, ignoring Kloss's defiant speeches. He threw away the enchanted sword with numerous serrations, unwinding the Grail chain from his forearm. Kloss had to reckon with such a weapon, carefully launching the boomerang into flight.

Kloss's confidence knew no bounds; he hadn't even used half the weapon's potential. Due to the attacker's carelessness, the boomerang spun in the chain, and Hans pulled it to the ground, quickly approaching

Kloss. Before the blade returned to him again, Hans slammed his chained fist into his opponent's face. The crunch of bursting cartilage reached his ears.

Without waiting for Kloss to come to his senses, Hans returned his earthen hands back to the wall, clearing the way to the priests. Eager to help Avalsa, Hans paused, assessing the situation. There was no one left to help. The mercenaries lay on the ground in various positions, like rag dolls. Avalsa neutralized the last priest with electromagnetic needles, and the singing stopped. It was all over. The pulsating circle of summoning will go out without replenishment, and the ritual can be considered failed.

In the center of the circle, Kloss's boomerang vibrated.

The vibration was accompanied by a hum and unstable gusts of wind. Hans barely managed to cover Chloe and Avalsa, who did not understand anything, with an earthen sarcophagus. The turbulence became increasingly stronger, with the boomerang serving as the epicenter.

"Now you will know the true power of the demon blade." The voice behind him seemed split, guttural. Hans turned around and saw the transformed Kloss, around whom boomerangs were circling, blowing streams of wind. On his face was a bone mask in the shape of the skull of some animal with fangs. His eyes blazed with hatred. The air, vibrating, lifted small pebbles above the ground. This was the first time Hans had seen such a mask, but he suspected that it was part of a demonic weapon.

"You can't protect these people, no matter how hard you hide them," Kloss rasped, sending his blades flying. Hans was enveloped in a strong whirlwind, lifting him several meters into the air. Trying to find balance, he felt his clothes, under the influence of an invisible force, being torn on his body, soaked in blood from numerous cuts. The elements cut through his skin like melted butter.

The tip of the tornado reached the edges of the canyon, rotating chaotically around its axis. Hans tried to escape from the "cutting centrifuge," which inflicted fatal wounds. The whirlwind stopped as suddenly as it began. After being high in the air, Hans flew down, losing consciousness. The bone mask on Kloss's face crumbled, and Kloss fell to his knees, breathing heavily.

Hans showed no signs of life. The blood slowly spread, forming a puddle on the roughened ground.

"Having renounced your own weapons, you cannot be one of us." No longer paying attention to him, Kloss entered the circle of challenge, filling it with strength. He did not notice that the sarcophagus protecting the warriors of the Raven Guild was still standing.

Kloss placed the weapon in the center of the design, again causing the lines to ripple. In time with the spoken words, small flames burst out from the circle. The fire grew higher and denser. Kloss was lucky; the priests did their job. All he had to do was saturate the circle with power, materializing a gate in this world.

There was a disgusting smell of burnt meat. The bodies of the priests, being on the lines of fire, began to smoke. However, Kloss didn't care about this circumstance.

Tiara, standing behind her teacher, watched in fascination what was happening. She was not afraid of the flames escaping, being confident in Kloss's strength. With huge tentacles, it tried to reach them, but it broke against an invisible barrier, like water against rocks. She smeared her hand with ointment and bandaged it tightly to prevent infection. She tried not to even think about the moment when she would have to remove the dried bandages.

Releasing the pent-up power, a pillar of flame shot into the sky. Toothed creatures with heads and bodies resembling dogs began to appear through the flames. One of them approached Tiara closely, extending her coal-black tongue, sniffing the girl. From its mouth came smoke and a stench that filled the insides. Tiara stood still, trying not to make sudden movements. Kloss, paying attention to them, kicked the creature in the face. The dog, growling angrily, rushed along with the others along the riverbed, in search of permitted prey.

A howl of agony was heard from the open gates. The minotaurs came out and cut the camels, feeding each other's limbs. The unfortunate animals, tearing the reins, tried to get out, but the hounds, overtaking them, knocked them to the ground, and the minotaur's axe ended their lives.

Kloss watched what was happening, holding Tiara close to him.

"Is there hell there?" She pointed toward the gate, trembling when her teacher nodded. The girl felt confusion spreading like jelly along the bottom of the canyon.

Kloss turned to his student, bringing her out of her daze. "Before the demon appears, four waves of lesser creatures will pass through the gate. The first wave is the hounds. The second wave"—he pointed to the bull faces with axes—"minotaurs."

A loud bell rang out from the open gate. Several creatures with webbed wings emerged from the flames. Their bodies, with powerful elongated winged arms, were somewhat reminiscent of human ones, with underdeveloped lower limbs. On the head, instead of eyes, hung a horny plate, turning into an ominous mouth, wide from ear to ear. Transparent skin revealed an ebony skeleton that hid its pulsating organs.

"These are the fallen." Kloss followed with his gaze the flying creature leaving the edge of the gorge. "The more a demon's body resembles a human's, the stronger and more dangerous the creature." Kloss smiled ironically at the girl listening attentively.

He noticed some movement behind him, forcing him to interrupt the description. Several hounds and minotaurs huddled around something. Signaling for Tiara to follow him, Kloss decided to take a closer look.

"I'm telling you for sure, he needs help. Do you hear how it rumbles and sparkles?" Jerome could not find a place for himself in the cramped shelter.

"Hans told us to appear only if the writing on the swords lit up." Seraph was adamant, but he was also worried about his friend.

The swordsman commander had not felt this way since he was a youth. Hans tried to prepare the party for everything, telling them what to expect; but rolling boulders, starting fires with the movement of a finger, creating cutting winds was too much for the aging mind. "Listening and imagining" is very different from "seeing and understanding."

221

It was difficult for Seraph's squad to wait in ambush. The commander protested the decision to send Chloe alone, firing from another hiding spot. With common sense, he understood that Hans's idea was not without meaning, but Seraph managed to become attached to the girl. Secretly, he considered Chloe to be the daughter who never existed. Fatherly feelings also surprised the old warrior.

The squad leader was perplexed that Ludwig was still with them. They had gone through a lot in the past, but what was happening around them did not fit into the framework of what they had experienced. Ludwig calmed Ishmael, who covered his ears with his hands, crouching to the ground. The potbellied Arab did not tolerate loud noises well— the consequences of an exploding shell on one of his missions.

Seraph felt it rather than saw it. Lloyd's exclamation was only confirmation.

"The letters lit up!" He looked at the axe in fascination, seeing such light for the first time.

"Come on, all together." Seraph leaned his body on the lid of the shelter, giving a signal by example.

The squad jumped out of the hole one by one, spreading out at the entrance with their weapons drawn. What they saw could have led everyone into numbness, but the commander issued a cry: "At least some variety, instead of stinking poachers!"

Without saying another word, he rushed at the nearest hound with a wild cry. It was a shame to show fear in front of his comrades, but the squad could not move, watching as Seraph entered into battle with the creature. The hound howled disgustingly, and the sand was sprinkled with coal-black blood. The dog fell dead from Seraph's quick blade. The commander turned to the squad. "Why are you stopping, girls?! We are working!"

Inspired by the personal example of the commander, they rushed into the attack with shouts.

Their accumulated experience of fighting with edged weapons formed the veterans into the usual battle formation. At the tip of the wedge was Ludwig, holding the creatures at a distance with a two-handed sword. On both sides stood Seraph with a bastard and a half and Ishmael, wielding twin swords. The Arab's plump arms rotated with amazing dexterity, inflicting deep cuts on the hounds. Along the edges were the "claws" of a fighting squad of swordsmen: Lloyd with a mighty axe and Jerome with a heavy two-handed saber. With large muscles on their arms, they wielded such weapons effortlessly.

Lloyd, faced with the minotaur, exchanged several swings of the axe, trying to reach its body. The bull's face roared, anticipating a bloody slaughter. Ishmael, sneaking behind the creature, inflicted several injections into the humanoid body. Without allowing the creature to recover from the pain, Lloyd ended the life of the hellish creature with a diagonal attack from his axe. Blood boiling like tar hissed underfoot.

Jerome heard Seraph's warning and crouched down, spreading out just in time. Claws closed overhead, and the flapping of membranous wings was heard.

"In the sky! About a dozen!" Ludwig cried, tackling another minotaur.

"Jerome, I'm bait!" Ishmael decided to use the proven maneuver, getting closer to the native. Jerome, understanding his comrade, nodded, continuing to fight with several hounds at the same time.

The fallen one entered a new circle and dived at the Arab. Finding the moment, Ishmael fell on all fours, covering his head with his hands. Using its back as a springboard, Jerome delivered a powerful strike with the winged creature's saber. It hissed and howled disgustingly. Before falling, the creature doused those around it with boiling blood.

Nobody felt pain. The squad fought, ignoring their wounds. This happened when warriors fell into battle fever. From the outside, it seemed that the veterans, like a precise mechanism, worked harmoniously and clearly, complementing each other. The years spent in the Raven Guild were not in vain. The morale of the detachment seemed unquenchable. They believed in their commander, who fought blindly along with everyone else. The squad stopped being afraid. They became convinced that Hans's words were true: the enchanted weapon wounded the creatures from hell.

Even though the veterans were tough, any long battle was exhausting. There was no end to the creatures. They all arrived through the open gates, attacking those resisting with renewed vigor. People's movements were no longer so fast; their hands became heavier.

Without knowing it, the detachment concentrated on itself all the creatures that came out of hell. The creatures were eager to get the head of at least one mortal who dared to fight them. They intensified the onslaught, mercilessly stepping over the dead.

Another bell ringing echoed along the bottom of the dry riverbed, heard from the open gate. The members of the squad, weakened from blood loss and numerous wounds, almost lost their balance from the vibration. The hound of the underworld, bending down, jumped from behind, biting into Ishmael's neck. Blood bubbled on his lips. The others noticed it when it was too late. With the last movement of his sword, the Arab took the creature with him to the next world.

Furious at what he saw, Lloyd cut off the hand of the nearest minotaur. With the next swing of his axe, he cut the hound in half. The Scandinavian blood boiled in the red-bearded veteran. He smashed, not paying attention to his own wounds.

In the heat of battle, Lloyd failed to hear the cry of warning. Something sharp pierced his back, and the next second he stopped feeling the ground with his feet. The flapping of wings was heard overhead. Lloyd tried in vain to reach his opponent with an axe. When another pair of claws dug into his chest, the weapon fell from the warrior's hands.

Jerome screamed exhaustedly into the air as he watched his comrade in arms being torn apart. The crunching of joints and the sound of tearing tendons was unbearable.

To prevent the remaining members of the squad from reckless behavior, Seraph barked at the top of his lungs, "Back to back!"

Accustomed to the commander's orders, Jerome and Ludwig stood in a stance.

The three warriors fought with all the fury of despair. The strength of the veterans left them, sweat poured into their eyes, and their lungs heaved like bellows. The hounds surrounded the squad. The warriors did not immediately notice that the creatures had stopped attacking. Without lowering his weapon, Jerome said, "They have surrounded us and are expecting something."

Ludwig thought the same, gloomily examining the hellish creatures.

Behind the rows of hounds and minotaurs, a human figure appeared. The fair-haired, short-haired guy looked rather tired, but there was no lack of authority in his voice.

"You did an amazing feat for ordinary people." He pointed to the pile of dead bodies of the creatures of the underworld. "I think the luminous writings were able to make your weapon deadly for them. It will remain a mystery to me where Hans got such knowledge from."

The creatures stood motionless, the smoldering fire in their eyes filled with hatred.

"You have no one else to fight for." Kloss turned to the squad again. "Your leader is dead, as is the archer, along with another girl."

The warriors' grip on their weapons weakened for just a moment but immediately became stronger, and their faces became more determined.

"Then don't hold these creatures, and we will fight them."

Kloss smiled. "The lack of fear against the creatures of hell is very impressive. Perhaps Hans had a hand in this too. But I'm not the one holding them back."

The answer to the silent question was a heavy tread behind him. Towering above the hounds and minotaurs was a mass of muscle and ferocity. The creature, three times the height of a man, stamped its hooves as it approached the squad. The lesser creatures gave way, the fallen greeted with guttural cries resounding in the heavens. A huge monkey's face, with long lower fangs, glared at the trio. Mighty webbed wings were folded behind its back, and in its hands, it held the stump of a sword. The blade seemed to reach the height of a man.

Three more appeared behind the creature.

"These are close associates." Kloss was overcome with inexplicable admiration. "The last step before the appearance of the demon. What a pity that you will not see this miracle."

The close one raised its hand with a sword high above its head. The circle of hounds closed, and the detachment could not miss the crushing weapon. Jerome closed his eyes, reciting a prayer in his native language. A bang was heard somewhere nearby.

Chapter

21

Darkness. He immersed himself, opening his consciousness to visions. It was filled with pain and suffering; every step taken was drowned in a river of blood. Hands emerged from the river and grabbed the body, pulling the head toward itself, in whose eyes madness was visible.

"For what?" the heads shouted in one voice. "You betrayed us! You let us die!"

Hans recognized these faces, remembered them from a past life. The darkness gave way to the glow of flames. Tongues mercilessly licked the face. Piercing pain pounded into the head along with the screams of the dead.

It all seemed unbearable. Hans screamed and shook his head, trying to drive away the nightmares. They laughed wildly at him.

A vision emerged from the flames. Three vaguely familiar people were surrounded by the creatures of hell. The picture changed, showing two girls suffocating under the lid of the sarcophagus.

A crash sounded overhead, revealing to the light a radiance that was deceptive in its holiness. The insinuating feminine whisper echoed clearly in his mind.

"Are you going to let them die too?"

His shoulders dropped, but his gaze did not lose determination. Passing all the pain, suffering, and curses of the past through himself, he uttered a single word. A word that evoked blatant horror in nightmares, the desire to kill. Vowing never to utter it, Hans whispered quietly, "Flamentia."

A wave of fire swept away the fallen, hounds, minotaurs, along with those close to them. The creatures of hell burned in their own fire, screaming in agony. The remaining close associate attacked the walker with the hatred of a beast. A piece of the sword, meeting a long blade of smoky steel, crumbled; and the giant's body was cut in half. An open fire of boiling blood breathed into his face.

Kloss looked dumbfounded at the weapon in Hans's hands. Complex patterns covered the obsidian-colored sheath and hilt. The semicircular hilt resembled an unopened moon. The long blade hid the wandering fog, absorbing sunlight. Kloss recognized the blade. Blade of the demon blade. The legendary weapon was in the hands of a legendary warrior.

Without wasting any more time, Kloss attacked first. His face was again hidden behind a bone mask, enveloping him with demonic power. He no longer thought about the consequences for the body. Kloss went on the attack. Boomerangs swirled around the enemy. The resulting tornado, as before, began to lift the inactive Hans into the air. Air blades formed in the walls of the vortex, cutting the enemy inside into small pieces.

Kloss was proud of this technique. It was considered the best achieved over the years of training and merging with demonic energy. The air blades inside the tornado were spinning too fast. Sharpened in the strongest technique, Hans deflected the blades into a whirlwind until the funnel dissipated. Refusing to accept defeat, Kloss threw boomerangs at unimaginable angles. Hans used the sheath, deflecting both blades.

He felt the mask on his face crack. Growling with rage, Kloss threw a boomerang behind his opponent's back and raised the second one for a diagonal attack. Hans took the handle of the katana.

Jerome, who watched the fight, did not understand what happened. Just one moment completed the outcome of the battle. With two quick blows, Hans dismembered his opponent. The boomerangs clanged to the ground, and the blade rested in its sheath again.

With his consciousness rapidly fading, Kloss heard the whisper of his conqueror.

"The difference between us is that you don't even know the name of your blade."

He tried to make out Hans's face, but his eyes were clouded with a hopeless fog, plunging him into the jelly of oblivion.

—∞—

Avalsa gasped for air, looking at her friend who was on all fours. She believed that they had decided to bury them alive, but suddenly a wall of sand appeared. Avalsa looked around, expecting an attack.

"How are you?" Avalsa asked Chloe. Chloe nodded in response, rising to her feet. She saw Hans approaching with a strange weapon in his hands. As far as Avalsa remembered, he did not have such a sword with him. A girl with a bandaged hand was crying over a mutilated corpse nearby.

"This is Kloss." Avalsa said and approached, examining the body closer. The crying woman did not pay attention to anyone, so Avalsa stopped calling out to her and asked Hans instead, "Where is our squad?"

Hans was about to answer but suddenly looked behind the girl with alarm. She turned around, also sensing danger.

The gates of hell, spitting out fire and clots of magma, still remained open. The breach lit up especially brightly, letting a unique creature into this world. Slowly, with appropriate grandeur, the creature walked, striking with unimaginable beauty, rhythmically clattering her neat hooves. Of all the creatures of hell that came out, she was the most humanlike.

Her skin had a smoky hue, highlighting her bare breasts and flat stomach of seductive shapes. Her luxurious head of hair was crowned with small twisted horns with swirling fire between them. Her smooth, tarry tail gently stroked her hips with its pointed, flat end. The creature's lower abdomen breathed fire of such strength that it was impossible to look at her, like the sun.

The creature paced back and forth along the circle, her hooves clicking like her heels. Looking at the challenge letters, she did not pay attention to those around her. Hans, standing behind Avalsa, whispered in her ear, "Go to the remaining members of the squad. Help destroy the rest of the creatures of hell. Chloe, is your alchemical mixture enough to keep the arrows lethal to the creatures?"

She did not immediately answer, staring at the grace of the creature with a sword in her hands.

"After Prague, I finalized the composition, but there was no opportunity to check it."

"Now you have it," Hans said, clearly nervous, looking toward the circle. "You can't let the creatures reach the villages. Innocent people should not die."

What they heard instilled determination in the girls.

"But what will you do?" At that moment the demon raised her head in their direction and smiled charmingly.

"I'll fight her." Hans shielded the girls with himself, and the pressure of fear squeezing his temples decreased. Avalsa wanted to object; but her friend, ignoring her resistance, dragged her by the hand.

—m—

A demon of amazing beauty stood in the center of the circle, waiting for Hans to approach and smiling carnivorously. There was playfulness and passion in her every gesture, voice, and movement.

"I remember this weapon." She spoke as soon as he came close to the circle. "It used to belong to one of us. His name was Flament. He was a mighty warrior." The next moment, hatred was already visible in the succubus's eyes. "You came to our kingdom to kill him, to appropriate the weapons for yourself. I don't remember how much time has passed since then, but I remember your name, Hans." The demon smiled charmingly, revealing pointed fangs.

"I remember you too, Ignessa." Hans tried to be respectful, assessing whether the succubus could hold the circle of challenge. "Flament was considered a ferocious warrior, but your dexterity, which knows no equal, complemented him."

Appreciating the flattery, Ignessa laughed.

Seeing the summoning priests on the ground, the succubus changed her face again. With a flick of her tail, she cut off the head of the nearest one and, as if from a goblet, drank the blood from a fragment of a skull. Hans tried to appear indifferent, although raging emotions prevailed inside.

"Cowardly worms." Ignessa killed the paralyzed old men one after another with visible pleasure. "They believe that they can steal our weapons without paying anything in return. A shameful sacrifice of blood only incites hatred." The demon looked at Hans with snake eyes, continuing, "Our weapons recognize only strength. You know that. It can only serve someone who has mastered someone else's will." She walked along the circle, getting excited. Indignation was visible on her beautiful face.

"Your companion learned to summon us to this world, knowing that in hell we are stronger," Ignessa snorted, flicking her tail. "He drew this circle, which serves as a cage for the demon, holding him in place. I've only heard of something like this. Demons who had their weapons stolen in your world were forcibly pushed back into hell. They raged, cursed, but could not prevent the writings. I watched them."

Ignessa paused and winked at Hans. "Your partner created a clan of thieves and impudents. I have been collecting information about this circle for a long time. I kept waiting for the gates to open to appear in the world of helpless lambs."

Approaching one of the lines, the demon hit it with her hoof. The calling circle, blinking its fire for the last time, went out. Ignessa took a confident, unhindered step toward Hans. He remained calm, holding back the raging hurricane of anxiety. Hans did not count on her finding a way to free herself from her shackles.

"Today I have an appointment with your companion." The demon reveled in her own victory and conversation with her old enemy. "It's clear from your eyes that you also want to meet with him. Have you ever wondered why he doesn't show up to any calls? Does he think that if his students can cope, then there's no point in getting their hands dirty?" Ignessa raised her head to the sky, screaming loudly, "It's time to show up now, because your subordinates failed!"

Naturally, there was no answer and no appearance. She laughed out loud.

Ignessa saw the disfigured corpse of Kloss and languidly licked her lips, running her hands along her stomach.

"Your skill, as always, is at its best. You may not have used a weapon for several centuries, but the blade does not forget its owner."

Hans slowly drew his katana, still not answering. Surprised by his determination, Ignessa said angrily, "Flament was my lover whom you killed. I accepted his death. Step aside, I need Reiza, not you."

"Your presence in this world upsets the balance of power. The weapons of demons constantly rock the scales, which are about to tip over."

Ignessa laughed ironically. "What loud speeches for the killer of an entire legion. By the way, do you still have nightmares?"

Without allowing Hans to recover from what was said, Ignessa struck. Her attack, like a fiery explosion, swept along the dry riverbed. Hans managed to block, and two demonic blades met, striking sparks.

Her weapon looked more like a long dagger than a sword. The absence of a guard was compensated by the bend of the blade, which protected the hand. The handle, wrapped in a leather braid, slowly flowed into the blade, the edge of which seemed to glow from the shine of sharpening.

Hans never took his eyes off the succubus's tail, using it as a weapon. Blows rained down from different sides. The air trembled and changed from the swings of swords. From Ignessa's sweeping blow, Hans sank into the sand, blocking. The speed of the attacks was amazing. They weaved patterns of a deadly dance, testing each other's defense. Ignessa's short blade was an advantage. Hans tried to impose his tactics, keeping the enemy at a distance. The tail snapped near the ear, miraculously not splitting the head. Ignessa moved in leaps and bounds, increasing the force of her attack with her body weight. Her swordsmanship was impressive. All of Hans's attention was focused on not missing the blow that could be his last.

Hissing from another failed attack, Ignessa threw the sword to the side, deciding to use force. Bringing her palms together in front of her, she threw a hot blob of magma at Hans. The ball grew rapidly, obscuring the enemy. He had no choice but to release his weapon. The blade, hearing its name, began to shine, changing. The fireball crashed into a fire wave of no less magnitude.

Ignessa, standing at a distance, applauded. "I thought you wouldn't use his power." She held her sword with her tail, quickly closing the distance.

Without answering anything, Hans launched another wave, covering the enemy. The modified weapon seemed too massive for a person. The blade, four palms wide, like Ignessa's sword, did not have a guard. A wide plate on the hilt served as a counterweight. The weapon, covered with writing, glowed with green flame.

Despite the weight of the massive two-hander, Hans repelled the succubus's attacks with amazing speed. Ignessa parried, passing the terrible blade, avoiding a frontal blow.

—ɯ—

The glow of two lights made it hard to believe that it was still night outside. Hans launched waves of green flames, trying to reach Ignessa. She released clots of magma, meeting Hans's attacks.

The two warriors, drawing closer, switched to fencing again, abandoning long-range attacks. They circled and attacked, hunting down each other's slightest mistakes. Although there were minor cuts, no one was seriously injured during the fight.

Once Hans began to tire, he returned the demon blade to its original shape. Ignessa's skin was damp with sweat, and her breathing was ragged. She fought with the man seriously, with difficulty repelling the deadly attacks.

The snap of her tail cut Hans's jaw. Hissing in pain, he was forced to go on the defensive, repelling the advancing enemy. Blood poured into his neck; his bloody T-shirt stuck, hindering his movements.

Feeling the smell of blood, Ignessa licked her tail, unable to resist the temptation.

"Your blood is still sweet." The flame in the lower abdomen flared up brighter. "I want to torture you so that the blood from the cuts slowly oozes, allowing you to enjoy the aroma for a long time."

Taking advantage of the respite, Hans did not answer anything, regaining his breath. He looked at the demon gloomily, squeezing the handle tighter. Ignessa, her face changing, barked, "Give up! I don't have time to bother with you. You are just a mortal."

She hoped to influence a person with the voice of suggestion, often using it against demons. Hans was glad to see the opportunity. Obeying her word, he lowered his weapon.

The blood stopped flowing, and he felt weak. Time seemed to slow down. Hans saw Ignessa approaching, holding her sword raised above her head. She decided to end the fight by piercing her opponent through. Meeting the succubus, he began to act at the last moment, banking on surprise.

Hans threw the scabbard in front of him, at Ignessa's feet. The demon swept away the obstacle with her tail, without slowing down. He saw the tip shining in anticipation of its prey. Spinning around its axis, Ignessa's sword barely scratched her back. Hans lunged.

Blood sprayed into the air. Falling to the ground in heavy drops, it hissed loudly. The demon's eyes widened in surprise. With one hand, Hans held her in his arms; and with the other, he clutched the sword, deeply embedded in the feminine body. Resinous blood dripped from the edge of the blade.

Hans pulled the succubus closer, whispering in his ear, "You too, Ignessa, mortal. But not every weapon can kill you."

Smiling with her lovely lips, she died in his arms without saying a word.

He carefully removed the katana blade from his body. The fire in the lower abdomen was quickly cooling down. Hans looked distantly at the closing gates of hell, forcing himself to rise by force of will. He carried Ignessa in his arms to her world, carefully placing her on the fiery ground. Next to the girl, without a bit of regret, he left Flamentia, saying, "You have no place in this world." He remembered this phrase uttered several centuries ago. "You only bring destruction."

Holding Ignessa's weapon in his hands, Hans hesitated. Having remembered something, he returned. He remembered boomerangs remained near Kloss's body, but they were no longer there. The student fled with the teacher's weapon. Hans made a terrible mistake by leaving

Tiara alive. A bright flash lit up the dawn sky. The rift connecting the two worlds closed with a bang.

—ɯ—

Hans sat down on a nearby rock, completely exhausted. There was one more thing left to do, but his strength was rapidly leaving his body. Avalsa ran up to him, swaying joyfully. Hans did not immediately recognize her alarmed, sweet face.

"Hans, you did it! You closed the gate!" The girl continued to talk, not letting him lose consciousness. "It sparkled, of course, notably. We were farther along the riverbed, but the flashes and heat of the fire reached us. Chloe killed the remaining creatures. Her chemical mixture had an amazing effect! The creatures were disintegrating right before our eyes. Hans, can you hear me? We won!"

He looked at her with a hazy look. Taking Avalsa by the shoulder, Hans tried to rise. She leaned over him, helping.

"Get up, Hans. Don't you dare lose consciousness, do you hear? Hang in there. We'll get through this."

Overcoming himself, he straightened up, pressed himself against her, and whispered, "Sorry."

Hans fell unconscious to the ground. Avalsa knelt down, staring in shock at the hilt protruding from her stomach. The pain spread throughout her body no worse than the blood spreading around. Her vision darkened. Avalsa looked at Hans in shock, unable to believe what he had done. Trying to get up on her knees, she became more weakened. The surviving members of the squad, seeing the tragedy unfolding, rushed to help in the hope that it was not too late.

Avalsa lost consciousness in a pool of her own blood, at the bottom of the dry bed of a deep river in Africa.

EPILOGUE

Autumn. A time when melancholy and apathy paralyze the flow of people throughout the world. The time of heavy rains and fallen leaves covering lawns, alleys, and gardens with a dense carpet. In late autumn, nature, following people, also goes into an indifferent state—it waits for the onset of winter.

For London, similar weather is typical at any time of the year. Smog, hanging over the royal country like an impenetrable gray cloud, is a landmark of the time. For residents of the hilly areas of London, morning fog appears more often than dawn sun.

On one of these foggy autumn days, there were especially many people on the streets of London. Barkers shouted, inviting people to visit newly opened establishments; sellers lured them to try the best goods of Foggy Albion. Someone was calling a taxi with a loud whistle; somewhere in an alley, a pickpocket robbed a drunk. The workers were in a truck on their way to work.

Life was bustling around Clark, and he was enjoying it. Gray tones had always occupied the imagination of the illusionist. To him, it was the color of a blank canvas awaiting the application of bright colors. The grayness of London life was the starting point for creating some kind of colorful illusion.

Clark enjoyed watching his creations. The flower shop at the intersection of two streets was fragrant with all kinds of plants. On glass display cases, vases of various shapes were arranged in several rows, in which blooming buds flaunted in a rainbow composition.

Farther along the street, in front of the arch of a residential building, there was a bakery, attracting numerous passersby with the smell of muffins, cinnamon, and almonds. No one left there indifferent. In everyone's hands, there was an airy, hot pastry.

Clark turned his head to the right and saw a bright window of a music store with soft music playing from the outdoor speakers. The store stocked all kinds of recording media: from CDs to vinyl records. Each one featured an image of the iconic performer. Anyone who entered could always cheer himself up with his favorite music, enjoying the purity of the sound of studio equipment.

Clark created illusions of the small pleasures of life. Let the flowers wither over time, the bun be consumed with coffee, and your favorite song eventually got boring; but in that one moment, a person was happy. He was delighted by the unearthly beauty of a flower, amazed by the spicy bouquet of baked goods, and satisfied by listening to legendary music. In one short moment, a person became happy. The illusion helped people smile sincerely.

He noisily inhaled the morning air. It was already feeling like winter outside, although there were still a couple of weeks of autumn left. Adjusting his medium-brimmed bright-red hat, Clark headed to the nearest bar.

The room was dim, and the air smelled of beer and fried potatoes. The illusionist thanked fate that at least there was no smoking in the bar. Clark maneuvered between the tables, deftly warming up to the visitors. The bar was crowded. Mostly there were working people here who liked to drink a lot, complain loudly, and fight a lot. And only in this sequence.

He felt the crowd staring at the red leather cloak, at the upright aristocratic posture. No one, not even the most inveterate fighters, tried to block the road.

Clark headed toward the corner tables. Three out of four were free. He stopped at the occupied one and looked at the visitor. His shaved temples had already turned gray. Silver was also visible in his long hair, tied into a ponytail. The face of a thirty-year-old man was sharpened by unnatural thinness; his cheeks were sunken. Brightly burning yellow eyes stood out in the twilight.

The head of the Raven Guild smiled welcomingly at Hans, taking off his hat.

"I'm grateful that you helped me get out. We would have died in that direction."

"Some did." Clark shrugged, and there was silence for a while.

Hans was the first to break the silence. "I have one more request. I need you to send me to Raven Valley."

Clark's eyebrows rose in surprise. "Do you want me to send you to the place where the illusionists imprisoned their worst enemies? Sorry, but you are not one of them. Besides, I don't even remember how to do it."

"I need to prepare a student." Hans's voice seemed tired.

"Prepare for what?"

"To the demon's weapon."

The head of the Raven Guild did not answer; he just sat down next to him, ordering a double whiskey.

February 2017–January 2018

Milton Keynes UK
Ingram Content Group UK Ltd.
UKHW010704220524
443011UK00010B/163/J